## *He heard the steady thunder of controlled cannon fire.*

The injured man howled with each jolt from the moving horse, his right leg nothing but a meaty stump, oozing blood.

Dudley felt his cheeks drain at the sight. He thought, *There, now I have seen the ugly face of battle, and it is nothing like seeing a sick man, even one who dies.*

He drew in a long breath, closing his eyes. The shock of seeing the wounded man passed.

He carried on in his search for stragglers. Now and then he glanced forward, toward the pounding of the distant guns. He hoped to catch a glimpse of what was happening.

That glimpse came when the army crested a low ridge. A wide river valley lay below. Moving across that flat, dead ground was the force that the Hussars and Artillery had encountered—columns of gray and brown Russian infantry, retiring south, away from the advancing British.

"My God," Dudley said.

# DUDLEY'S FUSILIERS

*Empire and Honor Book 1*

# HAROLD R. THOMPSON

ZUMAYA YESTERDAYS

AUSTIN TX

2010

DUDLEY'S FUSILIERS
© 2010 by Harold R. Thompson
ISBN 978-1-934841-72-3

Cover art and design © Gary Trow

"Zumaya Yesterdays" and the phoenix colophon are trademarks of Zumaya Publications LLC, Austin TX.

Look for us online at www.zumayapublications.com/yesterdays

Library of Congress Cataloging-in-Publication Data

Thompson, Harold (Harold R.)
Dudley's fusiliers / Harold R. Thompson.
    p. cm. -- (For queen and empire ; bk. 1)
Prequel to: The guns of Sevastopol.
 ISBN 978-1-934841-72-3 (trade paper : alk. paper) -- ISBN 978-1-934841-73-0 (ebk.)
 1. Soldiers--Great Britain--Fiction. 2. Crimean War, 1853-1856--Fiction. 3.    Great Britain--History, Military--19th century--Fiction. I. Title.
 PR9199.3.T4668D84 2010
 813'.54--dc22
                                2010001903

This edition is
for the JBF

# CHAPTER ONE

When I was a youngster gossips would say
When I grew older I'd be a soldier.
Rattles and toys I threw them away
Except a drum and a sabre.

T. S. Cooke
"Hey For the Life of a Soldier"


*It was October 14*, a month after Wellington's death. William
Dudley finished his breakfast, put on his best frock coat, and
tramped downstairs to the main door. After stepping into the
yard, he paused for a moment under the sign that read "Black
Horse Tavern and Inn."

A recruiting sergeant stood near the gate, haranguing a
small group of village lads with his parade-square bellow. The
sight of the sergeant made Dudley think of Wellington's passing,
of how the nation had mourned. He recalled a snatch of verse
and hummed to himself:

Come all ye valiant soldiers
And listen unto me,
Who has got an inclination
To face your enemy.
Never be fainthearted
But boldly cross the main,

1

Come and join Lord Wellington
Who drubbed the French in Spain.

The words belonged to one of the many soldiers' songs Dudley had learned as a boy. The men of the Royal Hampshire Fusiliers had often sung the song as they marched through the village, trailing barking dogs and excited children. Dudley had always followed close behind the regiment, marching as far as his short legs could carry him.

The recruiting sergeant spoke of Wellington now, attempting to entice the young men to enlist to honour the memory of the Iron Duke. Dudley approached the group and stopped to listen. He felt the force of the words. They stirred the old dream, his passion from boyhood, to "go for a soldier."

With some effort, he turned away from the sergeant and walked out of the yard. Following his usual route, he made his way through the village and toward Highwood Hall. He tried to forget what the sergeant had said. Someday soon, if circumstances allowed, he was to go away to Cambridge. The life of a soldier would never be for him.

Dudley gazed through the library window and waited for the arrival of his single pupil, young Jeremy Wilkes. As was his habit, Dudley had come to Highwood Hall early to enjoy a few moments of solitude. The library, with its shelves of leather- and cloth-bound books, was a welcome escape from the room he rented on the third floor of the Black Horse. At the inn, the constant noise from the taproom downstairs created an impression of perpetual company. Dudley enjoyed the presence of others, but he also relished silence, the chance to be alone with his thoughts and imaginings.

Today those thoughts kept returning to Wellington. The old general had died on September 14.

Dudley reached into the pocket of his frock coat and drew forth his constant companion and good-luck talisman. He turned it in his hand—a small tin soldier, the last survivor of a box of twelve. Dudley had named it after the hero of the Peninsula and Waterloo.

2

"Well, Wellington," he said to the soldier, "though your namesake has passed on, you're still here. Even after I've lost Bonaparte, and Meaney, and Sergeant MacDougal, and all the rest of your tin compatriots."

Dudley smiled at the recollection of those bygone imaginary friends. His father had given him the box of toy soldiers, a Christmas gift purchased in London.

The smile faded. Memories of the toy soldiers could be both pleasant and painful. The gift, though a gesture of caring, was the last such gesture. After that, the elder Dudley had forgotten his son, and had fallen into drink and despair.

Dudley's mother had died when he was an infant, her body yielding to a consumption of the lungs after a long struggle. For two years, his father had managed to cope with the loss, and Dudley had never known that something was amiss with his remaining parent.

But the coping had been an illusion, and the elder Dudley had begun to spend most of his time in local taverns. Neglected, little William had retreated into a private world, inventing fantasies based on the adventures of the toy soldiers. The true exploits of Britain's troops in the long wars against the French had provided the basis for those adventures. Dudley's fascination with the army had begun.

Then Dudley's father, in a drunken stupor, had toppled into the Test River and drowned in its shallow waters. This second tragedy had led to the release of seven-year-old William Dudley into the care of an uncle and aunt, the Reverend and Mrs. Robert Mason.

Reverend Mason managed a small public school in northern Hampshire. Dudley had attended that school until he was twelve years old. The reverend had then seen to the remainder of his nephew's education—and the education of Dudley's five cousins—personally. Reverend Mason had also obtained for Dudley the position of tutor to the young son of Mr. George Wilkes, the master of Highwood Hall. At Highwood, Dudley taught his pupil a full range of subjects, including mathematics, physical science, French, Latin, geography and, his personal favorite, history.

Perhaps a history lesson, Dudley thought, would serve to combat his growing ill mood. To indulge himself in one of his enthusiasms, with Jeremy as a subject, might raise his sinking spirits.

When Jeremy entered the room, Dudley had just finished planning the lesson in his mind.

"Good day, sir," greeted the small boy, bobbing his curly head.

"Good day to you, Jeremy," Dudley replied. "I have a treat for you today. I know that in history we have been learning about the Greeks and Romans, but I thought that we should look at some of the history of Britain." He paused, then asked, "Do you know who the Duke of Wellington was?"

Jeremy grinned, for he knew the answer. "He was a famous soldier, sir. You were fond of him."

Dudley returned the boy's smile. Already his gloom was lifting.

"Yes, I was. But did you know that he first became famous in India? You know where that is. Please go to the globe and show me."

In the afternoon, when the lessons had ended and the autumn sunlight spilled through the windows to pool on the carpet, Jeremy's oldest sister, Martha, came into the library. This was part of a daily ritual. When Jeremy departed, Martha came to take his place, though not as a pupil.

Dudley stood as she entered, and said, "Good afternoon, Martha."

She smirked at him. "Good afternoon? This is all the greeting I receive after all this time?"

"Forgive me. You make me feel quite humble. I'm almost afraid to ask if you would care to walk in the garden, while it's still light."

Their walks in the garden were another part of the ritual. Sometimes they even ventured past the garden, down to the brook with its stone bridge, or into the lane beyond. Today, they halted on the bridge beneath the golden beeches, elms and oaks.

4

Dudley leaned on the railing, staring at the flat-flowing water. Martha stood beside him, and he studied her reflection next to his. *How lovely she is*, he thought.

Their courtship had begun a week after Dudley's arrival at Highwood. Martha, it seemed, had taken to his good humour, while he had felt an instant attraction to her liveliness, her elfin beauty.

"We shall have the whole winter together," her reflection appeared to say, "and the spring and summer as well, if you do not go off to Cambridge until next Michaelmas. Almost a whole year!"

Dudley followed a yellowed leaf as it spiraled toward the water. His mood seemed to fall with it, threatening a return to his earlier state. Why should that be? he wondered. He knew the reason the moment the question entered his mind—Martha's mention of Cambridge.

"I don't really want to go," he said, thinking aloud.

Martha took his arm. "Oh, you are in a funny mood today, aren't you? It has always been your aim to go to Cambridge, your dream to study the law."

"That is not my dream, it is simply a plan. When my education is complete, an acquaintance of uncle's—a barrister—has agreed to take me on as his articled clerk." He sighed. "Another one of my uncle's plans for my future."

Martha turned from him and strolled along the bridge.

"You're frightfully gloomy today. I don't care to see you like this."

He watched her move away from him into the shaded lane. He had let his renewed melancholy show. That was unfortunate, for he could never explain to her why he felt this way.

How could he tell her that Cambridge held no interest for him? That he wished to pursue his childhood dream of leading men into the glory of battle? A foolish dream, for he could not afford the price of an officer's commission. His uncle had agreed to pay part of his fee for attending college but would never agree to his entering the army. And Martha would never agree to his enlistment in the ranks. Respectable men like him did not do such things.

His dreams must remain dreams, childish fantasies that had grown from his play with tin soldiers.

"I'm sorry, Martha," he called, catching up to her with a few long strides. "I don't to spoil our afternoon."

She halted under the oaks that bordered the lane and fixed him with her brown eyes. He stopped beside her.

"You're not spoiling our afternoon," she whispered, and he noticed how close to her he had come. He hesitated, then reached for her tiny hand and took it in his.

"You may kiss me if you like," she said. "If we are ever to be married, we must not be afraid of each other."

Dudley's heart quickened. He could feel the warmth of Martha's body where it pressed against him. Even through her thick dress and his woolen coat, he could sense her warmth. When he kissed her, he could not believe the softness, the sweetness of her lips.

When they parted a moment later, she repeated, "We shall have almost an entire year before you leave."

Dudley dismissed his inner protests of a moment ago. For this, he thought, he could forget his old dreams, take the respectable path to Cambridge, enter the Bar or even run for Parliament. For her he would do anything.

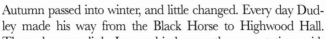

Autumn passed into winter, and little changed. Every day Dudley made his way from the Black Horse to Highwood Hall. There, he gave little Jeremy his lessons then spent time with Martha. On Sundays, he joined the Wilkes family for dinner, and these affairs became the high points of the season.

On one Sunday in February, Dudley was not the only guest at Highwood. Martha's cousin Edwin had arrived with a friend, a Lieutenant Jonathan Sackville of the 33rd Regiment. Edwin and Sackville would be staying the night, then resuming their journey to London in the morning.

Dudley looked forward to discussing matters of war with the young army officer. Over dinner, he asked him what he thought of Russia's apparent designs on Turkey and the Balkans. The lieutenant's response was disappointing. He explained that he knew little of Russia or the looming crisis with Turkey, and refused to discuss any other military subject. Instead, he described his father's racehorses, directing his conversation at Martha. He aimed a question at Dudley only once, saying, "Is it true, Mr. Dudley, if I may be so bold, that you are an orphan?"

"That is true, Lieutenant," Dudley said. "My mother died before I had the opportunity to know her, and my father drowned when I was seven years old."

"Ah, now, that's hard. Truly hard, sir, to grow up in such a state." He nodded with affected sympathy.

"On the contrary," Dudley returned, "my later childhood was far from dreary, for my mother's brother and sister-in-law took me in. Though my uncle can be stern and aloof, my aunt is a warm and maternal woman. I made many friends at my uncle's school, and my cousins are a lively crowd. I never wanted for affection and companionship amongst them."

"Ah, that's good to hear. There's so much misery in the world, such a story warms the heart."

Sackville's condescension was blatant, but Dudley did his best to hide his disgust. He glanced at Martha to judge her response. She was staring at the young officer. Staring, it appeared, with admiration. Surprised, Dudley turned his attention back to his food. Perhaps he had imagined it.

But as the dinner wore on, he decided that his original interpretation had been correct. Sackville monopolized Martha's conversation, and Martha returned the attention, absorbing every word the fellow said and laughing at his weak attempts at wit.

Dudley's ears began to burn with jealousy, and his head filled with questions and suspicions. He became deaf to the talk around him, and only awakened when someone mentioned the Duke of Wellington's recent death.

"Always an admirer!" Sackville declared. Dudley bristled to see that the fellow again directed his exclamation at Martha, who smiled as if to say *Bravo, Lieutenant!*

"Always!" the young officer repeated. "You know, Waterloo and all that. Our regiment's named for him, and I believe that he even commanded it once."

"I have always thought his greatest success," Dudley interjected, "was at Assaye, in eighteen-oh-three. He also considered it the best thing he had done in battle. A victory against such overwhelming numbers says great things for both the general and the common British soldier, I would say."

"Ah, yes, quite," Sackville replied. He cleared his throat. "I'm afraid, however, that I know very little about that engagement."

There was a moment of silence, a moment of satisfaction for Dudley. He spied Martha grinning at him, beaming with unabashed affection. With that, he felt a burst of triumph, and knew he had achieved a small victory. Martha must have been humouring the young officer all along. There had never been a reason for Dudley to feel jealous.

He went home that night ashamed of his suspicions. He resolved never to mention them to Martha.

Spring approached, and with it the promise of things to come, good and bad. Dudley tried to enjoy the routine of his days, though nervous thoughts of his future were never far away. He waited for word from Cambridge.

It seemed he was always waiting for something. During his childhood he had waited to become a man, passing the time in play and games. In play, he had escaped from the hopelessness of his father's home. In play, he had found a happy existence with his cousins and at his uncle's school. He had never bothered to plan, to take action, to consider the course of his life. He had come to rely on his uncle for that.

Now, he waited for Cambridge and the end of his term as tutor. The former was beyond his control, while the latter would come in July.

Then, in June, an unforeseen event occurred. Edwin Wilkes and his friend Lieutenant Sackville returned to Highwood Hall. They each brought several pieces of luggage, for George Wilkes had invited them to stay for an unspecified number of weeks.

To his shame, Dudley found that this situation made him nervous. The jealousy of that first meeting with Sackville returned. He hated the thought of Martha living under the same roof as the fellow.

He never mentioned his fears to Martha, but she must have sensed them. She made a point to convince him that she disliked Sackville, thought him foolish, a fop. He pretended to believe her, and almost convinced himself that he did.

On a morning in late July, a drum rattled outside Dudley's open window. He washed, dressed, ate his breakfast downstairs, then hurried into the yard. There, he found the drummer. The recruiting party, the same one from almost a year ago, had returned to entice young labourers and ploughmen to enlist.

Though tempted, Dudley could not linger to hear the recruiting sergeant's discourse. Instead, he began his usual journey to Highwood. Jeremy's lessons had ended a week previous, but Dudley had received two letters that he wanted Martha to see. They had arrived in yesterday's mail and now lay folded in his coat pocket alongside the tin form of Wellington.

The letters had come from his Uncle Robert. One was official notification of his acceptance into the undergraduate programme at St. John's College, Cambridge. The other was congratulations and promises of monetary aid. Martha would be pleased.

Yes, Martha would be pleased. Dudley himself was indifferent to these prospects, to the thought of a university education. His pleasure would lie in Martha's reaction. As he walked up the long drive to Highwood's front door, he anticipated hers expression when he showed her the letters.

The maid let him in but had disappointing news. Martha was not there.

"I'm sorry, Mr. Dudley," the maid said. "She went for a walk in the garden with the young Mr. Sackville."

"Thank you," he said.

He moved past the maid and walked through the house toward the back entrance. It was strange that Martha would go out with Sackville.

Dudley wandered into the garden to look for her. He clutched his uncle's letters in his right hand. Against his will, old suspicions began to form in his mind. Jealous suspicions. He told himself there was no need for them, that Martha barely tolerated Sackville. She was probably just being polite in spending time with him.

He could not find her in the garden. He made his way toward the brook. She was not on the bridge. He crossed over into the lane.

In a shaded nook beside the lane, he came upon Martha and Sackville. Martha and Sackville, arms encircling each other.

For a moment, Dudley did not understand what he was seeing. Then Martha noticed him, gasped, and leapt back behind her uniformed companion. Sackville glanced up, and his face split into a sheepish grin.

"Rather embarrassing, I'm afraid," the officer said, chuckling.

Dudley could not speak. He felt a constriction in his chest. His jealousy was justified after all. Martha's professed devotion to him was false, maybe always had been.

"You lied to me," he said to her.

Sackville frowned. "See here, what's this all about?"

"Couldn't keep your hands off her, eh, Sackville?" Dudley snapped, temper flaring. He took a step forward.

Sackville's face reddened. "I don't care for your tone of voice, sir."

Dudley ignored him and advanced on Martha, thrusting his uncle's letters out to her.

"I was going to Cambridge, Martha. Here is my acceptance!" Crumpling the letters, he cast them at her feet. Martha recoiled from him, tears rolling down her stricken face.

He felt a hand on his chest. The hand pushed hard, shoving him backward. Close to his ear, Sackville murmured, "Stay back, old boy."

Dudley reacted without thinking. His left fist smashed deep into Sackville's middle, then his right struck the officer full in the face. Sackville stumbled backward. His legs became entangled in his sword, and he toppled into the brush.

He did not wait to see what Sackville would do. Turning on his heels, he strode back the way he had come, along the lane and across the bridge. Martha called after him, but Dudley did not look back.

Sackville did not give chase. Martha may have held him back. Dudley assumed she had still meant to marry him, keeping her little fling secret. Such a marriage was impossible now. He was alone and betrayed.

As Highwood Hall receded behind him, he asked himself, *What am I to do now?*

When he reached the Black Horse, he found the answer waiting.

The sign showed a black horse rising on its hind legs. Beneath the signpost was the recruiting sergeant, a drummer boy on his right, a corporal and two privates on his left. They all wore elaborate uniforms, though none looked as splendid as the sergeant. The sergeant wore a scarlet double-breasted coatee, and a slung brass-hilted sword hung at his side. Perched on his head was a round forage cap with no peak, and attached to the cap was a little cockade of bright ribbons that fluttered in the breeze.

The sergeant stood on a crate above a small crowd of village and country lads, offering a description of military life. He emphasized its good pay, attractive uniforms, the ample pension on discharge, and spoke of the glory and horrors of war. Dudley joined the audience and felt almost drunk on the decision he was about to make. He hung on the sergeant's words, knowing that much of what the man said was exaggeration but not caring.

"I want able-bodied men of fine limb and martial aspect," the sergeant announced, "from five feet eight upwards, and not over thirty years of age. All must be of good character and free from any disease, blemish, or impediment. They must be fit to dig trenches and throw up breastworks, to work at a fortress, or haul big guns into position. They must have the courage to mount the scaling ladders and charge through a breach when storming a fort or citadel. They must be able to fight single-handed with the Indians, or capture the sword of the czar or the Great Mogul himself when so commanded.

"I want no lubbers, mind, but gallant fellows with strength, heroic minds and endurance, ready to volunteer for the greatest danger. Lads who will go anywhere, to freeze to death in Siberia, or to simmer on the burning sands of Arabia."

The sergeant smiled under his neat mustache, and his merry eyes twinkled as he described these adventures. Adventures, hardships and glory, just as Dudley had imagined in his boyhood games with Wellington and his tin comrades.

"Now, boys," the recruiting sergeant continued, "who'll enlist for this and a great deal more? You'll get double pay, double clothing, tools for nothing, superior bedding of long feathers, three square meals a day and two holidays a week. The army will teach you everything you need to know, such as how to turn properly on your heels and toes and to stand as stiff as starch. We'll teach you all the useful marches—the goose step, the balance step, the side step, the quick step and the slow step. We'll teach you how to step before the commanding officer if you misbehave, and how to step into the black hole if you don't act as a soldier and a gentleman should."

With this last, he stood even taller and straighter, and his comrades, including the drummer boy, all frowned and nodded to each other.

"Now, boys," the sergeant said, "I am ready to enlist as many of you as want to join, and treat you as gentlemen. There is no compulsion. You must all be free and willing. Remember that the regiment I am enlisting for is among the bravest and most honourable in the Service, with the best officers in the British Army. Why, did you know that the Royal Hampshire Fusiliers—or the Royal Hants, as we all like to call ourselves—fought the French in Spain? That they charged the breach at Badajoz, and stood with Lord Wellington at Salamanca, Vittoria, and then at Waterloo? It's a long history of guts and glory you'll be inheriting, and I can't help but give three cheers for it! Hip-hip…"

"Hurrah! Hurrah!" the corporal and privates cried. Those gathered, Dudley included, could not help getting caught up in the spirit, and all cried the last "Hurrah!" together.

"And God Bless Her Majesty, Queen Victoria," the sergeant added, stepping down from his crate. "Anyone who wishes to take her sacred shilling, follow me into the Black Horse. There I have a table prepared and a few mugs for those interested."

Inside the taproom, the sergeant moved to a table under a window and sat. His uniformed companions stood behind him. From a valise, he took a sheet of paper, an ink bottle and a pen.

A few of the country lads had the courage to venture inside, but they hung back, undecided. One, a chubby fellow with a bit of drool dribbling down his chin, turned to Dudley and said, "I always fancied I'd make a good soldier. But what would my ol' ma say to that?"

Dudley did not reply. He thought of Martha, conjured an image of her smile, her eyes, her hair, her lips. The pain that stabbed through his heart seemed to propel him forward, toward the sergeant.

"Sergeant," he said, "I want to enlist in the Royal Hants."

The sergeant grinned at him and exclaimed, "Bravo! You are just the young lad I want! Upon my reputation, there is not a gentleman in the three kingdoms does me greater honour than yourself by selecting the Royal Hants for your career. And you're obviously an educated fellow. I have no doubt you will attain the highest rung in the ladder of promotion, or the highest rung on the scaling ladder."

The sergeant told Dudley to sign his name on the form on the table. Then he rose to his feet and said solemnly, "Hold out your right hand and answer me this: are you free, willing and able to serve Her Majesty Queen Victoria, her heirs and successors, for a period of twenty-one years, or until your legal discharge?"

Dudley took one deep breath, let it out, and said, "I am."

With that, the sergeant placed something cool in Dudley's hand, saying, "I give you this in the name of the queen. You are now bound to her service."

Dudley looked at his hand, saw the significant shilling. He did not know what to say or think. He had at last made an active move toward his future, but had turned his back on the life that he knew. Turned his back on his uncle, on Cambridge, on Martha.

"Wake up, lad," the sergeant cried, chuckling and clapping Dudley on the back, "though I know it's hard not to be in awe. After all, you're a soldier now!"

Four others enlisted in Dudley's wake. The sergeant then led his catch into a back room where an army doctor waited to approve their physical appearance. As the examinations were taking place, Dudley experienced a moment of panic. What had he done? This was nothing but a fantasy, and he had just enlisted for twenty-one years! And in the ranks!

But it was too late for second thoughts. The Queen's shilling was in his pocket, jingling against the tin form of Wellington. He had chosen his life, and now he would have to live it. As a soldier.

———※———

The next morning at ten o'clock, the sergeant took his five recruits before a magistrate and had them sworn in. The recruits then had the remainder of the day to themselves to pack what they thought they would need and to sever whatever ties they had to their old life. Tomorrow, they would leave for the regimental depot in Fairbridge.

Dudley felt a mixture of excitement and dread. The excitement was at the prospect of grand adventures like those he had always wished for. Then he would remember Martha, and his spirits would plummet. She had driven him to service in the ranks. Dread would set upon him at the thought of those twenty-one years—twenty-one years of possible hardship and deprivation. Life could be cruel for a private soldier.

Yet it was not fair to blame his decision on Martha. He had enlisted as an escape. An escape from the pain of his discovery of her and Sackville. An escape from a path in life that he had never wanted to follow in the first place. Martha, by her betrayal, had not driven him to anything. Her actions had instead removed her from the original portrait of his future, and without her, that portrait was lifeless. There had been no other option but to pursue his dream.

In his room at the Black Horse, he examined his reflection in the mirror. A young man of nineteen, just over five feet, eight inches tall, with a slight build, thick blond hair, a boyish face— perhaps too boyish to be handsome. What kind of a soldier would he make?

"A damn good one," he stated.

That was his goal. He would be as good a soldier as he could.

Though, with that determination, he was left wondering just what he meant. What elements were necessary for being a good soldier? He considered the regiments he had seen marching through the village, or parading on the green, drums beating and bands playing. Regiments of steady men, moving as one when called to, their clothes and accoutrements gleaming just as the recruiting sergeant's had. To Dudley, they had looked like good soldiers. Men who knew their drill, who knew their duty, who understood discipline, who would uphold the values of Great Britain. Men who had reason to feel pride in what they did.

Then there were the many stories he had read and heard. Tales of great feats of arms from before Wellington's day and later. Tales of the soldier's loyalty to his sovereign and comrades, his sense of honour, his fighting spirit. Dudley had recently met an officer at the Black Horse who had told such tales.

The man had described the events of the Afghan revolt of a decade ago. The 44th Regiment had stood alone at Gandamak, surrounded by crazed rebels, fighting on to the last man. The courage of soldiers who could do such a thing—fight on without hope of rescue—had made an impression on Dudley. In his judgment, there was considerable glory in such a defeat. Those soldiers had retained their dignity, remembered their training, and had not given up.

"If I ever have to confront death or defeat," he said as he faced his reflection, "I hope I shall confront it as those men did—unflinching."

Perhaps he did not understand what he was saying. His notions of soldiering were, after all, mostly the gatherings of a child. It was possible he did not have the faintest idea as to what made a good soldier.

Well, that was of no consequence, he decided. He would soon learn.

He bid goodbye to his friends and acquaintances at the Black Horse. It had not taken long for the news to spread that William Dudley, former tutor to Highwood Hall, had enlisted in the army. Everyone was curious about that remarkable decision, and Dudley explained that he had always wanted to be a soldier. Some responded with encouragement, while others did not know what to make of it. A few thought he had made an absurd mistake. These last Dudley did his best to ignore or forgive. He did not need to be told he had been foolhardy.

Later in the evening, he returned to his room and packed a few belongings in a shoulder bag—books, stockings, an extra blanket, his toilet case. He did not need much, for the army would provide him with the essentials. When he had finished, he looked over the room in which he would sleep one last time.

There was no need to be sentimental, for he had been at the Black Horse for a scant fourteen months. It seemed like no time at all since his arrival last summer. He remembered the excitement of that event, of leaving the home he had come to know and venturing out into the world. Or so he had seen it at the time. The fact was, he had only moved a few miles away, had not even left the county.

To become a tutor, of course, had been his uncle's suggestion. A suggestion after the fact, since his uncle had made the appointment without consultation. He had told Dudley after the arrangements had been concluded.

Uncle Robert was an imposing figure, with the inherent strength of the preacher-turned-schoolmaster. He was confident, authoritative, a man who believed he knew what was best for others. He believed in punishing those who did not live up to

16

their potential, but he was not a cruel man. He believed in the purity of the human soul. He displayed kindness to those who worked to better themselves in a manner congruent with his conceptions.

Dudley remembered the interview in his uncle's darkened study. A heavy spring rain had been drumming a constant tattoo on the roof and windows. He had entered the study not knowing what he was about to hear.

Uncle Robert had sat in his leather chair, the air about his head thick with tobacco smoke from his heavy mahogany pipe. He had worn the tiniest hint of a smile on his thin lips.

"Sit, my boy," he had commanded and, as Dudley had taken the other leather chair, added, "though perhaps I should not call you 'my boy,' anymore. You're a young man now, William. You're eighteen. It is time that you embarked on a career of your own."

Always uncomfortable with this subject, Dudley had forced a smile and had replied, "I believe so, sir." In fact, he had felt it was past time.

"Yes, it is high time," his uncle had continued. "In light of this fact, I have secured for you a very respectable position with a Mr. Wilkes, an old friend of mine from my own school days. You shall be tutor to his young son, Master Jeremy. The term shall begin in September."

This had been a startling announcement, though Dudley's surprise had not been without joy.

"Thank you, Uncle Robert. That is…stupendous news!"

His uncle's face had glowed with pleasure at that response. "I am glad that you think so. The position is for one year. Now, we have spoken of Cambridge, and I shall work towards securing you a placement there. We have also spoken of pursuing the law, and we shall continue with that possibility. But after Cambridge we shall see what really strikes your fancy, hmm?"

This had been his way of telling Dudley he was free to choose his own life after all.

"Perhaps the bar will suit you, or perhaps the clergy. At any rate, we shall see. We shall see."

Dudley had liked that last statement. *We shall see.* First, he would have a year of employment, followed by a lifetime of possibilities.

The day of departure had arrived a few weeks after the meeting in the study. Dudley packed his trunk, arranged to have a few pieces of furniture sent on after him, then said his farewells. His aunt hugged him long and hard, just as she had embraced her eldest sons when they had left home. He shook his uncle's hand. His favourite cousin, Jane, kissed him and wished him good luck.

Then he and his trunk piled into a chaise that was attached to an aged pony and driven by the son of a local farmer. The pony strained and moved forward, and the chaise began to roll up the lane. Dudley's family stood waving as if he were going off to sea, or to India or some other distant colony.

He had shared that sense of great adventure, if only because this was a new experience. There had also been the added fascination, both wicked and thrilling, of living over a public house. That his uncle would ever suggest such an arrangement seemed incredible.

But the Black Horse had not proven to be so wicked after all. It was just the center where the villagers gathered to gossip, and a depot for the Royal Mail. He had even discovered that he enjoyed a pint of something before going to bed.

All in all, not much had changed from his life at home. He had not even had to prepare his meals, for the landlady usually provided that service. In fact, life became less exciting than before, for he missed his old friends and his relatives. Meeting Martha had been the only genuine adventure of his tutorship.

Now that his position had ended, maybe it was appropriate that his association with Martha should have ended as well, though it would not be so easy to forget her, to forget the dominant factor in his recent life.

He tried to keep his mind on other subjects, and concentrated on the task of storing whatever items of clothing he would no longer need, putting them away in his trunk. But Martha stayed with him. He could not help reliving his most prized moments with her, torturing himself with the memory.

There was a sharp rapping on the door, bringing him back to the present. He crossed the floor and undid the latch, expecting the landlady with his dinner. He instead found himself face-to-face with Martha, as if she had emerged from his imagination.

For a moment, he wanted to slam the door, but the impulse quickly passed. In his indignation, he did not want to talk to her but knew it was good she had come. If she had not, his last memory of her would have been of the episode with Sackville. After their time together, such an abrupt finish would never have satisfied him. There needed to be explanations on both sides.

"Good evening, Martha," he said.

"Is it true?" she asked, incredulous. "You've enlisted in the army?"

"Yes, I have. I have joined the Royal Hampshire Fusiliers, one of the finest regiments in the service."

"But how could you do such a thing? *Why* would you do such a thing?"

"Why would I do such a thing?" he cried. "How can you ask such a question after what you have done. After betraying me?"

"Betraying you? But it was innocent," she insisted, wringing her hands. "Simply an innocent display of affection…I…I don't know why…"

Tears welled in her eyes, and Dudley felt his anger diminish, his heart softening. He opened the door wider, beckoning her inside and showing her to a chair. He closed the door and sat at his writing desk.

"So, your rendezvous was innocent," he said. "Very well. I will attempt to be calm and reasonable and not put this in the worst possible terms. Those terms being that you would marry me, yet continue to have little trysts behind my back. Use me, in other words, for whatever purpose, though such a purpose eludes me right now.

"What I will say is this simple truth, which is enough to end our presumed engagement—I am not as important to you as I thought I was, and I cannot marry someone who will not give

19

me that devotion." He paused, then added, "What man would, under the circumstances?"

"But it was not how it must have seemed to you," she replied. "You must allow me to explain myself. I was confused—Jonathan said so many confusing things. It was simply a mistake."

"No explanation you can offer will excuse your actions, and that is that."

Martha bit her lip and would not meet his eye. "So, you will never forgive me?"

"Would you forgive *me*?" She did not answer that, so he said, "At any rate, nothing can be changed now. Don't you understand that? I've been uncertain all my life about what I want to do, and now I'm doing something. I've taken the Queen's shilling. My decision cannot be rescinded."

He studied her face, her exquisite face, her mouth drawn down in anguish. Perhaps her distress was every bit as great as his. He knew that, in the days to come, he would long for her, and that was dreadful to contemplate. He could not bear to lose her, but it was too late. She did not understand the finality of what he had done.

He leaned forward and took her hand, whispering, "I'm to go away, and not just to Cambridge. I could very well be posted as far away as Africa, or India."

"But I love you," she insisted.

He squeezed her warm flesh, remembering that day when they had kissed. He remembered it with regret and sorrow. He would never have that with her again.

"Maybe you do love me, in an odd sort of way," he said. How could she possibly expect him to forgive her? "I don't know. But things can't be how we thought they would be. That's a simple fact."

"Then it's goodbye," Martha whispered.

"Yes," he answered, standing. He looked down at her and said, "Goodbye, Martha."

She said nothing more. Composing herself, she rose from her chair, moved to the door and left.

Dudley watched her from his window, saw her climb into the gig that waited in the yard. He watched as it began to move, bumping away toward her home.

When the gig had disappeared, a wave of anger more intense than he had ever known washed over him. He wanted to scream, to smash the window, tear the bed apart, splinter his desk and chairs into kindling. Pounding his fists on the desktop, he told himself he could not have controlled what had happened. He could not change the course of events. And why should he really want to?

When the anger subsided, he slumped in his chair. He realized there was another painful task that had to be completed before the morning. He had arranged to have his few furnishings transported back to his uncle's house. He would have to write a letter to go with them.

Taking his pen, he dipped it in ink and collected his thoughts. "My Dear Sir," he wrote. "It is with great pleasure that I write to you with my news, though it is also with great misgivings. I fear that my motivation in this matter may not be readily comprehensible, that my judgment may be called into question."

He sighed and set down his pen. He could think of no possible way to help his uncle understand his actions.

"Uncle will never understand what I have done," he muttered. "Though he will have to accept it."

He snatched up his pen and finished the letter.

# CHAPTER TWO

Who is the happy Warrior?
Who is he
That every man in arms
should wish to be?

William Wordsworth
"Character of the Happy Warrior"

***The five recruits*** marched north along the turnpike, following the hawthorn hedges and tollbooths. An ancient staff sergeant served as their escort, a stooped and wizened fellow with enormous gray side whiskers and a spotless uniform that looked as if it had just come from the tailor.

"Call me Fair Willy," he told his charges. "That is what my comrades called me and continue to call me, for every man in the regiment knows that my words are fair and true."

The sergeant chattered as they walked, entertaining the youths with soul-stirring tales of his service under Lord Wellington in the Peninsula. Dudley listened and tried to forget about Martha, telling himself there was no need to dwell on the misfortunes of his past. His career as a soldier was off to a favourable beginning.

22

They came within sight of the regimental depot just after noon. The depot was on the outskirts of the town of Fairbridge, squatting in a barren field to the left of the road. It was a square enclosure of rectangular buildings built of red brick, each five stories tall with rows of white-trimmed windows. Narrow and blackened chimneys sprouted from the gray slate rooftops, and the place seemed anything but cheerful, despite Fair Willy's joyful exclamations.

"Your new home for the next six months, gents," he declared. "And before I settle you in, there are a few things I should tell you.

"There are two simple rules about barrack life. First, if a comrade's wife is in need of water or coal, or is about to go get it, volunteer to fetch it for her. Second, lend a helping hand to a sergeant, corporal or comrade without having to be asked. If you do this, you will have a host of friends and your name will circulate amongst the NCOs and officers. Hence, promotion. As well, you will become a boon to your Queen and country, and an everlasting monument of glory to your friends and relatives.

"It is my opinion that a man who does nothing extra and is always drawing a line to say where his rights lie will never be a success. Such a person will never be a commander—nor a master tradesman for that matter, nor a discoverer in science, nor a propounder of philosophy. You mark my words, young fellows, for I've lived a long and eventful life, and know this to be fact."

Dudley nodded and decided he would follow that advice, to always help those in need. To this, he added another clause—never complain, no matter how difficult or miserable the situation became.

But even as these thoughts entered his head, he understood their irony. Here he was, making these noble promises to himself, yet in reality he had not made the best of his situation. He had *fled* his situation, in effect betraying his uncle's wishes, ignoring his uncle's efforts to secure him a place at St. John's College.

"Ye look troubled, lad," the sergeant said, iron-gray brows meeting over his bulbous nose.

23

"Something *is* troubling me, Sergeant," Dudley admitted. "I was just thinking of how I've not followed your advice in the past."

The sergeant clapped him on the back. "Then there's no better time to start."

Dudley nodded again. The sergeant was right. There was only one course of action—recognize his hypocrisy and never repeat it.

The recruits came to an arched gateway in the nearest barrack building, the one that bordered the road. Set into the wall above the gate was a shield bearing the flaming grenade badge of the Royal Hampshire Fusiliers, tricked out in gold paint with a green border. Beside the gate stood a sentry, and when he saw the recruiting sergeant, he snapped to attention.

"Go right on in, Sergeant."

Fair Willy nodded and led the recruits into a dark brick tunnel with an arched ceiling. A moment later, Dudley and the others emerged to find themselves standing on the edge of a wide courtyard. This was the parade ground, he assumed.

Fair Willy beckoned them to the left, to a plain white wooden door adjacent to the tunnel entrance.

"Here is the orderly room," he told them. "And here is where I leave you, with the best of luck."

He saluted. With that, Fair Willy was gone.

For Dudley the next few hours were a whirlwind. The he recruits entered the depot, the staff sergeant led them to the orderly room and wished them good luck. After he had departed, the recruits received both a second medical examination and a haircut. An orderly corporal then took them out to the parade square. The square had been empty, but now it was becoming crowded with a growing host of other recruits, a shapeless gaggle of young and middle-aged men. Dudley noticed that most of those gathered wore filthy rags, and had sallow complexions and stooped shoulders. They were men of the working classes and the poor who had joined the army in desperation.

The regimental sergeant-major appeared and introduced himself as RSM Maclaren. He was a tall man with a barrel chest, oddly slender legs and a small round head like a cannonball. A thick comb of mustache obscured his mouth until he opened it to speak, and when he spoke his voice was a practiced baritone, thick and melodic and demanding attention. He welcomed the assembled recruits to the Fairbridge depot and explained that they would now form temporary companies.

Upon this declaration, a gang of sergeants waded into the mass of confused newcomers, shouting and pushing them into three large groups. Corporals took charge of smaller sections of each group and led them off the parade to the barracks.

A fellow named Corporal Trump took Dudley's section to Barrack Room Number Ten. Trump introduced himself as their barrack-room commander. He was the opposite to Maclaren, small and wiry, his arms a bit too long for his torso, his round face clean-shaven and apple-cheeked.

He said, "Now, there are twenty-four bunks in this here room, and only twenty of you. When we go in, I want you each to stand still next to one of them beds. Questions?"

There were none, so the new men filed in, coughing and muttering and cracking quiet jokes to hide their nervousness.

The room was rectangular, its walls whitewashed and the floor made of unfinished planks. Near the door was a potbellied stove, and in the far wall were a fireplace and two deep-set windows. Twelve folding bunks stood against either side wall. In the aisle between the bunks were two trestle tables.

Dudley chose a bunk and stood next to it. No longer would he have the comfort of a room to himself. From this moment on, he would live in a space less than six feet long and three feet wide, with a shelf and three pegs on which to hang his meagre belongings.

"The spot you have chosen," Corporal Trump said from the front of the room, "is yours for as long as you're stationed here. Except for you," he said to a man next to him. "That place is mine, and I'm afraid you'll have to move."

25

There were a few chuckles as the recruit obeyed, moving to an unclaimed bunk near the back.

"Good," Trump continued. "Now, stay here for the next few minutes and get to know one another. I'll be back in a few minutes for tea."

Once the corporal had left, Dudley turned to the fellow on his right and extended his hand.

"Hello, my name is William Dudley."

The fellow took the hand and shook it.

"Reginald Harris. Pleased to make your acquaintance, sir."

Dudley studied the man for a minute. He had a slight build, pale thinning hair and a narrow face. Unlike most of the other recruits, he stood erect, alert; and his coat, though a bit worn, was of good quality and fit well. He also carried a small bundle with him that, by its angular shape, contained books.

"You are a reader, Mr. Harris?" Dudley asked.

"Yes. Yes, I am. Of poetry, generally. I am an admirer of Blake and Shelley in particular, though you will observe that the two are very different."

"That they are," Dudley agreed. Here, it seemed, was another educated fellow, perhaps a bit down on his luck. Though he did not know the man, he felt an instant kinship.

"Rather Spartan accommodations," Harris said, glancing around the room, "though I should be thankful. A roof and four walls and three meals a day are more than many men have. More than some of these fellows have ever had, God bless them."

The other recruits were hanging up their coats or arranging the scanty contents of their pockets on the shelves above their bunks. Harris began to remove the books and other belongings from his sack. Dudley reached into his coat pocket and took out his tin soldier. Placing it on his shelf, he murmured so no one could hear him, "Well, Wellington, here is your new post. Guard it well."

At ten o'clock, a bugle sounded "lights out," and every man took to his bunk. The only lamps still burning in the depot were those in the orderly room. The clerks there had an extra fifteen minutes to finish the day's burden of paperwork.

26

Dudley lay on his back, blanket up to his chin, and stared at the gray smudge of the whitewashed ceiling. His iron-frame bunk was as narrow as a child's bed, the straw mattress thin and full of lumps. Around him were the sounds of a room full of men at night: shuffling, bedsprings creaking, smacking of lips, muttering, snoring. A young recruit was talking to his mother in his sleep.

Dudley felt as if he were back in his school dormitory, surrounded by the other children. There had always been those who would call for their mothers in the night.

He rolled onto his side, the bed groaning even under his trim weight. He knew how those children had felt, how the young recruit felt. Unwanted images of Martha haunted him, though he understood that losing her was not the only cause of his depression and loneliness. He had enlisted without the knowledge or sanction of anyone. Not his uncle Robert, not his auntie Bronwyn, not Jane nor any of his other cousins. There had been no goodbye kisses on the doorstep, no hopeful prayers or wishes, and no one to wave as he set off for Fairbridge.

His sole consolation was that he had posted his letter to his uncle. Maybe there would be a positive response after all. At least his family would finally know what had happened.

He closed his eyes and tried to relax, but his mind was racing. He worried about his uncle. He worried about the morning and what it would bring.

It was long after midnight before he fell asleep.

<hr />

The chirping of a bugle announced the beginning of Dudley's first day in the army.

"Right! Up, you lot!" Corporal Trump growled as he struggled out of his bedclothes. "Quick visit to the latrine, then I want a volunteer to fetch water for washing."

Dudley wanted to volunteer to fetch water, but Trump chose another who spoke up first. As the fellow scurried off, Dudley sat on the edge of his bed. It was five o'clock and still dark, and he watched the dim shapes of the other men, all fighting to shrug off sleep.

Corporal Trump lit the room's two candles, and everyone received a jolt of energy, Dudley included. The water buckets arrived, and the recruits washed and dressed. Corporal Trump then showed them how to make their beds.

"You'll be doing this every morning," he said, "and I'll be inspecting you, as will the orderly sergeant. Now, that's not quite right, there, soldier. Do it like this.

"Right. When the bugle sounds again, that'll be fall out for drill, in which case you'll all fall out for drill. Any questions?"

Drill was at six o'clock. The recruits from each barrack room filed onto the parade and settled into their companies. Dudley's was No. 3 Company. The others were Nos. 2 and 4. For no apparent reason, there was no No. 1 Company.

Sergeant-Major Maclaren stood as straight as a flagstaff before the three clumps of recruits. In a voice that filled the parade from one brick wall to the other, he shouted, "Tell off into squads."

The drill instructors split the companies into squads of eight or ten men. An instructor then led each squad to a different part of the parade. Dudley's unit followed a sergeant into a corner. The sergeant told them to halt and all face in the same direction.

"Right. My name is Sergeant Wellman," he said. Like Maclaren, he was the perfect picture of a soldier, back straight, uniform spotless and blond mustache trim, though Dudley thought he detected a look of eager hunger in the man's deep-set eyes. "Some of you may know me. Be that as it may, you won't get any favouritism. You're all recruits, and you're all equally ignorant in the eyes of the British Army. You know nothing!

"But I am here to remedy that situation! I am here to instruct you in a few basic matters of drill. It will all sound like bloody nonsense to you at first, but by the end of this hour and a half, it'll be second nature to you all. Keep in mind that the Royal Hants is one of the steadiest regiments in the service. We'll see you through, no matter how hard the next few months get."

From his inside coat pocket, Wellman produced a little wooden case. From the case, he took a piece of chalk. He then marked the toe of each man's right shoe with a large chalk cross.

This was for those who did not know their right from their left, which was Wellman's first lesson. His second lesson was the "position of a soldier."

"When you stand in this position," he lectured, "you are at attention. You will not look around with your head or eyes. You will not twitch. You will not speak, mutter, or utter the smallest unnatural sound."

So the morning went. Sergeant Wellman, with a mixture of firmness and patience, taught them how to stand at ease and how to ask their instructor questions. He then showed them how to dress in a line as infantrymen.

"The tallest men on the flanks," he said, "and shortest in the middle. That way you all look imposing, see? This here is how you'll march in line and into battle, at close order. Standing together like a band of noble brothers, each fellow touching the elbows of his comrades. And when you move forward, you'll move like an unbroken wall of men, a wall that no enemy can withstand."

These were impressive words, but Dudley knew he and his comrades had a long road to travel before they became such stern and steady warriors. They would have to learn to stand in a line with the enemy's fire raining down on them. To hold their ground and not run. That was their goal, for steadiness and discipline were the keys to victory, to life or death. A soldier had to kill the enemy while standing and ignoring the possibility of his own destruction.

How did that feel, Dudley wondered, to know that you had killed a man, another soldier with the same hopes and dreams of glory you had yourself?

The distress that question caused him was startling. He did not want to have to think about it. But he knew he had to, for it was part of being a soldier. If he was to keep his vow to be the best soldier he could, he would have to learn to face death. Death for his enemy, for his comrades, and for himself.

But he could not do that here, on the parade square. Only the actual moment, only the heat of battle, would prove or disprove his courage. Until then, he would have to concentrate on his drill and learn all the proper military procedures. Until war, he could ask no more of himself.

For the next five days, the recruits followed the same schedule: reveille at five, make beds, inspection, roll call, drill, breakfast, drill, dinner, drill, tea. Dudley began to hear parade commands in his sleep. He worried that he was not performing as well as he should. He began to dread making mistakes and having to hear the instructor scream his name in reprimand.

In the evenings, he calmed his nerves in either the depot recreation room, the soldiers' library or the barrack canteen. The canteen was by far the most popular spot for most of the recruits. A common phrase heard at the depot was that the recreation room and library were fine places, but one could not buy a drink in either. Even Dudley found himself going to the canteen more often than the other facilities, in keeping with the comforting habit he had developed at the Black Horse.

The canteen always held a mixture of drab recruits and uniformed veterans. The air was close, and a gray fog of tobacco smoke clung to the low ceiling. Dim oil lamps provided the only illumination. Chairs and benches flanking tables gave the men a place to sit, and there was a long bar at the back of the room. The bar was the home of the regiment's unofficial mascot, Blacky the raven. The bartender, Corporal Denny, was also the raven's keeper.

Dudley had seen Blacky fly about the room, land on shoulders and dip his beak in a mug or two. Some found this annoying, and they had forced Corporal Denny to confine his pet to a wire cage.

On Dudley's sixth evening in Fairbridge, he sat in the canteen with Reginald Harris, who had become his constant companion. Noticing the raven in its cage, Dudley commented, "I wonder if the bird really can talk?"

"So they have told us," Harris said. "But they know how gullible recruits can be."

Dudley wanted to find out, so he went to the bar and peered into the cage. The raven met his eye with one of its own beady black jewels and said, "Beer."

Dudley laughed. "So, it's true. He does speak."

"He's a friendly sort of crow," said Corporal Denny, big-nosed and bird-like himself. "Maybe he's axin' for your drink."

Dudley put his hand over his mug. "He's not going to get it."

"Ax him who's got the fattest arse in the regiment!" Denny said, excited. "Go on. Don't be shy, mate."

Dudley saw this was a joke directed at one of the other veterans, and he was curious to know the answer. He peered into the cage again and said, "Blacky, who has the fattest arse in the regiment?"

"Lance-Corporal Lloyd," Blacky stated. "Lance-Corporal Lloyd."

The men at the bar, all uniformed NCOs, burst into laughter. Dudley laughed as well, though he had never heard of Lance-Corporal Lloyd.

One veteran was not laughing—a red-faced man with a single white chevron on his upper-right sleeve. The fellow pushed past the others to stand in front of Dudley, then demanded, "Who the bloody hell do you think you are, laughin' at that, ye friggin' recruit. What's your name?"

Dudley's smile faded. "Private William Dudley, Lance-Corporal."

"Private bloody second class," Lloyd sneered. Then, before Dudley could react, he poured the contents of his mug over Dudley's shoes. Now it was his turn to laugh, and he declared, "That's what I call a fine joke!"

The others shared his delight in humiliating this recruit in civilian clothes. Dudley ignored their laughter and looked at his shoes, at the beer beading on the leather. His ears burned as they always did when he knew shame or humiliation. Or anger.

Fists clenched, he took a step forward. The smile on Lloyd's pockmarked face became a sneer.

"Just you try it, mate," the lance-corporal hissed. Behind him, the other veterans overcame their mirth and glared at this recruit who dared to threaten one of their own. Even Corporal

Denny, who had been so friendly a moment before, frowned in disapproval.

"Unfortunately," Dudley replied, unclenching his hands, "you have the law on your side, Lance-Corporal. Something for you to hide behind."

He turned his back. Partly he hoped that Lloyd would be moved to action by his remark, attack him in some way. He thought he would be justified in defending himself. But the lance-corporal let him go.

"Good thing you didn't hit him," someone at his side said. It was Corporal Trump. "Fighting with the older men, and you just in your first week of training. The colonel would have flogged you for sure, and pegged you as a wild one. A man to be broken."

"I thought as much," Dudley said. He had come close to committing one of the serious crimes in the army—striking a man of superior rank.

Trump nodded and moved off. Dudley waded back to his table.

"I saw that fellow spill his drink on you," Harris said. "It looked as if you wanted to kill him. I suppose it's good you did nothing."

"Yes, fighting in the barrack canteen would not have done me any good," Dudley understated. He was relieved he had managed to control his temper.

"You could have been injured," Harris went on. "These rough fellows are used to fighting, brawling in the gutter with their bare hands."

"I'm no stranger to fighting myself," Dudley confessed, "and of being in trouble because of it."

Harris seemed surprised. "Oh, really?"

Dudley did not elaborate, though he remembered one incident well. As a quiet and reflective child, he had been a natural target for bullies. A group of older boys at his uncle's school had decided to torment him. At first, Dudley had either run or submitted to their torture, but the continued harassment had eventually become too much to bear.

He had decided to attack, to strike out with his fists, a tactic that had astonished him with its effectiveness. He had won the respect of his tormentors, and the torment had ended.

He had also won the disapproval of the master of the school. He remembered his uncle's stern reproach, huge brows drawn down as he shook his head and said, "Fighting in the dirt like some common urchin—that will simply not do. Not for a Dudley or a Mason. Not for anyone, I might add. Fighting is the resort of beasts, William, of creatures that cannot settle their differences by reasonable means."

"But soldiers fight," Dudley had protested.

"Do you presume to question me, boy?" his uncle had cried. "Do you?"

Dudley had looked at his feet, concentrating on the buckles on his shoes.

"No, sir."

"Soldiers fight, indeed! That may be so. But soldiers are a necessary evil, my boy. A necessary evil but an evil, nonetheless, for their sole purpose in life is to make war, and war is destruction. I shall admit that Wellington is, indeed, a great man, and I know how you esteem him, my boy, but even he would not approve of your wrestling in the dirt. He fought to depose a tyrant who would not listen to reason."

For a moment, Uncle Robert had paused in his tirade, as if aware he was on the cusp of self-contradiction. He saved himself, declaring, "What is most important, Master William, is that you are not a soldier, nor shall you ever *be* a soldier."

Now Dudley was a soldier, and he was still encountering bullies. He looked over his shoulder, back towards the bar. The veterans there seemed to have forgotten him. To them, he had been just another of the recruits, someone who had not yet proved his worth and was thus worth nothing, a creature without rights.

"I almost believe they wanted to get me in trouble," he said. "Maybe breaking recruits is a pastime of theirs. Well, I will not play their game, Harris."

Harris lit his clay pipe, drew on it and blew a jet of gray smoke.

"I believe you're right. This army wants disciplined men who will follow orders. Perhaps scenes like this one of yours are an informal part of that discipline. To cow one into obedience."

"I am not cowed," Dudley stated, feeling his anger rise again. "I am simply following the rules. Those men tried to bait me into a fight, the blackguards, or use me as an excuse to exercise their puny authority."

"To force you to obey the rules in any circumstance, then, if you don't like the term *cowed*. And it worked. You didn't fight, even though you wanted to, because the man was of a superior rank."

Dudley pondered that for a moment. "You're right. But I don't have to like it or agree with it. We're supposed to be professional soldiers, a body of fighting men whose obligations are to each other. I believe that a soldier in any army has to know how to conduct himself properly, with honour. We are men of the Queen, pledged to uphold Britain's ideals of fairness and justice, and British justice is the best in the world." He nodded towards the bar. "That fellow with the fat arse and his friends didn't behave with justice towards me."

"Don't worry, old fellow," Harris reassured, "I'm sure they didn't mean it personally."

There was no drill parade for Dudley's company the next morning. Instead, the quartermaster issued the men their kit. This event could not have come at a better time for Dudley, for he was still smarting from the incident in the canteen. Maybe once he had a uniform, he would feel more like a soldier and less like a recruit.

The kit was extensive. The dress coatee was red, its buttonholes decorated with white lace, its collar and cuffs dark blue. The undress jacket was similar, though of waist length and without lace. There were two pairs of trousers, one dark blue and one gray tweed, and two caps. One of the caps was the stovepipe-shaped "Albert" shako, while the other was the round forage cap with no peak. There were also accoutrements: belts, pouches, knapsack, camp equipment and so on. Finally, the armoury issued each man a three-sided, seventeen-inch socket bayonet and an 1842-pattern "Brown Bess" smoothbore mus-

ket. The musket was heavy, outdated, and still the main arma-
ment of the British Army.

The morning of the first dress parade dawned crisp and
cool, unseasonable for August. Dudley awoke before the chirping of the bugle, and cried, "Good morning, gentlemen. It's
time for our first day as real soldiers." It was his most cheerful
moment since arriving at Fairbridge.

There was not so much idle time now. After washing, and
making their beds, the recruits had to shine their kit and dress
for parade. Dudley's Auntie Bronwyn had been fastidious about
personal cleanliness and grooming, so this was nothing new for
him. He polished his shoes, brushed his coatee and trousers,
chalked his waist belt a smooth white and shined its brass locket
front and back.

When he had finished dressing, he grinned at Harris in
satisfaction. Instead of returning the grin, Harris stared back in
panic. Harris could not get his stock—a leather neckband that
fitted inside the collar—to fasten.

"Let me get that for you," Dudley offered, fastening the
clasp for his friend.

"Thanks," Harris said, sighing with relief. "But I'll have to
learn to do that myself, before long." He was sweating in anticipation of being late for parade.

The bugle chirped again. Dudley followed the others
through the barrack-room door and onto the parade. He
dressed into the line and stood at ease. He noticed that the stiff-
ness of his uniform made it easier to remain steady, and his stock
and collar supported his chin and jaw. He felt a swelling of pride
in his breast. This was the true army life, here on the dusty parade in full uniform.

The orderly-sergeant of No. 3 Company, Sergeant Randall,
marched out to stand before them, then called them to attention. Randall was the only man at the depot, as far as Dudley
could tell, who wore spectacles. After forming the company in
two ranks at open order, he marched in and took the morning
roll call. He called every man's name and checked it on a list he
carried. When he had finished, he returned to his position be-

fore the ranks and did a smart right-about-face, turning his back to the men. After a few moments, Sergeant-Major Maclaren crossed the square and halted before him.

"All present and ready for inspection, sir," Randall said.

"Very good, Sergeant," Maclaren replied. "You may fall to the side."

The orderly-sergeant trailed Maclaren as the sergeant-major approached the company and began moving down the line, going from man to man, his long legs propelling him forward like some great crane wading through the shallows. When he came to Dudley, he stopped, frowning. Dudley felt a knot of alarm clench his stomach.

"Private Dudley," Maclaren said in his deep and resonating voice, "there is a splash of white dust on your right shoulder." He turned to the orderly-sergeant and said, "Place this man on dirty parade." Then he bent forward and spoke to Dudley as if the offending dust were somehow a personal insult. "When you are in uniform, Private, you represent Her Majesty Queen Victoria. When on parade, one's clothes must be free from any speck of dust or fluff. If you are carrying arms, every part of your musket and sidearms must glisten. Do you understand?"

"Yes, Sergeant-Major," Dudley replied. He tried to keep his voice from shaking.

Maclaren nodded and moved on. Dudley's ears began to burn. He could not understand how his coat could have become dusty. He must have brushed against something on his way out the door. Now he was on dirty parade, meaning extra drill following the usual morning period, punishment for slovenliness. He swallowed, hating that he had failed in this small way, and hating even more that those comrades near him had heard Maclaren's lecture.

Sergeant-Major Maclaren finished his inspection then approached the morning-duty officer to present the roll-call lists. The officer, Lieutenant Justin Coltern, was a sallow-faced, arrogant and uncaring man, and he studied the lists as if he found their content distasteful. Then, with a lazy touching of his cap in reply to Maclaren's snappy salute, he gave the usual order: "Fall out in squads for drills."

As the drill period progressed, Dudley tried to impress Sergeant Wellman and redeem himself for his mistake. But when the period ended, Wellman halted the squad before the barrack porch and said, "Privates Dudley and Anton, fall out."

Dudley took a side step to his right, and a second later, Wellman shouted, "Squad, dis—miss!" The squad broke off, and the men filed into the barrack rooms for breakfast. Dudley stayed on the square.

"Dudley and Anton, you will form here for dirty parade," Wellman said. Then, in a louder voice, he barked, "Corporal Lloyd, the punishment squad is yours."

As the punishment squad formed, Dudley saw that the drill instructor was none other than the man with the fattest arse in the regiment. Lance-Corporal Lloyd stood in front of the squad and looked from face to face, his expression displaying pure disgust.

"My name is Corporal Lloyd," he said. "Thanks to you vermin, I shall be late for my breakfast. You have punished me with your lack of discipline. I shall punish you back. That, I think, is only fair."

Lloyd's idea of punishment, it seemed, was to bore the men to death. For ten minutes, he marched the squad counterclockwise around the perimeter of the square. When he finally called the squad to halt, Dudley's mind had begun to wander, and he nearly missed the command. He took an extra half-pace and almost slammed into the back of the man in front of him.

"What the Christ!" Lloyd exploded. He stomped forward and screamed into Dudley's left ear, "You, Private, what's your name?"

"Private William Dudley, Lance-Corporal," Dudley answered.

Lloyd's face went from red with fury to purple with fury, and he shrieked, "You will address me as Corporal when on parade, you sack of manure! Do you understand that? *Do you understand that, Private?*"

"Yes, Corporal," Dudley said, voice neutral. He had not been aware of this bit of military protocol.

"Then correct yourself," Lloyd commanded. Dudley adjusted his feet. Lloyd stomped away.

For the next half-hour, Lloyd marched the men around the square, first at the normal quick step, then at the double. He roared every man's name at least once, most more than that. He did not mention Dudley's name a second time. Dudley knew then that Harris was right, that the abuse of recruits was not personal. It was all part of the training.

Lloyd dismissed the squad, and Dudley returned to his barrack room. He was coated in dust, soaked with sweat under his uniform and filled with self-disgust. One look at the flaking white paint on the door frame told him where the mysterious white splash had come from. For one second of carelessness, he had earned more than thirty minutes of torture and humiliation.

He would not let his discouragement show. He pretended to be cheerful as he ate his late breakfast, saying, "We have an advantage over you lot now. I am an expert at the double march."

Inside, he was still seething. He would never march on dirty parade again, he vowed. No corporal would ever again treat him as a misfit and a failure. He would not give anyone the chance.

As the weeks wore on, Dudley's passion to improve kept him motivated throughout the unvarying structure of his days. The depot band had taken to playing during the early-morning drill period, and he used its music as inspiration. Another inspiration was the omnipresence of Sergeant-Major Maclaren, who made the rounds of the squads. The recruits did not all learn at the same pace, and across the parade were different groups in different stages of instruction. The sergeant-major monitored them all, and sometimes offered suggestions and observations to the instructors. If he spied an outstanding recruit, he would send him to an advanced squad.

Dudley's recognition came during an afternoon drill period. Sergeant Wellman was taking the squad through the list of basic arms movements. Dudley threw his musket around his body, trying to outdo himself. There was a certain satisfaction in the feeling of the wooden stock crashing into his shoulder. He was oblivious to the sergeant-major's scrutiny.

"Sergeant Wellman," he heard the sergeant-major say, "you may excuse Private Dudley from your squad. He will report to Sergeant O'Ryan, who has the most advanced squad. You also may tell Private Dudley this—well done."

The sergeant-major marched off, and Wellman said, "Private Dudley, fall out. You will advance to Sergeant O'Ryan's squad. And the sergeant-major says to tell you well done."

"Thank you, Sergeant," Dudley blurted.

"Don't bleedin' thank me," Wellman rebuked, "just keep up the good work. Now, off you go."

Dudley moved across the parade towards O'Ryan's squad in a gratified daze. His labours were showing results. Sergeant-Major Maclaren had placed him among the top recruits, at least as far as drill went. That more than compensated for his one morning on dirty parade. It was an exhilarating moment.

O'Ryan was a flat-faced Irishman with flaming red hair and a continuous air of amusement, despite his often harsh words. In his squad, Dudley learned the bayonet exercise.

"Now, remember," O'Ryan said, "when I call point, thrust forward with your weapon, arms at full extent, straightening your right leg and throwing your weight forward onto your left knee. Squad—point!"

"Point!" every man in the squad cried, stabbing at an imaginary foe.

"Squad—two!" O'Ryan thundered, an angry edge to his Irish brogue. "Goddamn yer eyes, the lazy lot of you! This is to kill a man, not tickle 'is belly! Squad—point! Squad—two! Drive it out, Private Wilson! You've got to stick your weapon through 'is ribs, through flesh and bone! Squad—point!"

It was the most strenuous drill yet. Dudley decided that success had its price.

The last drill period finished at half-past three in the afternoon. It had been a special day, but it ended like any other. Dudley walked into Fairbridge for a newspaper then returned to spend some time in the canteen.

In the late evening, the men mustered for retreat and returned to barracks. There, they prepared for the next day, polishing their boots and cartridge pouches, keeping their muskets and bayonets well oiled. Dudley read aloud from his newspaper for the benefit of those men who could not read. Whenever he did this, he tried not to be patronizing. His middle-class upbringing had differed from that of almost all of the other recruits, but he did not believe he had a right to count himself better than they. He was a private soldier in the ranks, and so were the rest.

Of particular interest to the men were news items concerning the "poor sick man of Europe"—Turkey. The situation with Russia was becoming more critical.

Using the justification of protecting Christians in the Balkans, Russia had invaded the Ottoman provinces of Moldavia and Wallachia. In an attempt to have the Russians withdraw, British and French warships had sailed into the Black Sea. A day later, the Sultan of Turkey had formally declared war.

"So, we're helping the Turkies," someone said. "Do you think they'll be sending us? To war on Russia, I mean?"

"I doubt it," said Dudley. "For Britain, it's a naval operation so far. And the Turks seem to be in command of the situation."

"A pity," Corporal Trump commented. "I wouldn't mind having a go at the Russian Bear. Steal me the czar's sword, I would."

"You'll have to beat me to it, then!" someone else cried.

Trump chuckled. "Oh, I will."

In late November, the newspapers reported a great Turkish naval defeat in Sinope harbour. The British press dubbed it a "massacre." A Russian naval squadron, firing explosive shells instead of solid round shot, had slaughtered four thousand Turkish sailors. The wooden Turkish ships had stood no chance against this example of modern naval artillery.

Public opinion in Britain shifted from indifference to sudden outrage over the government's weak stance in the crisis. Dudley read a disturbing article in *The Westminster Review* that warned of the Russian threat to Britain's commerce and passage to India.

"What do you think?" he asked Harris one evening in the barracks. "The public is calling for us to send troops."

"I'm not certain we should involve ourselves more than we have," Harris replied. "Maybe there *is* justification for Russia to fear for the rights of Christians under Muslim rule. And didn't we fight the Turks ourselves some years ago, to prevent their domination of Greece?"

"Yes, but here we have the reverse. Russia now threatens *Turkey's* independence, just as Turkey had threatened Greek independence. I don't believe the Muscovites care about the Balkan Christians. After all, the czar can hardly be said to treat his own people well. This is a simple war of conquest. Russia wants a route to the Mediterranean. And if they threaten our passage to India, surely we should go? Maybe they have designs on India herself. Russia has always coveted that country." Dudley shook his head. "Russia is a barbarous nation. Its government holds the people in the thrall of serfdom."

"Are we going to be setting those people free?" Harris asked. "No. We shall be killing them. Those serfs are their soldiers."

"Then we shall be setting the Turks free from a similar fate, and weakening the power of the despot in the bargain."

Harris was cleaning his musket, and now he looked up and said, "It will be a tangled mess if we get involved. Russia is the most powerful nation in Europe, with a much greater army than ours."

Dudley glanced up at his little shelf. Wellington still stood guard over his bunk.

"We have done it before," he declared.

"You are a romantic when it comes to war and soldiering."

"Maybe that's so. But I also believe in the strength of British arms. Of British resolve."

Harris nodded. "I cannot dispute such beliefs."

It was a typical discussion, for Dudley and Harris often found themselves on opposite sides of an issue. But rather than drive them apart, these discussions had helped strengthen their relationship. Since their first meeting, they had become fast friends. This happened despite—maybe because of—the fact they were not alike.

Dudley was learning the ways and customs of the army, and had come to know most of the NCOs and even some of the officers. He associated with the other privates in the canteen every day. He exercised in the recreation room and had strengthened his body.

Harris, in contrast, kept to himself. He spent every evening in the soldier's library. He had no interest in visiting the recreation room, and visited the canteen only once a week. Yet he was kind, and willing to help a comrade without needing to be asked, in the true sense of the old staff sergeant's philosophy. He did his work and duty well, but not well enough to be noticed.

"I have no drive to work at being a soldier the way you do, William," he confessed. "You want to be promoted. I am content not to hope for such things—hopes breed disappointment. I will simply do my best, and take what they give me."

Dudley judged this to be the attitude of someone who had never had much luck or opportunity. Harris confirmed this conclusion when he explained why he had joined the army.

"My brother and I failed miserably at our business," he explained. "We tried to sell modern farm machinery in the North Country. God, it didn't take us long to go bankrupt! I guess I'm no businessman. But it was worse for my brother, who contracted pneumonia and died soon after.

"I was fortunate enough to secure a position as a clerk for the railroad in Yorkshire. I was, however, asked to leave, as they did not have sufficient funds to justify my continued employment. I spent months searching for a new position but found nothing. At last I decided to come south and beg the charity of distant relations. They were only willing to help me for a while, during which I continued to look for a position here in Hampshire, but again found nothing.

"I was on my way to London when I came upon a recruiting sergeant. Well, I was at the end of my tether at that point, and the army seemed as good a career as any." He sighed. "Maybe it was an impulse that made me enlist, but I have no outstanding regrets. Three meals a day, physical activity and discipline, and just enough time free from duties to pursue other interests."

"You say you have no *outstanding* regrets," Dudley interjected. "That must mean you regret something?"

"I dislike the monotony of our duties," Harris explained. "Most of our comrades seem to enjoy the structure, but any educated man in our situation risks going mad with boredom."

Dudley shook his head. "Not me."

"You have your goal of promotion. Every day is a stage in furthering that goal. For me, every day is just another day, and what will come will come."

"I see. Well, I suppose I have a regret as well. I'm not bored, but I do find the lack of privacy difficult at times. There is nowhere to be alone." He gestured around the barrack room where they were sitting. The place was full of men going about their tasks. "Not even the library."

Harris nodded. "I had not really thought of it, but you're right."

Dudley thought of the library at Highwood Hall, the morning sunlight streaming through the windows, the trees outside budding green with the spring. It had been a sanctuary. He missed it.

But it would be best if he forgot all about Highwood Hall, he told himself. The place had never been what the memories made it seem. There had been nothing there for him.

Forgetting about Highwood, however, was not easy, and one December morning two letters arrived to make that task harder. The letters made Dudley grateful his squad was to practise their musketry on the shooting range that afternoon.

He loved the violence of the shooting range—the noise and the flame and the sulphurous reek of the powder smoke. It was an excellent place to purge the frustrations the letters had brought.

Dudley loaded his musket for his first shot. From his ammunition pouch, he removed a paper cartridge. He bit open the tail of the cartridge and poured the powder down the musket's barrel. Taking his ramrod, he pushed the paper and bullet into the muzzle and forced it home. Pulling the musket's hammer back to the half-cock, he took a percussion cap from the cap pouch on his crossbelt. When he had fit the cap over the breach nipple, he pulled the hammer back to full cock.

Taking aim at the black bull's-eye in the white-paper target fifty yards away, he held his breath and squeezed the trigger. The hammer struck the percussion cap, the musket kicked and banged. He waited to see where his bullet had gone. Bull's-eye, he noted with satisfaction.

The smoothbore musket was an erratic weapon, so that had been perhaps a lucky shot. But Dudley scored more bull's-eyes than most. He paid as much attention to musketry as all other aspects of training.

"Well done, Private Dudley," Sergeant O'Ryan said from behind the squad. "A regular marksman! Ye must be of the Irish Dudleys after all."

Dudley did not smile. Nothing could take his mind off the two letters.

One was from his auntie Bronwyn, the other from Martha. Martha's letter was short and spiteful. She explained how she was going to marry a friend of her brother's, someone she had met soon after Dudley's departure. Then she had written, "You will never see me again. Goodbye."

It was obvious she had sent the letter as punishment, a deliberate attempt to further wound him. The attempt had succeeded. Dudley wished he could no longer care what Martha did or thought.

His aunt's letter had been even more distressing. He had been writing to her and his uncle Robert for months but had not received any reply until now. The letter provided the answer to why there had been such a long delay. It explained that Dudley's inexplicable actions—"this mad running off to join the army"—had "devastated" his uncle. He would no longer speak Dudley's name nor even acknowledge that he had a nephew. Whenever someone mentioned "William," his face would harden, and after a moment of silence, he would change the subject.

Auntie Bronwyn also explained that she had written several letters before this. Uncle Robert had destroyed them. But she assured Dudley they still loved him, that the difficulties were temporary. She wished him a Happy Christmas. She hoped he would come home soon for a visit. Perhaps then, she said, Uncle Robert would accept what he had done, when they saw each other again.

Dudley knew his aunt did not understand the army, that there would be no Christmas leave for private soldiers. There would be no chance for him to see Uncle Robert soon.

His musket kicked again, forcing a dull pain through his bruised shoulder. The bullet made a black hole in the white paper target.

The pain of the letters lingered for weeks, and the night after Christmas Day Dudley had a dream of home. It was a dream about his aunt, and the downstairs parlour in her house. It was also a dream of the high downs, that expansive landscape he had wandered and explored for most of his life. The dream was nothing but images of these places and people, the last being his cousin Jane, with her dimples and flaxen curls, laughing at something he had said.

He awoke before reveille. The image of Jane was still fresh in his mind, more vivid than most memories. Jane, five years his junior, who worshipped him, who had trailed after him on his romps through the countryside.

He lay on his back and listened to the chorus of snoring around him. It was Boxing Day morning. He wondered what Jane would be doing come sunrise, what the others in the house would be doing. Had they been thinking of him on Christmas Day? He had sent them all gifts—new mittens for Jane of bright red wool—but he had received nothing from them, not even a further letter. He wondered if his uncle would persist in forbidding correspondence with him, and try to intercept any secret correspondence.

He rolled onto his side and tried to go back to sleep. His uncle had blocked his family connections, cut him off. Some day that could change, but for now he would have to live with it.

He would make new connections, here with the army.

———

The new year 1854 arrived, and there was much talk of war. An Expeditionary Force of British and French troops would be going to Turkey after all, to join with the Sultan in his struggle against the Bear of Russia.

At the Fairbridge depot, the commanding officer announced he would select a strong draft from the three recruit companies. These men would accompany a number of officers and NCOs to Portsmouth to reinforce the service companies stationed there. There would also be promotions, for the regiment needed junior NCOs.

On a chill January morning, a clerk posted the draft and promotions on the board outside the Orderly Room. Many a soldier, swaddled in his greatcoat, crowded around to see if his name was there.

"My God," Harris said, reading the board, "they've raised me to lance-corporal."

Dudley's name was also on the board, as was his promotion. He was now Lance-Corporal Dudley. He read the board three times to make sure, but there was no mistake. After all his work and effort, his sought-after recognition had come. And Harris, too!

"It's our education," Harris said. "Our officers believe we will make better leaders simply because we can read." He sneezed, then wiped his nose with a greatcoat sleeve. "I fear they have made a mistake on my part. Imagine making me corporal!"

Dudley clapped him on the shoulder. "Nonsense! We're Chosen Men now, the best of the lot!" He could feel the joy, the excitement swelling inside him. His family troubles seemed far away at that moment. "Don't let me hear any of that deprecating stuff."

"Chosen men, that's true," Harris agreed. "Chosen as the first to go to war if, in fact, war does come and our regiment goes."

"Turkey," Dudley said with anticipation. "Off to see a faraway and foreign land. Don't tell me you're not thrilled at that prospect."

Harris finally smiled. "Well, I must admit that *would* be something to see."

# CHAPTER THREE

Ours is composed of the scum of the earth—the
mere scum of the earth.

The Duke of Wellington

***Dudley's new service company*** bore the same designation as
his pro tem company of recruits—No. 3 Company. By a fortunate circumstance, this was Harris's new company as well. They
would again share the same living quarters, this time at the
Portsmouth barracks. Dudley viewed this turn of chance as a
good omen.

One look at his new station proved the inaccuracy of that
interpretation. The Portsmouth barracks was a dismal place
located in a dismal and shabby part of the old town. Like the
Fairbridge depot, it was an enclosure of brick barrack buildings
arranged around a central square, save that these buildings were
a squat two stories high, and were ancient and dilapidated, their
brick walls soot-blackened and crumbling in places. Dudley's
room, Casemate 17, was smaller than his quarters at the Fairbridge depot, and its two leaky square windows, with their rotting and unpainted wooden frames, were not much larger than
loopholes. There was a coal-burning fireplace but no stove, and
the walls were slick with moisture. At night, rats squeaked and

47

scampered about, sometimes crawling along the sleeping forms of the men, gnawing at blankets and mattresses. Guards armed with sticks stayed awake for rotating periods to watch for and deal with the troublesome rodents.

The room was also full to bursting. There was a man for every one of the twenty-four bunks, and a few of those men were married. The married men lived in the back corners with their wives, their only privacy a few moth-eaten gray blankets strung like laundry. Dudley found the arrangement undignified, but no one else seemed to care. Some of these people had lived this way for years, he supposed, while others may have known far worse accommodations. They were a hardened bunch, of rougher character than the recruits. Their wives were not much more refined, their harsh and high-pitched cackles ringing in the enclosed space of the room.

Dudley remembered his vow to make the best of his circumstances and tried to settle in for his first evening. It was no different from a night at the Fairbridge depot, he told himself. He kept busy by cleaning his musket and polishing its brass furnishings. He tried to ignore the heavy press of bodies and clutter around him.

Unlike the recruits, his new barrack-mates had been soldiers long enough to collect small personal items, such as ornaments and pictures. This mishmash of objects did not make the room more pleasant but added to its atmosphere of oppression. If he let it, that clutter could make Dudley feel as if he were suffocating, and he took a few breaths to calm himself.

"Place is a bloody mess," he muttered.

Harris had his bunk next to Dudley's. He was browsing through a small volume of Blake's poetry. When Dudley spoke, he glanced up from his page.

"Perhaps in time it will seem cozy."

Dudley was about to disagree, but then his eyes fell on a hulking bear of a man, Private Brian Barker. Barker was wading up the center of the room from the corner he shared with his wife. He was massive, with thick black hair, shaggy whiskers and eyes that peered out from deep and purplish sockets. He was a loud and aggressive man, one who dominated half the men in the room. Dudley feared he would be trouble in the time to come.

Barker made directly for Harris and stopped beside his bunk, hands on his hips.

"Here, what's this fellow up to?"

Harris again looked up from his book.

"I'm reading," he said.

Dudley suspected Harris had not meant to sound facetious, but he had. Barker scowled.

"So, one o' the new boys is a reader, eh?" he rumbled. "Think that makes you special, do you? And a lance-corporal to boot, how about that?"

With one meaty paw, he snatched the little book from Harris's hands and held it out of reach.

Harris sprang from his bunk, crying, "See here," and reached toward the hulking veteran. Barker howled with laughter.

"You want it back, eh? Then, fetch."

Barker threw the book toward the fire. His aim was off— the book slammed into the wall.

"What do you think you're doing?" Dudley demanded, leaping to his feet. He glared at the huge private as Harris scrambled for his precious volume. Barker turned toward him, staring down in contempt. Despite Dudley's higher rank, Barker reached forward to push him back.

Someone grabbed Barker's arm. The big man whirled around to meet his attacker but saw that it was the aged Corporal Manning, the senior man in the room.

"Leave off, Barker," Manning commanded. "That ain't no way to treat the reinforcements."

"Ha!" Barker shouted. Then, to Dudley's astonishment, he threw his arms around Manning's body and forced him backward.

Manning snarled and pushed back, hands seeking Barker's head and neck. The two men collided with a table, springing the top from the iron frame, then crashed to the floor, where they continued to wrestle. Everyone leapt out of the way, wives scolding, a few men shouting in annoyance and others encouraging the fight.

Barker had the upper hand from the beginning. Still holding his opponent, he lurched to his feet then flung the struggling corporal across an empty bunk. The bunk springs groaned in protest. Manning bounced once then lay there like a sack of grain, not moving.

Barker stepped back, bawling in triumph, then returned to his blanket enclosure in the back corner. A few men slapped his shoulders as he passed, while others shouted curses. No one made a move to see to Manning.

Dudley stared at the defeated corporal. Manning remained on his back for a moment longer, then sat up and blinked his eyes.

"Are you all right, Corporal?" Dudley asked.

"Christ, yes," Manning whined, not looking at him. He rolled out of the bunk, muttering, "I'll beat him yet, I will."

"You aren't going to charge him with assault?" Dudley questioned, incredulous. The entire event had left him shaken.

"Mind your own business, Lance-Corporal!" Manning snapped. "You let me deal with Barker. Now, leave off."

Dudley cleared his throat. "All right. If that's the way you want it."

Manning glared at him from one eye. "It is."

Baffled and uneasy, Dudley returned to his bunk and his kit maintenance. Around him, the barrack room had resumed its normal hum of activity.

"I can see why Wellington," Harris whispered, "often referred to his men as the scum of the earth."

"Oddly enough," Dudley replied, "he meant that they were scum before they joined the army. Scum who became decent fighting men as a result of army life and training."

"God help us," Harris breathed. "How can a man of any sensitivity be expected to live in an environment such as this?"

Dudley wondered the same thing, but said instead, "Never fear. You'll find a way. As you said, in time it might seem cozy. When we get to know the company better."

"Perhaps I spoke too quickly," Harris muttered.

A moment later, they saw Barker emerge from his corner and again move up the length of the room. Barker noticed Dudley watching him and stared back. When he came abreast of where Dudley sat, he looked down at the kit, boots and belts arrayed on the bunk.

"Polish them boots with mud, Lance-Corporal?" Barker said.

Dudley maintained a level head. "I suppose you think that you've insulted me, Private?"

Barker's smirk widened. "Just making an honest observation."

He continued on his way, and Harris muttered, "What an ass."

Barker halted near the barrack-room door and began speaking to one of the senior men.

"I wonder what his story is?" Dudley thought aloud.

Harris, assuming Dudley had spoken to him, proclaimed, "I could not care less."

Dudley soon discovered that Corporal Manning was a notorious and confirmed drunkard. Every evening, the corporal returned from the town or the canteen shrouded in a dense cloud of alcohol fumes. He would crash onto his bunk and be unconscious and snoring before his body settled into place. Come morning he would still be drunk, and after dinner he was the first to the barrack canteen. Perpetual intoxication had become his normal state, and he had learned to control it. Thus, the officers never noticed when he was drunk on parade, which was always.

The scuffle with Barker was another common occurrence. Every third or fourth evening, usually after Manning's return from the town, a similar fight would erupt between the two men. Sometimes fists flew, and sometimes they knocked over a table, the precious candles scattered.

Sometimes, they would damage government or personal property. When this happened, others would intervene to end the fray, either with words or force. But the fighting would always break out again at some point.

51

The match could be initiated by either man. Barker would strike at Manning as the corporal stumbled into the room, while at other times Manning would seek out the hulking private, curse him as a bone-idle whoreson, and the fight would begin.

No matter who was to blame for starting the trouble, it was no secret that Barker was the company troublemaker. He taunted the other men in the barracks and canteen, challenged them with words and insults. This baiting often caused Manning to step in, just as he had when Barker had accosted Harris.

Barker appeared to regard the fighting as some kind of cruel game, to see how far he could push authority. He shook with laughter all during the fights and after. He laughed even when he received the worst of the pummeling, though he usu-ally won—Manning's age and drunkenness made him less effec-tive as a brawler. The corporal's one advantage was that he seemed not to feel pain. He never charged Barker with assault, either, nor with mischief or any other offence, serious or other-wise. No officer ever came to investigate the disturbances.

In response, Barker paid for all damages without complaint. He considered his bullying an amusement, a sort of boisterous humour. Many shared this attitude, or at least pretended to.

Dudley began to notice how many men were afraid of Barker, an observation he found disheartening. Imagine soldiers of the queen fearing one of their peers, and a big stupid brute at that! But these cowards and lackeys were there, and they fol-lowed along with whatever Barker said or did.

To be fair, some of Barker's supporters simply respected the man's size and strength. They respected his audacity. They ad-mired him and wished they could be like him, for he was brave and rebellious, with an uncanny knack for getting away with his numerous misdemeanors. To many, he was the most powerful authority in the company.

Prominent among those who followed Barker was Private Geary, another recruit who had arrived with the strong draft. He was the youngest man in the company; some said he was still only sixteen. He laughed loudest when Barker made a vulgar joke or hurled an insult, and was never far from the big man's side. Dudley often saw them together in the canteen. Barker would feed the youth tales of his own prowess, of how he was the true leader of No. 3 Company. Barker would say that the men respected him more than Colour-Sergeant Onslow, the senior NCO.

As for the company officers, they were hardly worth mentioning. The company commander, Captain Clarke, was little more than a gentle stripling, while his second, the horrible Lieutenant Coltern, was an incompetent snob.

Geary accepted these opinions as fact. He had become Barker's apprentice, while Barker had become his older brother, and welcomed his worship.

But Geary was one fellow Dudley could forgive. He was just a boy, and eager to please his peers. A sense of self-preservation compelled him to seek Barker's approval. If he could not defeat the beast, he would be its friend.

Others insisted that Barker was still a decent soldier. One veteran told Dudley, "For all that, Barker's a fine man to have in a scrap. Ye should have seen him against the Sikhs back in forty-eight. He proved his worth there, lad. And he helps out in ways you cannot see, or refuse to, for your first impression o' the man was his bad side."

The speaker was Daniel Oakes, a grizzled private who had served with the Royal Hants for almost twenty years. Oakes had not been young when he joined the regiment, and now his hair was like iron and his face like leather. He was an unobtrusive man and a stabilizing force within the barracks and the company, even in the battalion. He noted the goings-on in the barracks with concealed amusement, though he did not care for some of Barker's more outrageous displays. He had the power to step in, whisper a quiet word, and have Barker cease his taunts or ranting.

"Aye, Barker's proved his worth in the past," Oakes asserted, "and he will again, I'm certain." Then he clamped his clay pipe between his teeth and said not another word on the subject.

Oakes's wife Hester also helped to make life easier for the men. For a small fee, she washed clothing, cooked and mended, and offered simple and honest advice. She took a liking to Dudley, and told him he was "A sweet little dish, and with fire in 'is belly." Dudley did not mind her affections. In fact, he found them comforting, and one thing to offset the unpleasantness of Casemate 17. She sometimes did his laundry for free.

Barker's wife, young—and handsome for such a large-boned woman—did *not* like Dudley. She cast icy stares in his direction through a rent in her blanket wall. If he stared back, she would scowl before turning away. Dudley presumed her disfavour was because he did not cower before her husband. Instead, he stood his ground, answering Barker's comments with his own, or stepping in to try to stop the fighting. He defied Barker without invoking the authority of his rank of lance-corporal—in this social setting, that would have been the route of a man with no other options. Dudley knew this was the right course to take if he was to win the respect of the company, yet it did him no good with Barker's wife.

Two other men were also victims of Mrs. Barker's venomous glances. Both were fellows who ignored her husband, while, for different reasons, Barker stayed away from *them*. One was Private John Johnson. Dudley suspected Johnson had leadership qualities, though his character was a bit wild for the tastes of most officers. He had heavy eyebrows like twin caterpillars, a mischievous smile and was almost fanatical in his love for the army. He had modified his musket's stock to make it less bulky, carving away excess wood on the small of the butt, and was an expert marksman. He contained a reserve of pent-up violence, like the tightened spring of a musket's hammer, waiting to be fired. Barker thought he was a bit mad. Dudley thought Barker might be right for once, and felt that, if not for the army, Johnson could have been either a prize fighter or an inmate at Dartmoor.

The other man was Private Ronald Doyle. Doyle seldom spoke, but sat on his bunk watching the world with dark and sunken eyes. His expression was one of demented humour, an exaggeration of Johnson's grin. He only emerged from his shell of silence after a pint in the canteen, and then he would snarl and growl like an animal for everyone's entertainment. Someone would shout at him to "Do the lunatic!" At this, Doyle would perform his impression of a madman. He could turn bright purple at will, his eyes rolling into his head, while he frothed at the mouth. At the same time, he would shriek, gurgle in his throat and wave his arms over his head like an enraged ape. His audience would roar until their eyes streamed with tears.

"The poor fellow *is* a lunatic," Harris insisted, "and they exploit that for their own indulgence."

"He seems a steady man on parade, though," Dudley said. "He does his duty, and there is nothing mad about that."

Rumours of the proposed expeditionary force against Russia continued to circulate, though nothing was certain. Britain still hoped diplomacy could force the Russians to withdraw from Ottoman territory.

For the soldiers in Britain's army, the usual peacetime schedule continued. In Portsmouth, that meant alternating days of drill parade and guard duty.

Though parade was monotonous, Dudley found reasons to enjoy it. The martial sounds of the fifes and drums and the regimental band always plucked at his heart. A jaunty tune gave him the strength to keep his shoulders back, to move his musket about with precision and to march with spirit. Without the music, he would find himself slumping under the discomforts of his uniform and heavy kit. When this happened, he tried to steal a glance at the regiment's Colours. The Colours stirred him as the music did.

These silk banners, billowing in the damp winter wind that blew in from the harbour, encapsulated the soul of the regiment he had joined. The Union flag of the Queen's Colour reminded Dudley who and what the regiment fought for. The deep blue Regimental Colour, with its long lists of battle honors, displayed the regiments's history in bright lettering for all to see—Peninsula, Vittoria, Waterloo.

Whenever the Colours were on parade, so was the battalion commander, Lieutenant-Colonel Freemantle. Freemantle was a lean and gangly man, with a white moustache, soft blue eyes, and a dispassionate bearing. Though not a harsh disciplinarian, he favoured a policy of attention to detail. During the Peninsula campaign, the Royal Hampshire Fusiliers had become known as one of the best-trained regiments in the army. Not the best-drilled, but the best-trained. Since first taking command, Free-mantle had upheld that reputation.

Having the Royal Hants look good on parade was not Freemantle's goal; having them well prepared for battle was. That was the factor Dudley's instructors had emphasized during squad drill. *Do this well*, they said, *for you will need it when you march into combat. Learn how to load and discharge three rounds a minute to maintain a steady fire upon the enemy. Master the bayonet exercise so that you can kill your enemy before he kills you.*

Dudley was confident in the talents of his drill instructors, though he did worry his regiment was not living up to its reputation in other ways. The problems in Casemate 17 made him suspect that, in his old age, Freemantle was neglecting morale and discipline off the square.

This concern didn't mean Dudley did not admire the man. It was possible the problem with Private Barker was a singular case. In any event, the troubles in the barracks did not spill onto the parade. Dudley could still share the enthusiasm that most of the men had for their commanding officer.

Freemantle had served against Napoleon's marshals as a junior officer in the regiment under Wellington,. This fact made him a hero in Dudley's eyes, even if his abilities had begun to deteriorate.

The only escape from three drill parades a day was guard duty. Dudley drew this duty at least every third day, and he both despised and enjoyed it. Standing sentry for two hours at a time was so tedious it was no wonder men sometimes fell asleep. A sentry had to remain at attention, could march a fifteen-pace beat six times an hour, and could make a few limited arms movements. He could speak only to suspicious persons (who were rare) and the NCO of the guard.

No one liked standing sentry, and Dudley was no exception. But he leapt at the chance to post and change the sentries, a task he sometimes drew with another junior NCO. This was one of the few instances where the duties of a lance-corporal differed from the duties of a private. Though not an independent command, it was his first taste of authority.

Sentry change followed specific procedures, but it was still a rare opportunity for Dudley to have men react to his shouted orders. Commanding others brought an impression of freedom he had not known since before his enlistment. A freedom he had forgotten. When he had lived at home, he had been at liberty to come and go as he wished. Even during his employment at Highwood Hall, he had been more autonomous than he was in the army. He had not been aware he missed it, but he did.

With the modest freedom of a lance-corporal came an equal share of responsibility. Dudley was an assistant to Corporal Manning and the other company NCOs. He also had to set an example for the rest of the men. In a normal setting, this would not have been difficult—he was already doing his best to set an example of good conduct. But the presence of Private Barker sometimes threatened to ignite his temper and blast away all his resolutions.

The closest the two men came to open conflict was when Barker discovered Dudley's tin soldier. The incident occurred one evening in the barrack room...

---

"What's this 'ere?" an incredulous voice squawked from behind Dudley's back. He turned to see Barker holding Wellington in his thick fingers.

"What's this 'ere?" the huge man repeated. "A little toy soldier?"

"Give that to me, Barker!" Dudley cried, feeling swift and unexpected fury. He knew he could never win a scrap with Barker, but he had thought about how satisfying it would be to land one or two well-placed blows. After that he would take what he got in return, if Barker dared strike back.

"So, the gentleman plays with toys, does he?" Barker went on. He was always referring to Dudley and Harris as "the gentlemen." It was meant as an insult.

Dudley rose to his feet and faced the giant. He maintained a slight crouch, ready to strike. He decided that if he did fight here and now, the other men would not think any less of him. And no one of prominence need ever hear about the incident. Only Corporal Manning would know, and he wouldn't care.

"It's a good-luck charm, Private," Dudley said, tone as hard as steel. He moved forward. "Surely, with your ignorant and superstitious mind, you can understand that?"

The second he said the words, he regretted them. Petty insults were beneath him. But Barker began to laugh. He reeled toward the door, still clutching Wellington. Dudley stayed where he was, waiting to see what the man would do next.

Barker halted above the prone form of Manning, who for some reason hadn't gone out for his usual binge. The grizzled corporal had dropped onto his cot soon after tea, an empty gin bottle gripped in one bony hand.

"You hear what he said, Corporal?" Barker cried in mock indignation. "My superstitious mind?"

Manning didn't reply. Barker gave his bed a resounding kick and repeated, "Did you hear what he said? My superstitious mind?"

The old man still showed no signs of waking. Barker kicked the bed again.

"Get up, you old goat."

The corporal didn't stir. He hadn't even dropped his bottle. Barker jiggled him with one great hand. Then, carelessly dropping Wellington to the floor, he grasped his old sparring partner by the shoulders and shook him. With an uncharacteristic note of panic, he muttered, "Wake up, damn you. Wake up."

Manning, however, would not wake. As everyone gathered round, the truth became apparent. Dudley's outrage dissipated, for the old barrack-room commander had taken his final drink sometime in the late afternoon, and then he had died.

The toy soldier forgotten, Barker pried the bottle from the Corporal's lifeless hand.

"Manning, you drunken old bastard."

Then, in a burst of passion, he cast the bottle into the corner by the door. It shattered against the whitewashed brick.

The day after Manning's funeral, while No. 3 Company was on late-morning parade, Sergeant-Major Maclaren ordered Dudley to fall out and report to Captain Clarke, the company commander. Clarke was waiting with the duty officer on the edge of the parade. Dudley hurried across the earthen square, heart hammering within his chest. Had he done something wrong? He could think of no reason why the captain should want to speak to him.

He halted before Captain Clarke and saluted, his left finger-tips touching the sling of his musket. The captain was a quiet and aloof young man, not much older than Dudley, with a pink-ish complexion and wisps of pale-blond hair protruding from the edges of his forage cap. He returned Dudley's salute and said, in his usual gentle tone, "You may relax, Corporal Dudley. I have some good news for you."

Dudley took a deep breath; he was relieved.

"Good news, sir?"

"Well, good news that is the result of unfortunate circumstances, I'm afraid. Manning was a good man. Though he was not well, I understand."

"No, sir," Dudley agreed, puzzled, "he was not."

"At any rate, his position needs to be filled. When I asked Colour-Sergeant Onslow for recommendations, he gave me your name. I have decided to take that recommendation up, and have passed it on to the colonel." A faint smiled appeared on his lips. "So, he has agreed to your promotion from lance-corporal to corporal. His secretary is drawing up the orders now. I thought that I would like to tell you myself for, after all, you are one of my men." He extended his hand for Dudley to shake, an uncommon gesture for an officer in relation to an enlisted man, and added, "Well done."

Dudley shook the hand.

"Thank you, sir. I…I'm not sure that I'm quite prepared."

Clarke frowned. "You don't want it?"

"Oh, no, sir, that's not what I meant. I do want it, and I appreciate your telling me in person, very much. It's just that it's so sudden."

"Ah, yes. Well, a good man should not be surprised to find himself rising in the ranks. Most men are content to remain private soldiers, but the army recognizes those who do not. At any rate, you may carry on, Corporal."

Dudley grinned. "Thank you, sir."

He saluted again and returned to his squad.

His happiness persisted until the end of the day's official duties, but during tea his mood began to change. Now that he had time to reflect, he realized he had mixed feelings about this second promotion. Again he had achieved something sooner than he ever could have imagined, but one of the most important factors in that achievement had been good luck. The company needed a corporal. As Clarke had hinted, this opening was the result of another man's death. Dudley found that fact troubling and somewhat distasteful.

As the days went by, he discovered another unpleasant side effect of his new rank. Some of the older veterans, headed by Barker and his strongest supporters, resented Dudley's selection for Manning's position. They had known Manning for years, had stood with him under enemy fire in the Sikh Wars. Dudley was nothing to them but an upstart recruit, a new arrival who had not proven his worth beyond a competence for drill, procedure and book-learning.

Barker had never singled Dudley out before, but he did so now. His attacks were not physical but emotional. He was careful not to break any laws or do anything that could land him before the commanding officer. He did not dare to fight with the new corporal as he had with the old, but he threw angry scowls at Dudley from across the room and made a point of not speaking to him. He tried to destroy Dudley's credibility, criticizing him behind his back. Many of the other men, who had been warming to Dudley's good humour now refused to associate with him save in those situations required by duty.

Dudley decided the only way to combat this vilification was to earn the respect of the company. He made this resolution even though it caused him some anguish. It was not fair that he should be forced to engage in a war of wills with this Private Barker, this buffoon! It was so unnecessary.

60

"It amazes me," he said to Harris one evening, "how one man can sow such dissension. How one man can make life so difficult for so many others."

They sat under the light of an oil lamp in the soldier's library. This was a cramped little room with heavy brown bookshelves lining both side walls, the intervening space filled with tables made from plain wooden planks perched on wrought iron trestles. No longer comfortable in the canteen when Barker was there, Dudley had been coming here more often. For once, there was no one other than Harris present, and he felt a need to talk about his troubles.

"That is the way of the world," Harris said. "Individuals have caused much misery with their actions, and other individuals have gained greatness sometimes by combating them. Think of Bonaparte and Wellington."

Dudley saw no comfort in this. "I don't feel like combating Private Barker. He's an obnoxious fool. I don't understand why someone hasn't put him in his place."

"Then why don't you? Go to Colour-Sergeant Onslow and ask his advice. Report Barker as a disruptive force, a bad character."

"Yes, yes," Dudley said with irritation. He had already considered these actions but had dismissed them as whining and cowardly. He wanted to deal with the problem himself, not pass it on to his superiors. But he also did not like having to single one man out for anything, even if that man deserved singling out.

"I will have to let Barker trip himself up," he stated. "I don't want it to look like I'm merely using my new rank as a tool against him. And I don't want to lose face with the other men."

"You may be right there. But no worry. Barker doesn't have poor old Manning to protect him anymore. He will trip himself up before long."

The dilemma of Private Barker had become Dudley's primary concern, but with the onset of February, he was able to push it to the back of his mind. A shipment of new muskets had arrived—rifled muskets, of the Minie pattern. They were lighter and shorter than the smoothbores, with superior accuracy and three times the range. He was eager to give one a try.

"They're a French design," the sergeant-instructor of musketry told No. 3 Company when they formed at the shooting range, an open field on the outskirts of town. It was like a cricket pitch, just a narrow green lawn bordered by leafless winter trees. A hundred yards from the troops stood the row of targets—paper circles hung from wooden frames and backed by hay bales and bags of sand.

"Aye, a French design," the sergeant repeated, "but don't let that worry you." There were quite a few chuckles at that, and the sergeant grinned. "The procedure for loading is the same as you're used to, with one difference." He held up a tiny bit of lead—a Minie bullet. "As you know, Old Brown Bess fired a round ball. Not these here. The Minie balls are, as they say, conical in shape. That way, they grab the rifling on their way out of the barrel, see? So, the only thing I ask is that, when you load 'em, put 'em in the right way around." There were more chuckles, and the sergeant then added, "'O' course, I'm in jest, for that mistake can't be made with these prepared cartridges. But we'll see, eh?"

The practice began. The bang of the rifle was of a higher pitch than the old musket, and the degree of performance was higher as well. The rifle's supposed accuracy was no exaggeration. Man after man saw an improvement in his marksmanship, scoring more bull's-eyes than he ever had before, amid many cheers and smiles.

Dudley agreed that the rifle was impressive, though he was not so enraptured as others. He noticed Private Johnson staring at his new weapon with adoration, then stroking its smooth wooden stock with one hand. When Johnson realized that Dudley was watching at him, he grinned and hefted the rifle in triumph.

Dudley grinned back.

The next day was miserable, even for February, the slate-gray sky spitting intermittent rain. No. 3 Company drew guard duty, and Dudley was pleased to discover he and another corporal had a section of the guard under their charge.

One of his tasks was to make the rounds of the sentries, visiting every post that required a guard—the main gate, the secondary gate, the meat and bread storeroom, and the ammunition storeroom. Dudley spoke to each man, ensuring he was doing his duty and asking if there were any problems or complaints. He found them in a good mood despite the condensed mist that ran off their oilskin shako covers, soaked into the gray shoulders of their greatcoats and made the whitening on their belts run. The new rifles had catalyzed an improvement in their morale.

He was puzzled, therefore, when he came to the last post on his route and saw the sentry slouched inside the gray-painted sentry box. The sentry was Private Barker.

"What's the matter, Private?" Dudley demanded as he approached. The box was a shelter from the rain, but one had to remain at attention when inside. "Are you ill?"

Barker looked at him, and there were tears in his eyes. He opened his mouth to reply. Dudley smelled the sourness of drink.

"My God," Dudley said, "you're so drunk you can hardly stand, let alone take charge of this post!"

Barker sniffed. "Aye, Corporal."

Dudley wondered how this could have happened. Barker had been pale and glassy-eyed that morning when the new guard had come on, but he had insisted he was well and had definitely not been drunk.

"You filled your canteen with gin, didn't you?" Dudley accused, guessing the only possible answer.

"It's amazing, Corporal, but gin looks like water. A natural mistake."

Dudley saw no humour in the joke. "You've done it this time, Barker," he said. "Drunkenness on sentry duty is no small offence. What have you to say for yourself?"

Barker did his best to pull himself up and stand at attention. "With all due respect, Corporal, if you didn't have your rank and false gentleman's airs to make you feel superior, I'd doubt you'd have the courage to speak to me the way you do. Even if you did, I'd kick your gold-plated ass."

Dudley gasped in disbelief. Had Barker lost his mind? He had just added another offence to his first. He wondered if maybe the man had gone insane, madder than Doyle or Johnson. It was possible Barker did not understand what he was doing.

"That sort of language won't get you anywhere, Private Barker," he said, "save for a garrison cell, that is."

He walked away, sensing the beginnings of anger. Anger with himself. Filling the canteen with gin was an old trick, and he should have checked this morning. The sentries were his responsibility, and he should have caught Barker earlier than this.

It was with mounting dissatisfaction that he located a replacement sentry, posted him and marched Barker into the guardroom lockup. He went to the orderly room and reported the incident, charging Private Brian Barker with drunkenness on duty and insubordinate language.

"Barker drunk on duty, eh?" the orderly-sergeant said. "Well, he shall be flogged for it till his stubborn back runs red. What he deserves."

"Flogged?" Dudley echoed.

"Aye." The orderly-sergeant nodded. "That or shot. It's not his first offence, you know."

"I imagined it was not." He knew the sergeant was right, that it would be at least a flogging. He felt a strange sickness, as if he were to blame for condemning Barker to such a fate. Yet he knew as well that Barker had meant to do this, and the army was harsh with those who did not follow its rules. Did not Barker deserve it, after everything he had said and done? He would be lucky if the court-martial did not sentence him to death, or dishonorable discharge.

Barker had at last tripped himself up, and now he would pay the consequences.

———◆———

Another miserable day, a gloomy and overcast morning. The bugles called for morning parade, and the companies mustered in their respective positions on the earthen square, assembling in the shadow of the shabby barracks. Sergeant-Major Maclaren commanded the companies to form on the Colours. There would be no squad drills this morning.

Maclaren arranged the battalion in a horseshoe, positioning himself in its jaws. He then turned to the right-about, saluted the battalion's second-in-command, Major Willis. Willis was as handsome and agreeable as an officer could be, and on most days his manner was a combination of good humour and firmness.

But not this day. This day, his lips were tight and his eyes grim.

"Battalion formed to witness punishment, sir," Maclaren said.

Dudley had been dreading this day. He knew what was about to happen. The battalion was to witness a flogging. Private Barker's flogging. The regimental band was forming in the jaws of the horseshoe now, and Lieutenant-Colonel Freemantle approached on horseback. With Freemantle was the regimental surgeon and the adjutant, both on foot. The adjutant carried a copy of the *Articles of War* and a small leather bag.

Maclaren stood the battalion at ease, then stood them easy. The men were now free to watch the proceedings. Many had not heard of Barker's sentence, but as two sentries came onto the square bearing the triangle, that sentence became clear. The triangle was a tripod of long wooden poles, and its function was well understood. The sentries erected it in front of the band, and a low murmur rumbled through the assembled ranks.

"Silence!" Sergeant-Major Maclaren sang out. "Sergeants, take the name of any man who utters a single word."

"Bring the prisoner," commanded the adjutant, a haughty and impatient officer with a receding hairline.

Barker emerged from the guard room, a small square brick house to one side of the main gate. He was flanked by two more sentries. His hands were unbound, and he marched between his guards in step, as if he were part of a sentry detachment. His upper body was bare, the hard muscles standing out beneath his pale skin. The sentries took him to stand before the triangle, where he faced the regiment.

"Adjutant, state the charges and the sentence," Lieutenant-Colonel Freemantle ordered.

"For neglect of duty," the adjutant began, addressing the battalion, "drunkenness and insubordination, the prisoner, Private Brian Barker, is sentenced to seventy-five lashes."

Dudley let out a long breath. Seventy-five lashes would be enough to kill some men.

Upon the announcement of his sentence, Barker turned on his own accord to face the triangle. Dudley was shocked to see that his back was a mass of puckered scars. This was not his first flogging.

Barker spread his arms and the guards bound his wrists to the triangle. One guard placed a leather bit in Barker's mouth to prevent him from biting through his tongue.

From the band, a Goliath of a drummer stepped forward. Behind the drummer came the bandmaster, armed with a stout cane. The adjutant approached the drummer, opened the leather bag and took out the cat-o-nine-tails. The officer then passed the lash to the drummer, who took it and gave it a few cracks in the air for practice.

"Drummer, do your duty," the adjutant commanded.

The drummer raised his right arm above his head. There was a pause, and the men of the assembled battalion seemed to hold their breath as one. Then the cat came down on Barker's back with a sharp smack. Dudley started as if whipped himself. Barker did not flinch.

The drummer raised his arm and struck again for the second lash, and Dudley put his hand to his mouth. Seventy-three lashes to go.

Near the tenth lash, Barker's skin, already swelling with new welts, broke. The thin lines of blood glared cherry-red in the dull light of the late winter day. Someone collapsed in the ranks to Dudley's left, and he looked over to see that a middle-aged private had fainted.

The drummer paused for a moment, then struck again, and again. Behind him, the bandmaster raised his cane and dealt the drummer two hard blows across the back, shouting, "Lay 'em on harder! You're slacking, man."

The drummer stole a glance at the bandmaster, then, with a hard grimace, struck Barker with all his might. Soon Barker's back was running red, the flesh beginning to separate into gory ribbons. He gave a slight jerk with every blow now, though he remained silent.

Sweat pooled inside Dudley's coat, and he had to keep swallowing to fight down nausea. More men had fainted, dropping like potato sacks onto the parade ground, where the sergeants let them lie. A number of officers stepped out of ranks and went to the barracks veranda to sit, their faces pale.

Barker's back was now an unrecognizable mass. Dudley flinched every time the lash struck the lacerated flesh, spraying blood that spotted the drummer's face, arm and white coatee. He wanted to look away, but forced himself to observe the punishment. He might have prevented this from happening had he been more diligent, so now he would watch it through to the end.

After what seemed an eternity, the drummer dealt the seventy-fifth lash. His unenviable task finished, he stood back, massive chest heaving from the exertion. One of the sentries came forward and poured a bucket of water over Barker's mangled back, and the other cut him down from the triangle. The sentries then tried to take him by the arms, but he shrugged them off. Spitting the leather patch from his mouth, he growled, "I can stand on my own."

"Have you anything to say?" the adjutant queried.

Barker stared at the officer. He wobbled from side to side and said nothing for about half a minute. Then he licked his lips and grunted.

"No, sir. I was drunk on duty and disrespectful, and I suppose I got what I asked for."

The adjutant nodded, while Lieutenant-Colonel Freemantle gazed down from his horse, face creased with regret.

"I hope you have finally learned your lesson, Private Barker," Freemantle said.

Dudley heard this statement and thought of the old scars on Barker's back, now whipped clean away. Apparently, Freemantle was aware of Barker's shenanigans after all. It was a wonder the members of the court martial had not decided to drum him out of the service.

The punishment ended, the adjutant dismissed the prisoner. Barker took one step, stumbled, and the sentries leapt in, taking his arms again. With a growl, he shrugged them off a second time. He took another step, and then another. Then, with his head held high, he made his way to the infirmary as if taking a Sunday stroll. The sentries trailed after him.

The sergeants saw to the men who had fainted, pulling them to their feet. The squeamish officers left the veranda and returned to their positions. Major Willis turned to Sergeant-Major Maclaren and said, "Dismiss the battalion to breakfast. There shall be no drill this morning."

The attitude of the company changed in the wake of the flogging. The barrack room was more peaceful now that Barker was in hospital, but underlying that peace was a silent rivalry between those who believed his treatment had been unjust and those who were glad for what had happened.

Dudley was neither. He was too aware that those on both sides saw him as the principal actor in the drama of Barker's downfall.

After a few weeks, the tension began to subside. With Barker gone, his influence waned. The men were more agreeable toward Dudley than they had been in months. The one exception was Mrs. Barker, whose eyes spat daggers from behind her wool blanket. But that was the extent of her hostility. She did not complain to Dudley nor to anyone else, and he knew that even she sensed discipline had improved with her husband's chastisement.

Dudley would not believe he had broken Barker's power forever, but he knew he had given his own power a firm footing. His only regret, and it was a deep one, was the ugly incident that had brought him those results.

On the afternoon of the first day of March, the Royal Hampshire Fusiliers, with band and Colours, again mustered in a horseshoe formation on the parade. It was still winter; and the men dressed in greatcoats, the ranks as gray as the sky had been for weeks on end. Dudley stood with No. 3 Company and wondered what was happening now. Surely not another flogging, some poor defaulter from another company? He felt the continuing absence of Barker's tall form on the right flank of the company. The fellow remained on the sick list, though his back was healing well.

Into the jaws of the horseshoe rode Lieutenant-Colonel Freemantle, resplendent in cocked hat and gold lace. With him were the scowling adjutant and a beaming Major Willis. Sergeant-Major Maclaren positioned himself on their left.

"Men of the Royal Hants," Freemantle said, "I have glorious news."

Dudley breathed a sigh of relief. It was not a flogging. Then he understood what that "glorious news" must be.

Freemantle announced that Russia would not back down, and continued to menace poor little Turkey. As a result, Britain was going to the sultan's aid. These facts everyone already knew, but no one had been certain whether the regiment would be joining the expeditionary force or not. Freemantle's announcement could only mean that they would. Dudley felt a bubble of joy rising within his breast, and a strange weight lifted from his shoulders.

"As you all know," Freemantle continued, "British troops have already departed for Malta. The Second Battalion of the Rifle Brigade left this very city to join them only a few days ago." He raised his voice and said with emphasis, "Now the Royal Hants will get their turn!"

The regiment would depart in a week, he explained, to join the Army of the East as part of Brigadier Codrington's brigade, in General Sir George Brown's Light Division.

It was incredible news. With three cheers for the queen, the men of the battalion cast their shakos into the air.

As Dudley looked aloft and watched the leather hats fly, he noticed the dense clouds beginning to part. A moment later, sunlight bathed the parade square in its golden radiance. He continued to gaze up at the blue sky, still cheering, not even certain why he felt so elated. All of the worries and adversity of the last months burned away. He felt a sense of liberation.

He was going to war.

# CHAPTER FOUR

Cheer, boys, Cheer!
No more of idle sorrow.
Courage, true hearts, shall
bear us on our way.
Hope points before, and
shows the bright tomorrow,
Let us forget the darkness of today.

Charles Mac Kay
"Cheer, boys, Cheer!"

***Dudley leaned on*** the ship's railing and watched the Spanish coast slip by. Beyond the approaching headlands rose the sharp wedge of the Rock of Gibraltar, Britain's guardian of the Mediterranean. Gibraltar was the first port of call on the voyage to Turkey, the first alien shore Dudley would ever tread. He watched its approach with growing anticipation. In stark contrast to the blue water, the land was dark and rolling, a series of gentle brown hills divided by green hedgerows and clusters of tiny white houses.

Dudley looked forward to the landing. After the storms and seasickness of the journey thus far, it would be a wonder and a relief to steam into that famous harbour. Not that the seasickness had spoiled the adventure of sailing abroad. It had provided an unpleasant interlude, but now that the interlude was over, his happiness came flooding back.

That happiness had begun on the first day, when the regiment marched through Portsmouth, the band playing "Auld Lang Syne" and "The Girl I Left Behind Me." The men sang along as they marched, while the people of the city lined the streets and cheered, waving their hats and handkerchiefs. Dudley had often imagined such an event, himself part of a regiment marching off to glory. Now, he had experienced it in reality.

The battalion had boarded a paddle steamer in Portsmouth harbour. On this strange modern contraption, they had set out to rendezvous with a motley collection of steam and sailing vessels serving as troop transports. Then, guided by a Royal Navy escort, the little fleet had charged away south. Dirty weather descended as they crossed the Bay of Biscay, condemning most to misery, but Biscay was notorious for its storms and the troops had expected a rough passage. Their morale remained high, though their stomachs had churned, and the seas had improved as the fleet moved farther south.

The first landfall had brought a tremendous thrill after so many days at sea. For Dudley, the historical significance of the cape that had first risen over the horizon added a further dimension—Cape St. Vincent, where Britain had won a glorious sea victory half a century ago.

The officers on board had examined it with their telescopes and binocular field glasses; and as they drew nearer to the point, its features became plain to the naked eye—a little detached rock of an island, then a high bluff on which perched a white lighthouse and a convent. Both buildings looked set to topple into the sea at the slightest disturbance.

Dudley would never forget the sight.

Now he stood at the railing and watched the advance of Cape Trafalgar, the setting of another battle from the old wars. In these waters, Nelson had known his greatest victory and met his end.

Dudley wondered if any of the other men shared his historical enthusiasm. He hoped they did. They lined the larboard railing, pointing and exclaiming as the fleet steamed toward the strait. The gateway to the Mediterranean beckoned. The high brown coast of Morocco, rising hundreds of feet above the water, made the southern gatepost. The northern gatepost was the Rock of Gibraltar itself, an astonishing lopsided peak rising from the end of a flat spit of land, its forts and batteries built right into the cliffs on the western face.

Under the shadow of the massive Rock, the town stood behind its ancient Moorish walls. Dudley was about to ask an officer for the loan of a telescope when the thud of a gun made him jump. The naval escort was saluting the batteries. As the escort and transports slid into the harbour, the batteries saluted back, the steady pounding of the artillery disturbing the flocks of gulls that trailed the ships.

The sulphurous cannon smoke still hung in the air when Dudley heard the anchor chains grind, then the splash as the larboard anchor slipped into the water. A multitude of local bumboats swarmed alongside, their owners offering oranges, dates, figs and other fruits. Dudley ignored the boats and the activities of the sailors around him. Here he was, in Gibraltar.

This voyage was like a holiday, the only true holiday he had ever had, for he had never been out of Britain. And what a place to choose for his first journey abroad! Gibraltar, a name from British history and legend, with the towering Rock and its silent, impregnable fortress. That fortress had withstood more than its share of conflict in its long watch over the interests of the Empire. Dudley anticipated the chance to explore its lengthy walls. He knew he would have the time, for the regiment would remain here for several days before continuing on to Malta. In Malta, they would join the rest of the expeditionary force under the command of the aged Lord Raglan, Wellington's successor and a veteran of the Peninsula. In the interim, the men would have some free time.

Dudley meant to use that time to its fullest.

***

Dudley, Harris, Oakes and Johnson climbed the main street to the bazaar. They shared the brilliance of the morning, the clear sky with its narrow line of fragmented clouds gathered on the mountainous horizon. Other groups of men were scattered about, for the Royal Hants had dispersed throughout the town.

"I have a few coins saved," Oakes said as they made their way up the steep cobblestones. "Maybe I'll find something for my Hester."

Dudley had a few coins saved, too. More than a few, for the money from his tutorship had not gone to college tuition as expected. This made him richer than most enlisted men, including senior NCOs.

"I feel generous," he said. "If anyone spies anything they want that is beyond their means, I'll either make you a loan or make you a gift, depending on what I think are the merits of the purchase."

Harris laughed, then said, "That sounds like a dangerous offer."

"Dangerous or not," Johnson said, "I'll take it."

They came to the market, a broad enclosure of square stalls intersected by narrow alleyways. The stalls were just tent canopies arrayed on poles, some of plain sail canvas and others of colourful silks. Inside each stall were wooden tables heaped with merchandise on display. The stalls always seemed crowded, and the air was noisy with conversation and shouting in many languages. Gibraltar was British, but it had more in common with its Iberian neighbours.

Oakes had been here many times, and he described some of the town's workings. Every morning, he said, the Spanish merchants with their loaded mules crossed the neutral ground to the gates of the town. There, they assembled with a host of other "foreigners" under the drawbridge, waiting for the firing of the morning gun from the fort. After that, the drawbridge would be lowered in welcome. Once inside, the Spanish joined the other merchants who crammed the port—English, Irish, Italians, Moors and Jews. Gibraltar was a place where cultures met and made exchanges.

A wealth of cultures also made for a wealth of goods, all welcome to the men of the Royal Hants. The soldiers found tobacco for their clay pipes, jewelry and ornaments for their wives or sweethearts, and luxuries like soap for their personal comfort. There were also oranges, grapes, figs, lemons, dates, olives and other fruits, all at prices a private soldier could afford. Most favoured, however, was the cheap wine.

"This is what I've come for," Oakes said, making for an Italian wineseller. He had apparently forgotten his idea of buying something for Hester.

The others joined him, though a Moorish jeweler in the adjoining stall caught Dudley's eye. The Moor was decked out in fez and turban, wide breeches, a long loose gown open in the front and yellow Moroccan slippers. He squatted down in the midst of his merchandise, smoking a long pipe. He grinned as Dudley approached.

"Ah, English soldier man," he said. "How can I please you?"

Dudley reached into a pocket and took out Wellington. He held up the tin soldier and asked, "Can you attach this to a chain?"

"Very easily, sir," replied the jeweler, "and it shan't take any time."

The jeweler stood and took the toy from Dudley. Working quickly, he punched a tiny hole in the tin shako then fed a length of fine metal chain through the hole. Dudley took the toy soldier back and paid the agreed-upon price of half a shilling. Holding Wellington up, he whispered, "You've brought me luck, little friend, I'm sure of it. May you continue to do so."

He took off his cap and draped the chain around his neck, thrusting the tin soldier inside his coat and shirt. The charm would hang there from now on, cool against his skin.

He turned back to the Italian wine merchant, but Oakes, Harris and Johnson were gone—wandered off in their excitement without waiting, he assumed. He started to look for them, pushing through the dense crowd. Three times he mistook other groups of red-coated soldiers for his comrades, and then he gave up the search. It didn't matter that he was alone. In fact, he was glad for it. Now he could enjoy his own thoughts, take in the surroundings without distraction.

And there was plenty to see. The Moorish merchants made an exotic spectacle all by themselves, with their exotic baggy trousers and brocaded vests, an early glimpse of what he would find in the Turkish empire.

He made his way round the market a few more times. After buying a bag of oranges, he decided not to spend any more money and turned his attention to the Rock. He shaded his eyes and studied its nearest face, a cliff pressed up against the rear of the market. He wanted to climb to the top. For such an endeavour, company would have been welcome, but there was no sense in wasting time making a further search for Harris and the others. He would ascend the Rock by himself.

Beyond the market, a winding path led along the base of the cliff. Dudley followed it, climbing past the high medieval walls of the fortress. The path was steep, and he had gone only a little way before he felt the temptation to unbutton his coat. To do this would be in violation of Lieutenant-Colonel Freemantle's dress regulations, but the heat was almost too much to bear.

As he stood on the path torn between comfort and duty, he heard the grinding of footsteps from above. Around a stand of shrubs came three figures—Privates Geary and Barker and Mrs. Barker, the latter shading herself with an umbrella.

Lieutenant-Colonel Freemantle had permitted one in six soldiers' wives to accompany their husbands on the expedition. Mrs. Barker had been among the chosen. Dudley tensed when he saw her and her companions. She still blamed Dudley for her husband's flogging, and Dudley still felt uncomfortable in her presence. He also dreaded the return of Barker's nonsense, the taunts and divisiveness within No. 3 Company. So far, this fear had gone unrealized, but he couldn't guess how long the peace would last.

Barker had been careful since returning to duty, on his best behaviour, but there was no indication the flogging had left him a humbler man. His resounding and boorish voice could be heard every time he dared raise it in company of friends and supporters, which was often.

Dudley moved to one side as the party approached. A quick nod was the only greeting he could manage. Barker, on the other hand, smirked and said, "Good day, Corporal."

"Good day, Private Barker," Dudley returned, then added with a second nod, "Mrs. Barker."

Mrs. Barker wrinkled her nose as she passed. Dudley watched her back as she and her husband followed Geary down to the town.

"What a pair," he said to himself, then turned and continued on his way.

At last he reached the summit. There, he was surprised to find an open expanse of greensward and shrubs gently sloping away from him. The place was crowded with other soldiers and civilians, sitting in the grass or wandering the paths. Barker had just been here, enjoying the view with his disagreeable wife. Dudley shook his head as he thought of Mrs. Barker's sneering face. The encounter seemed more comical than hostile. He thought of the size of the woman, her black rain umbrella grasped in one powerful hand, and chuckled at the picture.

He shaded his eyes. The view impressed him at once. He could see the piled snow-capped mountains of Spain in the north—brown, purple, deep blue and white, fold upon fold receding beneath the massive sky. And when he turned to look south, there was the blue of the strait, and beyond that the green coast and yellow sands of Africa.

He removed his sweat-soaked shako and stared. He was looking at *Africa*.

He drew in a deep breath of sweet sea air.

I am a part of the world, he thought. Never mind Barker, his wife, or anyone else. Today, on this summit, I am truly alive.

Dudley savoured the time in Gibraltar. At one point he said to Harris, "The army has proven itself to me again, for here I'm experiencing the world. Here I'm learning things Cambridge could never teach me. Would I meet such people at Cambridge, see such famous and historical sights? No, I wouldn't."

The port so enchanted him that he wrote a letter to Uncle Robert, though doing so gave him cause for bitterness. He knew there was little hope he would receive a reply. His only prospects lay in a further two other letters, one to Auntie Bronwyn and one to Jane. All three letters contained the same thing—descriptions of his adventures so far, and assurances about his health and safety.

He placed the letters on board the packet bound for home, and then the regiment left Gibraltar for Malta. The huge paddle steamer chugged away from the harbour then set all plain sail in open water. The steam engines died, allowing for some respite from the mechanical din and the filth of the coal smoke.

The short passage was as pleasant as the last had been unpleasant. Every morning brought the usual inspection parade, though now the regiment formed on deck instead of on the square. After this short bit of military protocol, the men idled away their time above or below decks. The regimental officers amused themselves shooting at porpoises with their revolvers, a pastime that brought them great merriment, though it made Dudley uncomfortable. The poor creatures were so willing to make friends, only to receive so rude a welcome. He dared to voice this opinion, but the officers insisted the porpoises were merely dumb fish.

Most of the enlisted men agreed. Some privates and NCOs even tried to catch a few of those dumb fish, since the things made decent eating. To this, Dudley relented, for he saw merit in the sport of fishing. But he did not join in himself. Instead, he spent his days gazing across the sea from the rigging, and looked forward to the evening entertainments on the quarterdeck. At these, the regimental band played a medley of tunes, after which informal groups of men sang comic and sentimental songs.

It was in this high spirit that the fleet raised Malta after four days, then sailed in past the tiered batteries flanking the harbour of Valletta. The men on Dudley's ship crammed the rail again, gazing at the Italianate domes and spires and terraced houses of the town. As the vessel steamed toward its anchorage, the guns of the main fort and leading man-of-war fired their salutes.

This was the first time the bulk of the British force would be assembled in one place. Beyond the cannon smoke, Dudley could see the masts of another fleet of transports and men-of-war that had arrived earlier. When the smoke cleared, he saw the soldiers of other regiments had formed on the quay. As the new arrivals approached, these troops began to cheer. The men of the Royal Hants cheered back and waved their caps.

Malta proved even more exciting than Gibraltar. He met members of two of the other regiments in Codrington's brigade—the 7th and 23rd Fusiliers—and was witness to an impressive array of uniforms from the other divisions. There were kilted Highlanders, Guards in bearskin hats, blue-coated gunners of the Royal Artillery, fanciful Hussars, Lancers, Dragoons, and Riflemen in their distinctive green jackets and black leather belts. Dudley began to feel part of something grand, something vast and epic.

This was the largest assembled British army since the struggle against Bonaparte. And this time, the French would be on their side, as allies in the field. The British would join the French army in Turkey, and that would be a sight to see.

But Dudley had not counted on the slow pace of war. As the balmy days came and went, thoughts of Turkey began to fade into the background. The war itself began to seem like a remote possibility. With the attractive buildings, the clean campsites and barracks, the mild spring climate, and the endless flow of cheap wine, the stay in Malta became a holiday in the true sense.

The army began to relax. The men remained cheerful, though they were no longer so excited. Only a few outbreaks of dysentery and diarrhea marred the situation, but these could be blamed on the wine, which was not always of top quality. Life was comfortable, much more so than in Fairbridge or Portsmouth, and speculation began to circulate that the Russians would back down. To Dudley, this possibility was both attractive and disappointing. No danger, yet no chance at glory.

Then, with the passing of March, the speculation ended. Orders came, and the regiments again boarded their steamers.

After a nine-day voyage, the army arrived off the port of Galli-poli. This new venue shook off the near-lethargy, and the ex-citement returned. From the deck of his steamer, Dudley saw a truly foreign land, a city of red-roofed houses and tall white minarets, like something from his childhood storybooks.

"I feel as if I have leapt into the *Arabian Nights*," he said to Harris before their disembarkation. "I half-expect to see a magic carpet wind its way between the spires."

He did not see magic carpets, but he did see the French, who had arrived a few days before. When the Royal Hants went ashore and formed up, Dudley spied a group of French officers watching the drill. The officers stood near the pier in their fine, modern-looking uniforms—single-breasted frock coats and kepis, little peaked caps with sloping crowns and gold edging.

"What do you think of that, eh, Wellington?" Dudley mut-tered to his tin-soldier charm. "Your old enemy is now our friend against this new menace."

It was a moving moment, but the reality of Gallipoli soon dealt his enthusiasm a crushing blow. Turkey had none of the qualities of Gibraltar and Malta. Gallipoli might have looked exotic and beautiful from the water, but on closer inspection it proved to be filthy and dilapidated, the streets narrow and cracked and filled with rotting sewage. To make matters worse, the French army had beaten the British to the best food and the best areas of encampment. The British had no choice but to cram into tiny campsites on the outskirts of the town, with no decent water supply nearby.

"This place is a miserable and villainous hole," Harris pro-claimed at the end of their first week, voicing the disillusionment of the entire army.

Villainous hole or not, the tiny port had to accommodate the needs of 18,000 British and 22,000 French. This sizable force remained in Gallipoli until early June when, with great relief, the British sailed north to Scutari and Constantinople. There, everyone thought, things would be better.

Dudley again looked forward to experiencing history first-hand in the Turkish capital, once such a powerful bastion of Christian society. Constantinople had been the center of the ancient Byzantine Empire, and now it was the center of Ottoman power. He watched the approach of the city as the fleet steamed up the Bosporus Strait. It was an impressive sight, a sprawling jumble of buildings in all shapes, sizes and colours. Some of the structures he knew from engravings he had seen in books. He recognized the Seven Towers, then Seraglio Point and the sultan's palace. Pictures come to life.

Soon, the fleet steamed into the Golden Horn. The Horn was jammed with shipping, everything from steam ferryboats of the British type to little Turkish caiques that flitted here and there. The caiques were long and slender craft, similar to North American canoes. Dudley watched as they passed back and forth from one side of the strait to the other. Some of them carried groups of Turkish women. The women wore flowing white robes and stared out at the soldiers from the gaps above their yashmaks. Dudley waved, but none of the women waved back.

"Part o' someone's harem," Oakes said, chuckling.

"Harem?" Dudley echoed, a little shocked by the implications of that word.

"Some Turkish gentleman's wives," Oakes continued. "One for every night of the week."

Dudley watched the caique he had waved to move off. "What a disgusting though fascinating idea."

"Which part do you find fascinatin'?" Barker shouted from his place at the rail. "I like the bottom part, meself."

Dudley ignored him, trying not to acknowledge that his face was reddening.

"Look! There beyond the Arabian shore is Mount Olympus."

Oakes looked, as did others. A moment later, the pale yellow medieval walls of the imperial palace obscured the mythic peak. The men watched in silence.

Then the steamer came alongside Hagia Sophia. Above its high dome were the forts, the muzzles of their ancient artillery commanding the water. Behind those crumbling walls was the Imperial City, rising from the Golden Horn in multicoloured

81

terraces of red-tiled rooftops, gardens, cypress trees, mosques, palaces and slender minarets of white stone with golden turrets.

"So, this is Constantinople," Dudley said, satisfied.

But the satisfaction did not last. After the regiment set up camp, Dudley had the opportunity for a closer look at the city. He discovered it was just like Gallipoli, though on a greater scale. Much of the Turkish quarter, as well as Scutari across the strait, was crumbling, dirty and stinking, the streets strewn with waste and filth. To make matters worse, the heat was intense, aggravating the stench.

Within days of the landing, many of the British began taking solace from the bottle. They condemned Turkey as vile, the people lazy and uncaring. Time and again, Colour-Sergeant Onslow gave Dudley the task of taking a squad to round up drunks.

Dudley did manage to salvage some of his hopes. He and Harris passed their free time sightseeing, perusing the buildings and monuments. He also never tired of watching the veiled Turkish ladies, so mysterious and alluring. He decided this visit to the ancient seaport was worthwhile, even though he and Harris had to make their way back to camp over the filthy and broken cobblestones, stepping around the worst messes and trying to ignore the array of bad smells.

The stay in Constantinople was brief. The British command established a permanent base and hospital in Scutari, then decided to move on to the next port. That port was to be Varna, in Bulgaria. There they would rejoin the French close to where most of the fighting had so far taken place.

The men of the regiment were glad to be moving again as the fleet made its way up the Bosporus towards the Black Sea. Dudley stared at the Turkish houses that lined the shore, the Turkish men sitting cross-legged on their verandas, smoking their long pipes and swatting at flies. The windows of these low houses were latticed and fastened, though here and there a beautiful unveiled lady in a colourful costume would peer out.

"Another glimpse of the harem," Oakes said to Dudley when they had spotted one of these graceful visions.

"A flash of fairy story," Dudley replied. His middle-class country morality found the concept of a harem perverse in reality, but what he had encountered on this journey was not real to him. He had seen so much in the last weeks his mind could not absorb it all.

The quality of the departure from Constantinople added to the effect of unreality. There was no cheering from the dockside, no music to see them off as there had been in every other port thus far, save for Gallipoli. The Turks did seem lazy and indifferent. They had paid no attention to the British soldiers, granting them no cheers and no evidence they cared that the British force had come to help them.

With no crowds to see them off, the idlers along the rails turned their attention to the shoals of dolphins and porpoises that followed the ships, leaping and chirping in their strange language. It seemed that these friendly sea creatures were the only ones with a mind to say farewell, and the troops were appreciative. For once, there was no target practice.

"Perhaps Varna will be better" was the refrain heard again and again on the voyage. Hopes ran high. Varna would be better, and within striking distance of the enemy. Maybe the expeditionary force, British and French, would even see some action at last.

Like Gallipoli and Constantinople, Varna seemed delightful from the ocean, with its bright houses and tile rooftops. Once on land, though, a close inspection shattered the illusion, just as it had twice before. Varna was not better. The buildings were not so bright, and had dirty walls with chunks of plaster missing. The streets were full of potholes, and each angled toward a central drain that was little more than an open sewer.

With sinking spirits, the men of the regiment recognized that this was the most unhealthy spot yet. And again the French army was here ahead of the British. They had taken the most convenient campsites and the best food—though these things were, in fact, just the most tolerable pickings from a bad lot. The British changed campsites several times, but every location proved just as bad. Decent food and drinking water were scarce. The weather continued to be unbearably hot.

But the Allied Expeditionary Force was here to stay. Days flowed into weeks, and weeks flowed into months. Months of idleness, while the Turkish army continued to battle the Russians alone.

Dudley found himself staring at a spring and early summer with nothing to do but wait. The joy he had first felt in Portsmouth began to slip away until it was just a memory. On some days, even that memory was impossible to recall.

Then the sickness began.

On a scorching July day, Dudley and another corporal helped a dying man to the hospital tent and laid him down in the crowded shade. The Light Division camp wallowed in disease now, as did the other camps. Several men in Dudley's company had died. He had helped bury them.

He looked at the rows of wretched forms under the long awning of the tent. He knew those already dead would soon be joined by many others. Casualties in a campaign before a single shot had been fired.

An army surgeon approached the groaning man Dudley had just brought in. Dudley did not know the man, but could tell at a glance he was overtaxed, his thinning blond hair piled in a knot on his head as if he had been grasping and squeezing it in exasperation. His eyes were red and sunken behind his spectacles, his mouth set in grim resignation.

"It's the cholera, of course," he said, looking down at the unfortunate patient.

Cholera. Dudley shuddered and eyed the weak and waxen forms at his feet, most of them curled up with intestinal cramps. The place reeked of their illness.

Rumours of the disease had germinated in the French camps, and the disease had not been far behind. Sickness had spread through the British tent lines and, before long, had even reached the men-of-war anchored in the harbour.

Dudley's eyes wandered to the form of another casualty he had brought in earlier that day—Mrs. Barker, lying on her side on a gray woolen blanket, shivering and sick. Her knees were drawn up to her belly, and a cloud of flies buzzed about her head. He still didn't like the woman, but her suffering made him sympathetic. He would not wish this fate, this painful and un-dignified decline, on anybody.

"You'd best be on your way, Corporal," the surgeon said. The other corporal had already departed. "This is no healthy place to linger."

"*Is* there a healthy place near this town, sir?"

The surgeon grimaced. "No. There you are right. This heat, contaminated water, bad food. It's a disaster, an outrage!"

Dudley nodded. Conditions had gone from bad to worse, and there was nothing he could do to help.

"I wish I knew the answer," the surgeon murmured. "I wish I knew—hello, what's this?"

Dudley followed the surgeon's gaze back towards the far end of the tent, where Mrs. Barker lay. An orderly was shouting at a soldier who had just ducked under the tent flap. The soldier was healthy, and when the orderly moved to one side, Dudley saw it was Private Barker. Barker stood over the dying form of his wife and shook his fist at the orderly.

"I'll look after her meself!" he was saying. "I'm not leavin' her here in this sick place. She needs air, you bloody fool."

"There's nothing you can do for her," the orderly insisted. "She could spread the sickness—"

"It's already spread. It's in the damned water. I'm takin' her, and you can't stop me!"

Barker scooped his wife up from the ground as if she weighed no more than a child. When he carried the groaning woman outside, the orderly gave chase.

"Let him go!" the surgeon called, his voice heavy with ex-haustion. He turned to Dudley, and his eyes were bleak, hope-less.

"We'll have to move the camps again," he said.

Moving the camps again proved ineffective, and the ranks of the sick grew. The army needed decent food and, above all, clean drinking water; but the latter was difficult to find, while fire destroyed a warehouse full of the former.

Dudley did his best to keep the sickness at bay. He boiled his drinking and cooking water. He took long walks away from camp. He volunteered for work parties whenever possible, even though those work parties were often set to the unpleasant task of digging graves. Digging graves at least provided exercise, and the work could be done in shirtsleeves. So far, these precautions had worked, and he remained healthy. Healthy despite the heat and stink of Varna.

Heat and stink—those two words best described this place. Dudley wondered if the commanders of the Allied forces, Lord Raglan and Marshal St. Arnaud, really knew what they were doing. Since Gallipoli, they had moved the army from one vile hole to the next then stood motionless in each. The Turks fought the Russians along the Danube while the British and French forces sat in frustration, surrounded by plague and misery. The men grew sullen, demoralized by death from disease, this foe at which they could not strike.

Even Dudley found it difficult to uphold his philosophy of conduct. To work within the bounds of the situation had been his vow. To never let anyone see him complain, for complaints were a further drain on morale. But it was difficult not to express what seethed under the surface of the army's ordered exterior.

As Dudley walked between the even rows of tents in the Light Division camp, he reflected on the distress those tents hid. He had seen and touched the artifacts of that distress. He had just dismissed another squad of gravediggers, and the odours of death and decay were still fresh in his nostrils.

His mood was not one of optimism. His emotions were in a dull, deadened state. He had witnessed mass death from disease once before, when an epidemic of typhoid fever struck one horrible year at his uncle's school. The outbreak had almost ruined Uncle Robert, until he discovered the source—a polluted well. Dudley had grown used to death then—hardened to it, as he became hardened now.

"It's not good to have that happen," he said, thinking out loud as he neared his own tent. "It's the beginning of not caring, a kind of surrender."

Harris sat under an awning in front of the tent.

"What surrender?"

Dudley noticed him for the first time. Harris wore his undress jacket and forage cap, and was busy polishing his bayonet. Dudley nodded at the weapon.

"Are you expecting to be using that soon?"

Harris set down his cleaning rag.

"My, you're sounding bitter. One grave party too many, I think."

Dudley took off his cap and wiped his brow. It was so hot sweat had soaked every inch of his cotton fatigue shirt. His body felt foul.

"This sitting and waiting as we die one by one is not my idea of soldiering," he snarled. "It's not what I bargained for. Not what I hoped for. Have you heard the news? The Russians have lifted their siege of Silistra and are beginning to withdraw from Moldavia and Wallachia. And here we sit and sweat and sicken and die."

"Oddly enough," Harris drawled, "this sitting and waiting in filth does not surprise me. It is something I always associated with army life. I like to think of it as a kind of perverse stability. We know what tomorrow will bring, and as long as we keep our own health, we have that comfort." He shook his head. "The pleasantries of Gibraltar and Malta are long over. From now on, I fear we are in for some hard campaigning." He swatted at a fly in sudden irritation. "God! But I shall go mad with boredom soon, with nothing new to read."

"We are all mad," Dudley muttered. "Mad to be here at all."

———◆———

Then, without warning, the mood changed dramatically. During a routine morning inspection parade, Lieutenant-Colonel Freemantle made an announcement that brought ecstatic relief. The regiment, he explained, would soon be on its way to the Crimean Peninsula in the Ukraine, on enemy territory. The Allied generals had decided the important Russian naval base at Sevastopol must be destroyed. This would prevent the enemy from threatening Turkey and the Mediterranean ever again. Even now, reconnaissance parties were planning the operation, examining the terrain for a landing area.

The men celebrated, singing songs and dancing jigs to the sound of fiddles and fifes. No. 3 Company shared that joy, though for them bad news followed the good. Later in the day, they heard that Barker's wife had finally succumbed. She had lasted longer than most.

Her funeral would be held that evening. Barker had maintained his good behaviour since Gibraltar. At least, his behaviour had been good for him. His aggressive teasing went on as usual, his coarse laughter ringing through the camp, but he had not picked any fights nor caused a major disturbance. He had even managed to abstain from excessive drinking.

This control remained with him through his wife's funeral. All of No. 3 Company attended that somber affair, including Dudley, despite Mrs. Barker's animosity towards him. After the service, Barker announced his thanks to everyone for showing their respects. Then he and a few of his closest mates visited a tavern in the town.

The next morning Barker did not appear for roll call. Captain Clarke ordered Colour-Sergeant Onslow to send an armed squad into the town to retrieve him. Onslow gave command of that squad to Corporal Dudley.

Dudley marched the squad along a twisting waterfront street, keeping it to one side of the putrid drain. He was not happy at being chosen for this duty. It pitted him against Barker again. Again Barker would suffer as a result of Dudley's actions. He would not suffer as he had under the flogging, but he would be punished. It was another chapter in the competition between the two men, a competition for the hearts and minds of No. 3 Company.

Dudley knew the competition existed, that it was not in his imagination. He had always stood up to Barker, and that had made him the champion of others who wished they could have behaved as well. At the same time, Barker's supporters watched him with suspicion. He feared a return to the tension that had existed just after Barker's flogging. If that happened, something might break.

His squad found Barker slumped in a chair in a cramped and murky hovel. The huge private was snoring with his face in a small puddle of his own vomit. One of the men in the squad dashed a bucket of water over the man's head. The big private awoke with a cry, flailing his arms and searching for assailants.

When he recognized Dudley, he blinked a few times then roared, "What the Christ are you at now?"

"You were not present at morning roll call, Private," Dudley stated. "You could be charged with desertion. However, I appreciate your grief at the unfortunate loss of your wife, and so I will do my best to present this incident in a light favourable to you."

"You will present this event in a light favourable to me?" Barker exclaimed, wiping his jaw with one hand. Then he clutched his head, groaning, and muttered, "How the bloody hell was I to know I'd miss assembly? The bastards I was with last night knew I was here. It's their damn fault for leaving me."

Dudley took a deep breath to help curb his impatience.

"You can't lay the blame elsewhere, Private. We're all responsible for our own actions, and you of all people know the consequences of heavy drinking." He paused, then remarked, "I believe you may be a hopeless case, Private Barker. The sorriest example of a soldier I have ever seen."

"The sorriest example?" Barker repeated, lurching to his feet. Dudley smelled his foul breath. "And I suppose you think you're something sweet, eh? What do you know about it, anyway? You think a good soldier is someone who drills smartly and looks fine in a uniform—"

"Unlike yourself, a soldier is one who knows his responsibilities, who fights and stands up for what is right—"

"No, a soldier is one who fights, and that is simply it." Barker glared down at him. "Fights because he's told, and dies because he's told. Who gives up everything because he's told. And what do you know of that? Oh, you do what you're told, all right, to a sickenin' degree, but do you know how to fight? Have you ever stood in a line under fire, elbow to elbow with your friends, and then one second you feel the fellow next to you ain't there anymore, that you've lost a comrade, and then someone comes and takes his place? Have you ever killed a man?"

Dudley did not have an answer for any of these questions. While he searched for something to say, Barker placed himself in the custody of the squad without further complaint. But as he moved past Dudley, he added, "You know nothin' about bein' a soldier."

"When the time comes," Dudley spat, "and I do see action, I believe I will prove more useful than you, Barker. Now come along."

Barker chuckled as the squad led him up the stairs, out into the merciless sunshine.

Being late for roll call could be a flogging offence during wartime, but in light of Barker's losing his wife, Lieutenant-Colonel Freemantle opted for mercy. Barker's sentence was nothing more than a period of extra drill every day until further notice.

———⚓———

While the summer waned, though the heat continued unabated, the armies boarded their transports and made the voyage across the Black Sea. Their destination was the Crimea.

On September 14, they landed in Calamita Bay, on the west coast, north of the port of Sevastopol. The Light Division was the first to go ashore, and as the boats put in Dudley studied the approaching beach, a long strip of yellow sand below a crest of thick grass. The land all around was open and featureless.

Dudley leapt from the longboat onto the wet sand. He held his rifle above his head and made his way up the beach to higher and drier ground. His pack, weapons and uniform weighed him down, while the shifting surface underfoot made walking difficult. Yet nothing could spoil this moment for him. He had allowed himself to forget the last horrible months. The waiting was over.

At the top of the beach loomed the grassy crest. Dudley noticed three brown-coated horsemen on it about a mile distant. Their dress and position confused him until Private Johnson, walking beside him, said, "Look at those cheeky bastards."

Dudley knew then who the horsemen were—Russian observers. He was seeing the enemy for the first time. Two salt lakes protected the bay, so the Russians could not oppose the landing. But they could watch.

He stared at them, fascinated. He felt a tingling along his spine. The enemy. An entity he had thought and heard about for so long. An entity that had become half-forgotten in the long journey to this place, to this beach in some obscure speck of land called the Crimean Peninsula. Now, there he was. At last, the enemy was in sight.

Dudley thought of what Barker had said in the Varna tavern, about how he had never been in battle, never faced death. Never killed anyone. He wondered if he could really meet those brown-coated men on the field. Could he remember his training and do his duty without flinching?

"I bet I could empty their saddles from here," Johnson said, unslinging his beloved Minie and pulling the hammer back to the half-cock.

"Don't bother, boy," said old Oakes, who was leading his gray-headed wife up the beach by the hand. "They may complain about your acting without any sort of orders and discharging a weapon on the crowded strand. There'll be time enough for that later."

Johnson did not agree, but his respect for the older man made him ease down his hammer anyway. He would get his chance later.

Dudley tore his attention away from the Russian cavalry and looked behind him. Most of the men of the Light Division had arrived, all eight battalions. Now the other divisions were coming ashore. The beach swarmed with men who moved between the barrels, crates and great piles of baggage that littered the sand.

It must seem formidable to the observing Russians, Dudley thought. Countless longboats pushed up on the strand, disgorging company after company. Groups of sailors in white duck frocks and straw sennet hats worked to land guns on artillery rafts. The great fleet of navy and transport vessels clogged the waters offshore. Above the beach, the battalions formed up to the rattling of field drums.

Dudley rushed to find a place with his regiment, thinking what fools the Russians would be to attack, even if they could.

All afternoon and evening the unloading of equipment continued. The marines and sailors towed in huge landing rafts loaded with horses, guns and detachments of blue-coated Artillery, all amid a heavy swell that grew heavier. The sky began to darken with cloud as evening fell, and horses could be heard screaming in panic as they kicked and plunged into the waves. The surf pounded a few boats and rafts to pieces, and a number of men must have drowned, though Dudley never learned for sure. He only saw the evidence of these small disasters after the fact, when he and several others gathered driftwood and bits of the broken boats and rafts to build their campfires.

The army would camp in the open, for the tents had not come ashore. Neither had the officers' horses and much of their personal baggage. As Dudley gathered his firewood, he saw the division commander, Sir George Brown, eating his dinner on a blanket under a gun carriage.

If such a proper gentleman can make do, Dudley thought, then the rest of us can. The tents will come off tomorrow.

With his bundle of fuel, he returned to his bivouac.

That night, the skies opened, and the rain came down in torrents, extinguishing the fires and making sleep and comfort impossible. The next morning, the troops sat sodden and miserable, though they did their best to dry their coats and blankets by hanging them out in the powerful sun.

The navy men continued to offload the horses, guns and equipment from the transports. By the second evening, the tents had still not arrived. The French troops, coming ashore a few miles along the coast, had received their tents the first day.

Five days passed while the British struggled to land their expeditionary force. All during that time, the men had to contend with no shelter and no fresh water. Many were still sick from Varna, and now the exposure made their condition worse. New maladies—colds and chills—erupted. To complicate things, the Russians made a number of appearances, nipping at the flanks of the invader. Dudley heard of such encounters, though he did not see the enemy himself nor further evidence of their presence. His discomfort, and the discomfort of the others in his company, was foremost in his mind.

"Someone has been blundering," he muttered to Harris one evening.

By September 19, the operation was complete. In the morning, the regimental bands struck up and the march began, south for Sevastopol. A detachment of cavalry and the Light Division marched in front while, away to the right, the French column marched closer to the sea. For a brief few hours, with the bands banging and crashing, all seemed right again. Right and ripe for glory.

Dudley tramped to the beat of the music, rifle sloped on his left shoulder. It was a relaxed march, so he took the time to examine the landscape of bleak and barren hills, all yellowish grass with hardly a tree to be seen. He wondered how anyone could live in such a place. It was almost a desert. He felt as if he were marching on the moon.

Harris walked beside him. Dudley could feel the touch of his friend's elbow in dressing. Harris's breathing was ponderous, and he kept clearing his throat. He stumbled several times. After about half an hour, Dudley turned to him and murmured, "Are you all right, old fellow?"

Harris made no reply for a few moments. Then, between breaths, he said, "I'm afraid the thirst and exposure are having their effect on me. I believe I may have a touch of fever." His face was ashen, despite being sunburned, and sweat ran in rivulets from under the rim of his shako. "I am not a strong fellow to begin with."

"Hang on," Dudley said, though he felt a jolt of alarm. He had seen men die of fever in Varna, joining the cholera victims, but he tried to believe himself when he stated, "Things will soon get better."

Harris managed a grin. "They can hardly get worse, now, can they?"

But when the bands stopped playing, things *seemed* worse. Gone was the encouragement of the music, its call to move forward. Now the army marched for the sake of marching. No one spoke. The only sounds were the crunch of thousands of pairs of boots on the stony ground, the clumping of hoofs, the creak of leather belts, the jingle of horse's harness and mess tins, the rumbling of gun carriages and oxcarts. Now and then someone coughed or groaned or muttered or sighed.

Dudley watched a private in the line ahead of him remove his shako, tear out the peak and throw the rest of the cap to the ground. The man then pulled his forage cap from his knapsack, slid the shako peak into its inside rim, and plopped this more comfortable rig on his head. Seeing this, the man marching next to him did the same.

Dudley knew that later the two would claim to have lost their shakos. He was about to tell them to fall out and recover the discarded pieces of kit, but changed his mind. The shako was a stiff and cumbersome headdress, and one less thing for the soldiers to carry. Dudley's own cap felt like a ring of hard leather around his skull. Sweat soaked every inch of his body, and a fine layer of dust covered his face and hands. His knapsack straps bit into the flesh of his armpits, while a burning thirst seared his throat. If the other men felt as he did, why should they not modify their uniforms to make them more practical? And if the quartermasters and generals who planned this expedition did not like it, then let them explain why their mistakes had forced the army to live without shelter for five days.

With this bitter thought, Dudley unclipped his leather neck stock, tore it from his collar and let it drop to the ground.

A dull thud made him look around, and he saw that a soldier had dropped to his knees. The man was struggling to rise, his comrades marching by and ignoring him.

Dudley's instinct was to help, but he would not break ranks. He hesitated, torn, until one of his old drill instructors, Sergeant O'Ryan, came jogging along the side of the column. Sweat glistened on the Irishman's ruddy face, and when he saw Dudley he stopped, gasping for breath, and said, "Corporal Dudley, fall out and follow me."

O'Ryan explained that Sergeant-Major Maclaren had detailed several senior NCOs to look after stragglers. The cholera was still taking its toll, as were thirst and exhaustion. The NCOs were to leave the hopeless cases, if need be, but help anyone who could be salvaged.

Dudley moved to the fallen private and tugged him to his feet. The man stood leaning on Dudley, and made a feeble attempt to brush the dust from his gray summer trousers.

"Can you carry on?" Dudley asked, and the fellow nodded. "Then hurry along and take your place, man."

The soldier hobbled off. Dudley walked back along the column, staring into the haggard faces of the men he passed. He found another soldier who had fallen behind, though this one was still on his feet, shuffling outside the ranks. It was old Oakes.

"Oakes," Dudley cried, finding the strength to hurry to the veteran's side. "Are you all right?"

Oakes nodded and held up his right hand. "I'll be okay, Corporal. Slipped gettin' off the boat, back there in Calamity Bay. Sore old shin, makes it a bit hard to walk. But I won't drop out. You look to Mrs. Oakes, though, if ye can."

"She's riding back there in an oxcart. I thought you had placed her there."

Oakes smiled. "No, not me. But you know the esteem the boys feel for my Hester. Someone has done her a kindness, for which I am heartily grateful. Now you run along and find some real stragglers. I'm fine here."

Dudley touched the old fellow on the arm, then resumed his search for others in need.

All afternoon he darted up and down the column, pushing and prodding men back into ranks. A few he came across could not rise. One near-hopeless case he and a private slung onto the

95

top of a baggage wagon. Another was dead where he lay, doubled up with cholera.

Then, as Dudley was moving back to check on Oakes again, the troop of 11th Hussars that had been riding in the fore galloped out ahead of the army. A moment later, in a whirl of dust and wind and noise, a column of Royal Horse Artillery dashed up from the rear. They rode forward to join the cavalry, their light bronze six-pounder guns bouncing along behind. Dudley soon lost sight of them, but a moment later, he heard the steady thunder of controlled cannon fire.

"They're pounding away at something," he said to himself, and found the inner strength to feel some excitement. It was the first time he had heard shots fired in anger.

But a few minutes later, a hussar came riding back, a wounded comrade draped across his saddle. The injured man howled with each jolt from the moving horse, his right leg nothing but a meaty stump, oozing blood.

Dudley felt his cheeks drain at the sight. *There, now I have seen the ugly face of battle, and it is nothing like seeing a sick man, even one who dies.*

He drew in a long breath, closing his eyes. The shock of seeing the wounded man passed.

He carried on in his search for stragglers. Now and then, he glanced forward, toward the pounding of the distant guns. He hoped to catch a glimpse of what was happening.

That glimpse came when the army crested a low ridge. A wide river valley lay below. Moving across that flat, dead ground was the force that the Hussars and Artillery had encountered: columns of gray and brown Russian infantry, retiring south, away from the advancing British.

"My God," Dudley said. It seemed a great host, though it was in fact just a small advance force. The movements of the columns were slow and ordered. There was no fear in their retreat. It was a tactical withdrawal.

Which meant that somewhere, a larger force lay in wait.

The retiring Russians disappeared as night fell. The British column halted and settled down to bivouac, sick and exhausted. The men gathered what they could from the bleak land to build their fires. When the cavalry returned from their forward reconnaissance, they brought intelligence that soon filtered through the ranks. A strong enemy force was entrenched along the heights beyond the Alma River, directly in the path of the advancing allies. The British column would reach them some time tomorrow.

The men of No. 3 Company huddled in their blankets and tried to absorb this news. They sought the warmth of the fires and of each other's camaraderie. The nearness of battle set the veterans to discussing home and friends far away. They needed to think of these things now, in case it was the last chance they ever got.

Dudley could not put a name to how he felt. A new weight had settled on his shoulders, but he remained calm. He was not afraid, but felt trapped in the path of an approaching event of great and grave importance. An event that could crush him with its momentum.

That feeling strengthened when the conversation ended and everyone prepared to bed down for the night. Dudley did not think he could sleep. He wrapped himself in his greatcoat, blanket looped up around his head, and stared into the twisting orange-and-yellow contours of the fire. Around him, a great stillness settled.

Harris broke that stillness. He raised his head from the ground and whispered, "Dudley, I have had a premonition. I am going to fall in the first action."

Dudley glanced down at his friend. A sudden constriction gripped his throat, but he managed to squeeze out, "Nonsense. What do you mean, a premonition? You're just feeling a little ill. Your fever is making you imagine all sorts of strange things."

Harris shook his head, features distorted in dancing light and shadow from the flames.

"It's true that I am ill. Very ill. But after tomorrow, I shall have no more need to worry about it." A hand shot out from his blanket and gripped Dudley's arm. "But I am determined to do my duty. Do not doubt me! I have not been an exemplary soldier, despite my early promotion. I have let things go by me, as I always do. That's how I have lived my whole life, never coming forward and taking an active part. Now, this early death shall be my reward for that failure."

"Harris—"

"No. I know what will be. I felt fear today, when I heard the guns, saw those wounded cavalrymen. I was never afraid of disease, but today I was afraid of battle. But let the dear Lord give me strength tomorrow to face my fate, and do my duty for my queen and country. For there is one thing I shall take an active part in—I refuse to be remembered as a coward."

"You are not a coward, Harris. And tomorrow, who knows what will happen?"

Harris looked at him for a moment in silence, then released his grip.

"I know what will happen," he said. "But I am content. I am content." He pulled his blanket close around his chin and went to sleep.

# CHAPTER FIVE

The trumpets sound!
The colours they are flying, boys,
To fight, kill or wound.
May we still be found,
Content with our hard fare, my boys,
On the cold, cold ground.

"Why, Soldiers, Why?"

**The 20th of September.** A day of cloudless blue sky above a vast and rolling land of jumbled stone and yellow grass. Across this unsheltered terrain marched the British force, an army of dust-covered men with stomachs half full. They marched in a double column, the Second Division leading the right, the Light Division leading the left. The piercing music of the fifes and drums carried them forward, despite the rumour that Lord Raglan did not care for the sound of those instruments.

Lord Raglan was a gentle old fellow who had lost an arm while fighting the French in the Peninsula. He rode at the head of his army, invisible to most of his men. He trusted that those men needed no encouragement from him. There was no question they would do their duty today.

Another officer took it upon himself to ignite the fire of the British army. This was a little man who cantered along the British lines on a fine big horse. The man wore a blue coat that

99

sparkled with gold braid and huge bullion epaulettes, and he grinned between his little upswept mustache and trim goatee. As he held his cocked hat aloft to the British troops, Dudley recognized him as Marshal St. Arnaud, the French commander-in-chief. The Royal Hants gave him a thunderous cheer as he passed. Dudley cheered with them.

"I hope you shall fight well today!" the French general called in English.

"Yes, we will," someone replied from the ranks. "Don't we always?"

Dudley smiled at the irony of this remark. The last time a British army of this size had "fought well" had been at Waterloo, against Arnaud's countrymen. That fact made this an historic occasion, the bonding of two mighty nations that had been foes for centuries.

A shiver of awe tickled the back of Dudley's neck. It no longer mattered that this expedition had not lived up to its initial promise. He was where he wanted to be, standing in the midst of what he considered fantastic and earthshaking events. France and Britain, hand-in-hand.

Brigadier Codrington approached the regiment on his gray Arab, and Dudley waved and shouted in his excitement. The general returned the wave, and the entire division began to cheer again. Forgotten were the fears and miseries of the previous night. That was all behind them now. The men faced battle and possible violent death, but were glad for it.

Battle would be better, Dudley thought, than the slow demise, the wearing away they had faced for months. Even now, as they marched ever south, men were dropping from the ranks, cramped or feverish. But those who remained moved forward with a single-mindedness, seeking the fire and destruction of battle. That cataclysm would purge them of all frustrations. The heroic deeds of this day would purify the army in spirit, remind them that they were Soldiers of the Queen.

The column moved along a narrow road that led through a small village of low plaster-walled houses. Beyond the village ran the Alma River, pouring out to the sea on the right. The river flowed slim and shallow, and green trees grew along its banks.

The far bank rose at a steep angle toward a long and even crest. The crest made a natural wall, barring the Allied advance. There the Russians had decided to make their stand to repel the invader.

Dudley caught his breath when the Russian positions came into view. They stretched for miles along the heights of the Alma. On the left of the Allied column was a large field fortification, a redoubt of low earthen walls and embrasures for heavy field guns. To the right of this great redoubt, columns of drab gray Russian infantry waited for the attack. Farther right was a smaller redoubt containing more heavy guns. Below the redoubts was a line of earthen-and-brush breastworks guarding more infantry.

There were so many of them—men in long gray or brown coats. Column after column waited, each like a solid block of stone. Stone armed with muskets and supported by the gaping black mouths of the entrenched cannon. The Russian position looked impregnable.

Yet, that was what they were to assault, and it seemed to Dudley the Allies would march straight on, without a pause. In a moment, they would cross the river and mount that slope, and there they would face a storm of lead and iron.

Dudley's cheers faded. For the first time that day, he noticed his throat felt dry and sore. He suddenly thought of the wounded hussar from the skirmish yesterday. He knew then that his notions of battle, even those of a few minutes ago, were fanciful. They were wishful thinking to keep his mind from the reality he could very well die in a few minutes. Or he could be maimed, which was worse. And even if he came through unscathed, others would not.

"A bleak place," Harris said beside him. "A hard place to have to die."

"I don't want to hear any of your premonition nonsense," Dudley snapped, anger rising to mask his sudden and unexpected fear. "Don't you realize we're part of the greatest infantry in the world? We'll shift those buggers up there. Just you watch what you're doing, and stay close by me."

"We will have to shift them with the bayonet, then," Harris added.

Yes, Dudley thought, almost convinced by his short speech. They would shift them. He recalled Barker's words—*a soldier fights*. There was no need to be afraid if he remembered that.

In front of the marching column, a dense pillar of black smoke rose into the air. The little riverside village was burning. The enemy had probably fired it as an obstacle.

"They think that will stop us?" Dudley heard someone scoff from the rank behind him.

Captain Clarke came scurrying along the edge of his company. Worry creased his youthful face, but he spoke with confidence, saying, "Look sharp, lads. We're going up and over that hill, and we're not stopping for anything."

The company veterans grinned at these brave words, for they knew Clarke had never seen action before. But the captain was right. There would be no pause in the advance.

Lord Raglan had fallen out, and sat his horse to the left of the British column, surrounded by his aides. He raised his cocked hat to his army as they marched past and descended into the little valley.

Dudley gave himself to the stirring notes of the fifes and drums. He tried to concentrate on his drill, on the feel of the rifle sloped on his left shoulder. Colour-Sergeant Onslow barked the order for the company to fix bayonets on the march, and Dudley focused on the procedure. He tried to ignore the sight of the Russian works, the dark muzzles of the guns. He paid no notice to the smoke and flame from the burning village, now far off to his right.

A loud bang made him start, heart leaping inside his chest. Something came skipping along the ground, throwing up great chunks of dry earth. It went by on the left, a rolling ball of solid iron. Russian round shot.

The ball did not seem real. It was almost like something from a story come alive, a piece of some favourite old book of adventurous tales of Wolfe or Wellington.

But it was real. The Russians had fired the first shot.

More cannon shots followed, scattered blasts sounding high and sharp in the dry air. More round shot came bumping along the ground. Dudley saw men of the 7th Royal Fusiliers open their ranks and let the balls go by, as polite as can be.

Nervous laughter bubbled up from his chest. He bit his lip to stifle it, and took deep breaths. He would not fail this test and show himself to be a fool or coward. He would *not* fail this test. It would be better to fall, he told himself. It would be better to die doing his duty than to run from the glory he had always sought.

The burning village was behind them now, but the Russian firing had escalated. The heights beyond the river barked and blasted in one unbroken tooth-jarring roar. There was no stepping around the iron balls now. Dudley saw two shots strike home, a file of men in the battalion ahead knocked down like bowling pins. When he heard the shriek of a fallen man, cold shivering waves ran up and down his back and neck. He thought he might be sick to his stomach, but a bugle call gave him something else to think about.

The bugle call was the order to deploy from column into line. Colour-Sergeant Onslow relayed the order to the company. The men halted and performed the necessary procedure, and then Dudley stood elbow-to-elbow with Harris on his left and another man on his right. The battalion had deployed in two ranks. Dudley stood in the front rank, a single brick in a solid wall of men.

Ahead, the 7th and 23rd Fusiliers also halted and formed two ranks. On the right, the Second Division did the same. The completed formation covered a frontage of about two miles, a broad but shallow target for the Russian gunners.

Out before the lines, green-coated skirmishers of the Rifle Brigade scurried to cover the advance. They moved in pairs, one loading while the other dropped to one knee to fire. They used what cover they could, knolls or rocks or shrubs, and aimed at the heads of Russian soldiers that showed above their fieldworks.

In the fore of Dudley's brigade sat Brigadier Codrington. To the brigadier's left rode the Light Division commander, General Brown. Brown waved his arm, and commands began to ring out.

"By the center, quick—march!"

The division moved forward as one, the drummers behind the ranks beating out the step. Shells whistled and burst, in the air and on the ground. Dudley saw one explode dead on-target within the two-deep line of the 23rd, scattering men and bits of men. It left a five-foot gap, but the line closed and continued forward.

Captain Clarke marched in front of No. 3 Company, his sword held at the slope. Without warning he turned and cried, "Lie down," gesturing with a leveled hand. The order must have come from Colonel Freemantle, for the entire regiment dropped, the men falling to their chests. Dudley could see the other battalions in the brigade doing the same, trying to avoid the next salvo of artillery.

As he lay waiting, Dudley tried to count the muzzles of the heavy guns facing them on the heights. He got only as far as fourteen, then flame and smoke blasted from those muzzles. The noise and shock wave followed a second later, the shot passing overhead.

As the Russian gunners reloaded, the battalions rose again and resumed the advance. The river was before them now, ten yards away. A few men surged forward. The long formation broke up when it came to the water, sergeants shouting at the men to mind their dressing.. Dudley saw some men preparing to swim, taking off their knapsacks and camp kettles, but that did not seem necessary to him. The river looked shallow, the rocky bottom visible through the clear water.

Holding his rifle and cartridge pouch above his head, Dudley leapt in. He sank to his armpits, gasping at the sudden cold, but he kept moving. His fear and sickness were gone. In their stead was a rushing excitement, a nervous need to move on.

The Russian gunners switched to grape and canister shot as Dudley neared the far bank. The air shrieked and roared with the passage of the small bits of metal that could rip a man to pieces. And joining the artillery fire now was a crackling of musketry from the entrenched infantry. Bullets whined and smacked against the trees along the river.

"Good God, good God," Dudley heard himself muttering. Something flung the man next to him backward, blood spraying from the fellow's chest. Grape shot puckered the water with little bursting fountains. For a fleeting moment, he wondered where Harris was; then, he scrambled out of the river and up the muddy bank.

The other fusilier regiments were already reforming and moving up, but every few seconds a gap in their ranks opened. Balls came bouncing through, knocking men aside and ripping off limbs. Shells burst overhead, and a thick curtain of smoke descended, making it difficult to see far in any direction.

Dudley moved up the slope. There were still men on either side of him, trying to dress in a proper line; but as soon as a line formed, it became broken and confused as the company passed through a vineyard. They crushed and pushed the vines out of their way, emerging to catch up with Captain Clarke, who had gone too far ahead.

The young officer halted then motioned for them to lie down again. The men crouched or knelt or lay on their chests as more shot and shell and bullets tore apart the air overhead.

"Prepare to fire a volley, at one hundred yards," Clarke screamed. "Ready!"

Dudley's reaction to the command was automatic. He pulled the hammer of his loaded rifle back to the full cock, then reached under his body to his percussion cap pouch. Pulling out a cap, he fitted it in place on the breech nipple, somehow managing not to fumble.

Clarke crouched low so the men could aim and fire over and around him. He shouted the order, "Pre—sent!" and every man brought his weapon to his shoulder, sighting on the enemy breastworks. Thick smoke screened the target, but Dudley could see the flashes of Russian muskets as they discharged. When Clarke gave the order to fire, Dudley squeezed his trigger. The rifle bucked, but he could not see whether he had hit anything. He rolled onto his side to reload.

The entire battalion, though disordered, now reloaded after firing by company. Section by section, the men rose to their feet to continue the advance. Captain Clarke stood first in No. 3 Company, and then his men were up and resuming their progress. They had gone three paces when Captain Clarke's head exploded in a red spray of blood, brains and bone. His body remained on its feet for a few seconds then flopped to the ground.

Without faltering, the men marched over it, as if nothing out of the ordinary had happened. For a fleeting moment, Dudley wondered why he was not shocked. As he passed, he saw the dead officer's shako wedged against a small boulder. The cap lay unscathed, the badge gleaming.

Generals Brown and Codrington still rode in front. They encouraged the men to move on, shouting and waving their hats. Then General Brown fell, his horse collapsing, its legs folding under its body. Brown managed to jump clear, and a second later, he was back on his feet. A bullet had killed his horse.

He waved his sword, and Dudley heard his voice over the din.

"Fusiliers, I am all right! Follow me, and I'll remember you for it!"

Brigadier Codrington, cocked hat raised, rode straight at the enemy breastwork and leaped his horse over the obstacle. Seeing this, the decimated ranks of the fusilier regiments charged forward. The first line of Russian infantry did not wait to meet them. They abandoned their positions and fled toward the larger redoubt.

This was but a small triumph. It was the redoubt battery that was the true objective. Lieutenant-Colonel Freemantle rode along the ragged front of his battalion, shaking his unblooded sword and crying, "One more brave push, lads! We're almost there! One more push!"

The men of the Royal Hants screamed and cheered in response, even as the bullets and shot smacked into their flesh and bone. Without thinking, Dudley screamed with the rest. The battalion began to run. Wailing at the top of his lungs, Dudley doubled forward with his rifle and bayonet leveled. He jumped the abandoned breastwork and moved up the far slope. On his far left, he could sense the regiment's Colours, now ragged and shot-torn. They drew the regiment onward, a beacon, a rallying point above the dense smoke.

The muzzle of a Russian gun loomed not more than ten yards away. Dudley was at the crest. The gun blasted fire and smoke, but Dudley had approached the gun from an angle, and the shot went by on the right.

The earthen gun embrasure here was less than two feet high. With one more step, Dudley had climbed on top. Below stared the astonished eyes of the enemy gunners. Dudley pointed his rifle at one pair of eyes, blasted a hole between them, and jumped down into the battery. He thrust his bayonet at the coat front of another man. The bayonet penetrated without much resistance, and blood gouted from the triangular wound when he tore the weapon free.

More fusiliers scrambled into the redoubt, firing their rifles in every direction. The other Russian gunners went down.

The battery was now full of red-coated infantry. Some pounded spikes into the vents of the artillery pieces to render them useless.

But the success was illusory. Behind the redoubt, the Russian reserve battalions waited. As the fusiliers milled about in disorder, those battalions advanced.

Dudley watched as a fresh block of men goose-stepped toward him like a machine of war, drums beating. There were too many. There was no way the remaining fusiliers could hold the captured battery.

A Russian volley blasted wind and smoke and bullets. A few fusiliers fell, while the others turned to withdraw. They flowed out of the battery and back down the hillside a few yards, hesitating, not wanting to run. On the left, Dudley saw part of the Light Division in full retreat. The sight dismayed him. Surely it would not end like this? He stood frozen with indecision.

Then he heard Lieutenant-Colonel Freemantle's voice calling from somewhere, "Reform! Reform!"

The call brought Dudley awake. He climbed out of the battery and stumbled down to where his comrades had halted in a tattered line and were reloading their rifles. Finding a position, he pulled out a cartridge, bit it open and rammed it down his rifle's bore.

"Set your sights for forty yards!" a voice behind the line roared. He knew it was Colour Sergeant Onslow, moving behind what was left of No. 3 Company.

The Russians marched over the crest of the hill, stomping over the low parapet.

"Pre—sent!" came the order. Dudley aimed.

The company volley came as a single sharp crack. Almost the entire front rank of the Russian column fell, pierced by the Minié bullets. Those in the ranks behind stopped short, slamming into each other, losing their momentum.

"For independent fire," Onslow shouted, "commence firing!"

The tattered British battalion banged away at point-blank range, blasting the thick enemy column. The Russians held up their arms, as if screening themselves from blowing dust. Man after man went down. The enemy column could not advance any farther.

On the left of the Royal Hants, the 7th had also rallied. They fired as fast as they could load. Amid their independent fire, a few ragged company volleys also let loose.

Dudley saw the face of almost every man he shot. He aimed with purpose, choosing a flat-nosed fellow in the front of the column. The man seemed bent on urging his lads forward. Dudley squeezed the trigger, felt his rifle kick and saw its billowing smoke. When the smoke cleared enough to see, the Russian was gone.

He reloaded, ramrod slipping in his fingers. From his position, he could look down part of the ruined slope up which they had fought. What he saw took his breath away.

Ordered lines of red-coated men in bearskin hats advanced to the aid of the decimated fusiliers. Behind them marched lines of kilted warriors, bayonets leveled. The Guards and Highlanders of the First Division. They advanced through the fog of powder smoke, Colours flying and bagpipes wailing.

Dudley's throat was dry and swollen, but he managed to croak, "Here they come!" Without aiming, he fired his rifle. He thought he heard fifes and drums again, but wasn't sure.

The brigade of Guards moved past the exhausted Light Division, on up the hill toward the battery. The Royal Hants, much reduced, followed to the crest of the hill and back into the redoubt.

The Russians retreated, running. Dudley leapt into the battery again and stabbed his bayonet through another man. He saw the fellow clearly, a man in a brown greatcoat with a red collar. The man wore a floppy forage cap with a red band and had a neat little mustache. There was fear in his brown eyes. He did not want to die, but Dudley killed him. Killed him and moved on, though now he could not find anyone else to fight. Everywhere he looked there were cheering soldiers in red coats, green coats, or kilts and feather bonnets.

He moved farther into the great redoubt, searching for the enemy. It took some time before he realized they were gone. Beyond the heights he saw them, their drab ranks fleeing south. Some British cavalry charged in, running down a few of the stragglers. Dudley began to understand the battle was over.

He stood in the captured redoubt, breathing hard and holding his heavy rifle over his head. They had done it. Exhausted and filthy with powder residue, he took up the cheer, joining in with his comrades.

This was victory!

The confused euphoria that had gripped him during the last part of the battle was gone, dissipating with the powder smoke. In its wake, it left an absence of emotion. He made his way back down the slope, indifferent to the slaughter surrounding him. Somehow, he had survived, with not even a minor wound. This had been pure luck, for the Russian artillery and musket fire had mauled the British divisions.

The artillery had done the greatest damage, cutting great swaths through the attacking lines. In places on the churned and blasted earth of the hillside, dead or wounded British soldiers lay in groups of six, or ten, or twenty. Those still living tried to move, their feeble calls for help mingling to form one continuous plaintive moan.

Bandsmen swarmed across the hillside. They carried stretchers to bear off the wounded and spades to bury the dead. Dudley made no move to help them. He picked his way through the wreckage of bodies and bits of equipment, pausing when he came upon the twisted form of Lance-Corporal Lloyd. His tormenter from the Fairbridge canteen now wore two lace chevrons on his right arm. Lloyd's glazed eyes stared at the sky, and one side of his face was dark with crusted blood. Dudley wondered how long the fellow had enjoyed his promotion to corporal.

"You never even knew me," he whispered. He was sorry Lloyd was dead.

He carried on down the hill. He still had a task to perform. Harris had not been in the great redoubt after its fall, and Dudley needed to find him. He remembered seeing him last at the riverside, before the company had become entangled in the vineyard.

The river stretched across the plain below. Dudley followed its blue trace with his eyes, out to the western sea. The little wave crests danced and sparkled in the afternoon sun, like a band of earthbound stars. Above these stars moved the masts and sails of ships, so graceful and at peace. Gulls wheeled and dipped overhead. Away to the southwest lay a small seaport of tiled rooftops that might have been Sevastopol itself.

The unexpected beauty of the view made Dudley stop. He felt a sudden aching in his heart, an aching for something he could not name. He thought of Martha, then of his aunt and uncle's home in northern Hampshire. Two things he had lost.

"Corporal Dudley," someone said behind him. He turned to see Corporal Trump, his old barrack commander, approaching from higher up the slope. Trump was filthy, hands black with powder residue, a spattering of blood ruining the white lace on the front of his coat. He appeared distressed, lacking his usual confidence.

"Corporal Trump," Dudley greeted.

"Have you seen my mate, Davey Chandler?" Trump asked. "He was with us when we went into that vineyard there. Then we got all mixed up with the Ninety-fifth, from Second Division, and I lost him."

Dudley did not know Private Chandler, but he knew what he looked like. He had not seen him, and said so. Trump nodded, and the two men stood in silence.

A voice spoke, a dry croak from somewhere. A voice speaking in Russian. A second later the voice changed to English, saying, "Water."

A wounded Russian lay in the dirt nearby. Dried blood crusted a trouser leg that had once been white. The man looked at the two corporals with pleading eyes, one hand outstretched, the other locked on his musket.

Trump opened his canteen and went to the wounded man's side. He poured a few sips of water into the Russian's parched mouth.

"There, you poor fellow," Trump said, stopping the canteen and rising.

As the corporal moved away, the Russian raised his musket and shot him in the back.

The bullet threw Trump into Dudley's arms. Dudley held him and watched as the Russian struggled to his feet and began to hobble away.

Dudley lay Trump down as gently as possible and unslung his rifle. He took his time loading. The Russian had not gone far when Dudley brought the rifle up, aimed and fired. The Russian's hat leapt from his head, and his body pitched forward to fall flat on the dry ground. It did not move.

Dudley turned back to Trump. A small trickle of blood ran from the corporal's mouth, and his laboured breathing gurgled. The bullet had gone into one of his lungs. Dudley put him in the most comfortable position he could but knew there was nothing he could do.

"You hang in there, Trump," he said. "The bandsmen and sailors are coming to carry you away to hospital."

Trump moved his head from side to side and waved one hand, but he could not speak.

Dudley left his old corporal's side and continued down the hill. For some reason, he could not summon the outrage the incident demanded. He just wanted to locate Harris.

Ten minutes later, he found him.

Harris lay on the edge of the river. He had not even made it into the vineyard. There was not a mark on him. Nothing to explain what had killed him.

Dudley sank to the grass and looked down at his friend's face. It was the face of a man who had thought himself a failure. The face seemed to smile. Dudley remembered some of their conversations, and the things Harris had said the previous night. He sensed a great emptiness, an almost total lack of feeling.

A footstep crunched on the river gravel. Dudley glanced up to see Barker standing nearby, watching him. Barker's uniform was a mess of dirt and blood, and there was a bullet hole through his shako plate. The corners of his mouth curled up in a smirk, and he said, "Now you know what it's like to lose someone you care something for."

Dudley could not believe his ears.

"Damn you, Barker!" he roared. He welcomed the burst of anger. It was at least a feeling of some sort.

Barker said nothing. His eyes flitted from Dudley's face to that of Harris, then he shook his head.

"Help me bury him, will you?" Dudley muttered, lurching to his feet.

Barker did not object. He and Dudley scraped a shallow trench with their bayonets, then dug it deeper when a bandsman brought them both spades. Then they wrapped Harris in his greatcoat and lowered him into the grave.

On the riverbanks and hillside, countless similar scenes took place. Marines and sailors helped carry off the wounded. Detachments of infantry rounded up Russian prisoners and held them in the vineyard. Others buried the dead. A few soldiers placed their friends and close comrades in separate graves, as Dudley did for Harris. Large common graves sufficed for the rest, though not before the sergeants had stripped the bodies of their canteens and haversacks.

Dudley and Barker stood with their heads bowed for a few minutes. Neither spoke. When an appropriate time had passed, Dudley nodded at Barker once, crammed his shako back on and turned to move up the hill.

Halfway up he found that no one had carried away Corporal Trump. No one had buried him, either, so Dudley did it.

Not since Waterloo had the British Army fought such a major engagement. Not since Waterloo had there been such a glorious victory. Not since Waterloo had so many sons of Britain died in a foreign land.

Dudley turned his back on the graves and returned to the crest of the hill. Fatigue flooded every muscle, and his rifle and knapsack seemed to weigh three times their actual mass. He saw that his regiment was already preparing a camp in the area of the captured Great Redoubt. Men had stacked their rifles in tripods and had collected wood for bivouac fires. Dudley wandered about until he found the men of No. 3 Company.

Lieutenant Coltern stood in the midst of them, smoking a slim cigar. As Dudley approached, the officer said, "Ah, Corporal Dudley? We have been looking for you."

Dudley snapped to attention and saluted, his right index finger touching his right eyebrow, his palm flat. Coltern touched his forage cap in return, then said, "You are promoted sergeant, by order of Colonel Freemantle."

Dudley stared at him. The announcement took a few moments to sink in. When it did, he replied, "Thank you, sir."

"Er, yes. Quite," Coltern said. "Well done, I suppose I ought to say." He took a pull on his cigar.

Well done. Dudley thought of Captain Clarke. Clarke had used those same words upon Dudley's last promotion.

A mass of sobs began to well up from deep in Dudley's chest. Somehow, he managed to hold them in until Coltern had departed. After that, there was nothing he could do to keep them from bursting forth.

The army camped on the captured heights of the Alma. Dudley sat with Private Oakes and stared into his fire. He tried not to listen to the cries and groans of the wounded. He reminded himself he was sergeant now. It usually took a ranker ten years to make sergeant. Such regulations sometimes mattered little in war, but the field promotion was still a notable achievement.

The flames of the campfire twisted and shifted. Dudley thought of last night's fire, of Harris insisting he would fall. Now it was a day later, and Harris *had* fallen, his awful vision come true.

Dudley remembered an incident from his fifteenth year, a day spent on the downs with Cousin Jane. He had been reading to her snatches of a book that he carried around with him, *The Book of Famous Battles*. Jane had frowned at one point and said, "Mummy says that war is wicked."

"War can be wicked, yes," Dudley had replied, beginning one of his frequent lectures. "Soldiers are killed in wars. And not just soldiers, but innocent people who find themselves in the way of history. But war, my little cousin, is a natural process which comes about when people cannot agree, or when dark forces must be destroyed, as in the case of Bonaparte. War is what uncle called a 'necessary evil.'"

"What does that mean?"

"It means something that is bad, but cannot be avoided, for it serves to counter an even greater and more destructive evil. You see, as long as Britain has enemies, powers who would dominate us, there shall be wars. That is the only way to prevent foreign domination. It is the same for other nations, as well. When evil threatens them, they must strike back, for evil will not listen to reason."

Jane had accepted this little speech. Dudley had believed it himself. He still believed it, but now he wished he did not. He wished that war were not necessary.

He covered his eyes so he could no longer see the fire. The myriad horrors of the day intertwined and settled down upon his exhausted mind. His shock, grief, shame and guilt all blended into a single inner torment.

114

He had suspected war would be unpleasant, but it was worse than he had imagined. Far worse.

This is victory, he thought. If this is victory, what must defeat feel like?

But he knew. At least, he had an inkling, for Harris was dead. So many others were dead as well, or maimed, and each of those casualties was a defeat. Defeat was death.

Dudley had caused death. He had exulted in the destruction of other men, men just like Harris. He had killed and seen the eyes of the slain as they died, as they knew their lives were at an end. Now he knew what it felt like to kill a man, to kill men, and he did not like it. It brought none of the glory he had wanted.

Perhaps the glory would come later. It had been a great victory, after all. An amazing triumph in the face of heavy fire and heavier odds. Dudley had felt a wild joy at the time, the ecstasy of battle he had often heard described. It had brought a sense of focus that fostered a belief in his invincibility.

Perhaps that was the glory, though now it seemed like madness.

Someone nudged him. He took his hand away from his eyes to see Oakes holding out a mess tin. The tin contained a steaming liquid resembling tea.

"Have a cup of this, lad," Oakes said. "It's a poor brew, something I've had stored away for a long time, but it'll warm your insides."

Dudley took the tin. The heat on his hands was a comfort, as was the old private's commonsense presence.

"Do you suppose anyone heard my blubbering earlier?" Dudley asked, adding, "I won't do it again, if I can help it. I must have sounded like a complete fool."

"Don't you worry on that, lad," Oakes reassured. "Ye weren't the only one to show how he felt."

That was true. Others besides Dudley had sobbed and wept. Most had never before seen action. They had sat trembling beside the bivouac fires until the close companionship of their comrades had brought them back to life. Many older soldiers and their wives had tried to comfort the grief-stricken. No one accused anyone else of being soft, for so many friends had fallen this day there was plenty of cause for sorrow.

With that sorrow went celebration. Groups of men had also gathered to sing triumphant songs of past British victories and to praise the dead. Dudley wished with all his heart that he could feel as they did. He wished he could join them, but he could not.

"You think too much, lad," Oakes said. "I can tell, watching you staring into the fire, twisting yourself into knots. It'll only make you sick. Remember this—every soldier expects death at some point. To die in battle is honourable, for it's the risk we take. It means we have been doing our duty. So much better 'n wasting away like so many good men did back there in stinking Varna! Listen to that song they're singin' over yonder. The men who died today went well, there's no doubt about that."

"I suppose," Dudley said.

"Aye. Death is part of our living, if I may say so. A soldier's living. Death is the living of those we fight. The enemy has no right to blame you for killing him. No ghost of a soldier has a right to complain about dying, unless his life was thrown away for naught. And that didn't happen today."

Dudley sighed. The old veteran's words were comforting. He knew exactly the right things to say.

"You're a wise old fellow, you know that, Oakes?"

Unaware of Dudley's promotion, Oakes said, "Thank ye, Corporal." He chuckled. "Don't I wish that were true, though?"

Dudley grimaced. "I wish I hadn't wept. I wish that had never happened. But it was all my worry draining out at once, you know."

"There was no shame in that." Oakes sipped his weak, muddy tea, frowned at the cup, then added, "You fought like a tiger today. We all did, were damned ferocious. Ye lost a friend, young Harris, and that's surely hard." He sighed. "I must admit, this was the most horrible day I have ever known. All the lads agree that never has there been such a murderous fire." He put his arm on Dudley's shoulder. "And we survived it. It didn't stop us, and that is cause for pride. It was a great thing done here today."

116

"But what a price we paid for it!"

"Aye. There's always a price, that's for sure. Ye know that now. And the greater the deed, the greater the price, leastways in this instance." He looked into the fire, then said in a lower voice, "Many of them that fell today contributed to the greatness of that deed before they caught it."

Neither man said anything for a few minutes. Then Oakes looked up at the clear sky, at the stars overhead. He said, "We'll be moving on tomorrow, or soon enough."

"Yes." Dudley tried to put some strength in his voice. "On to take Sevastopol."

"Aye. And then this little war will be over, and we'll all have something to sing about it."

# CHAPTER SIX

To conquer without risk is to triumph without glory.

— Pierre Corneille, "Le Cid"

***Gentlemen in tall*** hats and ladies with parasols had come out of Sevastopol to watch the destruction of the Allied army at the Alma. Captured Russian officers admitted they had planned to hold their position for several days until the arrival of reinforcements. The ferocity of the British and French attack left them shocked and amazed. The civilian observers, disappointed, snatched up their picnic lunches and wine glasses and fled. Sevastopol, they feared, was a doomed city.

The Allies did not march straight on to Sevastopol. Instead, they passed by the city, the British continuing on south until they reached the little seaside port of Balaclava, a cluster of whitewashed cottages crammed into a little valley at the foot of two rocky headlands. The houses were all low single-story dwellings with crumbling greenish slate roofs—nothing but mean hovels, Dudley thought, compared to English cottages. After firing a few shots at the ancient towers that were all that remained of a Genoese castle that guarded the harbor from atop the eastern headland, the Royal Navy secured Balaclava as a base of supply. Shipping soon clogged the ramshackle wharfs.

Meanwhile, the French made their base of supply at the village of Kamiesch some ten miles to the north. The two armies then advanced on Sevastopol from the south. This so-called "flank march" was at the behest of General St. Arnaud. The French commander had argued the Russians expected the Allies to approach from the north; therefore, the southern side of Sevastopol would not be as well-defended. Lord Raglan had wanted to attack from the north without pausing to secure Balaclava and Kamiesch, but politics had won him over. In the interest of Anglo-French relations, he had agreed with St. Arnaud's plan.

It would soon become apparent that St. Arnaud, on the decline with cholera, had been wrong.

---

The Allies arrayed their encampments in the barren hilly country south and east of Sevastopol, creating a great half-circle of tents, guns, horses, carriages and supply depopts. The French concentrated on the left of the half-circle, the British on the right. The Light and Second Divisions of the British infantry held the northern flank.

The Light Division made its camp on an open ridge the army dubbed "Victoria Ridge." The navy transports had at last landed tents in Balaclava, and supply parties brought those tents to the camps in hired wagons. In every camp of the British army, the air rang with the slap of thousands of mallets striking thousands of wooden pegs. The sound was a beautiful percussive music to those soldiers who had gone without shelter for so long.

The Royal Hants raised their tents in perfect rows. When the task was finished, Dudley stood back and admired the military symmetry. Each tent was circular, bell-shaped, supported by a single pole, and designed to accommodate sixteen men. He worried the tents would be scant protection in the coming months. It would soon be October, and the Russian empire was infamous for its harsh winters.

He also worried about the lack of available firewood, the land being so barren. The regimental quartermaster had promised to issue each company a ration of firewood that would have to be brought up from Balaclava. There was no telling how long that ration would last, nor when the next ration would come. Dudley felt a need for No. 3 Company to get the jump on the rest of the regiment, to stockpile what they could in case combustible materials became scarce.

"With your permission, sir," he said to Lieutenant Coltern, "I would like to take a party of men into the ravine below the ridge and cut some fresh firewood."

Coltern had suffered a bout of fever in Constantinople, and it had left him yellowed and gaunt, his uniform bagging on his spare frame. He stared at Dudley as if he had not heard, then sniffed once and said, "Certainly, if you like. Carry on, Sergeant Dudley."

Dudley chose the men he knew best, those who had shared his Portsmouth barrack room, and led them down a newly worn path on the northwestern slope of Victoria Ridge. The ravine below was not as barren as parts of the uplands. Stunted oaks that looked more like shrubs grew among the rocks on the lower slopes and bottom. Dressed in trousers and fatigue shirts, the men set to hacking these down with their hatchets, as well as collecting whatever deadwood they could find. The competition was fierce, for the ravine was full of other parties from the regiments in Codrington's Brigade

"A popular resort, this ravine of ours," Dudley said to Oakes, pausing in his labour to watch the host of other axe-wielding soldiers. "Do you suppose it has a name? With so many ravines and dry stream beds in this country, we can't go on calling this 'the ravine.'"

"Heard some of the officers callin' it Careenage Ravine," Oakes said, "so that must be it."

"Careenage Ravine," Dudley repeated as he stooped to gather a bundle of sticks.

When he rose with the sticks in his arms, he regarded the other men of his company, some of them gathering their own bundles. This was his first independent command, he realized, since his promotion to sergeant. His first mission—to lead his men in a glorious charge for firewood.

Laughter and a rustling in the brush to his left drew his attention. He saw Barker at the head of a group of men sprinting toward a stand of larger oaks. From the other direction, a work party from another regiment was approaching at a run.

"We've got them by a mile, boys!" Barker cried, and his followers gave a cheer.

Barker's group won the race and began furious efforts to gather the best deadwood and hack down the largest trees. Dudley marveled at Barker's ability to rouse the men to action. If he were not such an aggressive boor, such a bully to those who opposed him, he would have made a good corporal, or even a sergeant.

"Barker would make a decent NCO," Dudley said to Private Oakes. "It's a pity his character is so flawed."

"His character wasn't always so bad," Oakes replied after a pause.

"Oh?" Dudley said, curious. "You've said so before."

"I think he made a conscious decision," Oakes added, frowning thoughtfully.

"Why would anyone do that?" Dudley wondered. "Why would anyone neglect their duty on purpose?"

Oakes continued to frown and seemed about to say more when a voice hailed from the edge of the ravine.

"Sergeant Dudley!"

Dudley glanced up to see Lieutenant Coltern standing at the lip of the ravine.

"Sir!" Dudley barked.

"If you are finished here," Coltern said, "I have volunteered Number Three Company to bring further supplies from Balaclava. You shall head the supply party. Twenty-five men, your choice."

"Yes, sir," Dudley said, unable to salute for the bundle in his arms. Not that it mattered, for Coltern had already gone.

---

Dudley stood on Sapoune Ridge and gazed across an expanse that would soon become a battlefield. There in the distance lay Sevastopol, a city of white buildings built in the Italian style, many with arches and columns and tall windows, their tile roof-tops red and orange and rust-coloured. In contrast to the sur-rounding land, great clusters of tall trees grew along the streets and plazas, and here and there the gleaming white spire of a church or public building thrust upward through the lush foli-age. The city was like another world, an elegant world of civili-zation hidden behind miles of rough earthen ramparts and bris-tling cannon.

Dudley turned north to gaze at the Tchernaya River, a slender vein of silver. South of the town was a wide plateau, the Uplands of Chersonese, an open country of low hills, ridges and ravines. Here and there grew stands of cypress, juniper and more twisted oaks, but for the most part the land was covered in scrubby brush, yellowish grass and bare earth and rock.

Dudley knew this place would be his home for many months. Those who still hoped for a speedy conclusion to this campaign were fools, in his opinion, for the flank march had given the Russians time, and they had not been idle.

On September 25, their main army moved out of the town and into the interior. From there they could strike at the Allies in the open, and on ground they knew better than either the French or British. At the same time, their engineers in Sevasto-pol had thrown up that great line of earthworks, trenches, rifle pits and gun emplacements that ringed the city. Their guns were already at work firing ranging shots at the Allied encampments.

To the right of the Redan, Dudley could see another large set of works that resembled a shapeless mound of earth. He knew the mound was, in fact, another block of trenches and batteries. This was the Malakoff, or "White Tower," so named for the semicircular masonry tower that stood above its earth-works. The tower mounted five heavy guns, but would make an easy target for British artillery. The earthworks would be another matter, their soft sides able to absorb much of the shock of shot and shell.

"Seems to me," Oakes said from Dudley's side, "that we have our work cut out for us."

"That we do, Private Oakes," Dudley agreed. "So, we'd best begin. Let's be on our way." He turned to his supply party and called, "Form back up in two files!"

Dudley had chosen his twenty-five men from the same group that had gathered wood. They had charge of two pony-carts with which to bring up camp supplies from Balaclava. Dudley did not think the carts would be enough to carry what the regiment needed. At least not in one trip.

This would become a chronic problem, for the quartermaster's department had provided the regiment with few carts and wagons. The Light Division camp was miles from the supply base, and delays and shortages were inevitable. Trying to deal with those delays and shortages would be an ongoing chore, and Dudley knew this was not the last supply party he would lead.

The members of the party wore their undress uniforms, shell jackets and round forage caps. They marched south, guiding the ambling ponies. The supply route followed one of the main "highways," the Woronzov Road, a dirt track that ran from Sevastopol into the interior. The route then turned right, off the highway, onto another road that was little more than a mule path. This road led to the small village of Kadikoi, then to Balaclava and the sea.

The Woronzov Road continued southeastward after the supply route left it, climbing the back of a ridge called the Causeway Heights. The Heights made a natural barrier that guarded the southern edge of the Allied position. Along the crest, the Royal Engineers had built four small redoubts, each a square earthwork enclosing a battery of field guns. A sergeant of the Royal Artillery commanded each redoubt and its tiny garrison of Turkish gunners. Two more redoubts, both unfinished, lay farther west. Dudley thought the little forts would prove flimsy protection against a determined attack, but their importance as observation posts was obvious. Lookouts on the Causeway Heights could see an approaching army hours before it could come close enough to threaten Balaclava.

That was the function of the infantry now—standing lookout, picket duty, and taking part in supply parties to and from

Balaclava. Other tasks soon to fall to the soldiers would involve digging and fortifying trenches and artillery batteries, then manning and guarding those trenches and batteries. Dirty, heavy and tedious work, lacking in glamour.

There was nothing romantic in this hot trudge along the supply route, but in time, Dudley's squad marched away the last two miles to Balaclava beneath their booted feet. Seagulls wheeled overhead as the party neared the coast, and the smell of salt water drifted up to meet them. Here the steep and rocky bluffs descended to the sea, and at their bottom, on the south side of the harbor, lay the collection of shabby houses that was Balaclava. Looming above on a rocky crag, like some scene from the tales of King Arthur, stood the jagged and half-ruined towers of the castle, crumbled yellow-stone walls that had proven a poor defence against modern artillery.

Soldiers, curious local civilians, horses, carts, guns, limbers, baggage and supplies all clogged the little port. It seemed every regiment in the army had sent a supply party to Balaclava at the same time. Dudley had to wait his turn in order to obtain the equipment he needed. He told his men they could roam about as long as they returned in half an hour, entrusting Private Oakes to ensure no one wandered off.

After fifteen minutes, the men came back with another empty cart that they had scavenged. With the cart was also a bundle of overcoats—"discards from the battlefield," as Oakes put it.

"They'll be handy if we're still here come winter."

Dudley help up one of the coats. It was of thick brown wool, and its length and width could be adjusted by a system of drawstrings. It was certainly an ingenious garment, and much sturdier than British coats.

"Where did you get these, Private?" Dudley asked. "And the cart?"

Oakes shrugged. "I met an old comrade, a quartermaster assistant. Had some old junk lying about. Nothing untoward."

Dudley was uncertain, but decided their claim to the cart and the coats was as good as anyone's. The coats had been taken from Russians to begin with. Dead Russians.

124

"So, you're sergeant, now," Oakes said, changing the subject.

Like most men in the company, Oakes had first heard the news of Dudley's promotion earlier that day. Dudley did not bother to correct anyone when they still called him "corporal." He found it difficult to get used to the idea he was a sergeant. Of course, it didn't help that he still wore a corporal's two white-lace chevrons on his upper right coat sleeve. His single-breasted coat was also wrong. If he were to be a proper sergeant, he would have to look the part, if only to remind himself of his new authority.

"Yes," he said in response to Oakes's statement. He looked into the veteran's wrinkled and smiling face. "Unfortunately, I am your sergeant now because so many sergeants were killed at the Alma. I was needed as a replacement." He folded the coat and placed it in the cart. "Both my recent promotions have been the result of someone's death."

"No shame in that. Quickest way up the ladder. You may find yourself general, soon, the way the boys are droppin'. Ha-ha!"

Dudley smiled at the grim jest, but the smile was short-lived. The conversation reminded him how death had become such a fixture in their day-to-day experience. A fixture the survivors could only laugh at, and hope they would not have to join their unfortunate comrades anytime soon.

He heard the plaintive cry of a gull overhead, like a cry of mourning. He cleared his throat and said, half to himself, "We try to forget about death. We try to ignore it. I thought I had become used to it in Varna." He did not look at Oakes. "But death from disease is not quite like death in battle. Somehow, sickness seems natural, as if when one dies of disease it was meant to be. But to be killed, one's life cut short so suddenly, does not seem natural."

He let out a long sigh, then said in a stronger voice, "Then again, maybe I'm foolish. After all, I lost no one close to me in Varna, while Harris was killed back at Alma. Perhaps that's what's different for me."

"Could be," said Oakes.

"Not that Harris and I were really very close, I suppose. Not like family. We had only known each other a year, of course, and we were different in many ways. I don't believe I knew him long enough or well enough to truly need to grieve, but we had many good conversations." He paused, then added, "And I have no right to feel any worse than anyone else. We've all lost friends, haven't we?"

"Oh, aye," Oakes said, nodding patiently. "More 'n I care to recall. Soldiers know all about loss. It's hard, lad, it truly is. But soldiers know all about carryin' on, too."

"Yes, I suppose," Dudley agreed. "But we must learn the hard way, it seems."

He looked over to where Barker was standing with Private Geary. Barker talked to the younger man then laughed his usual guffaw, slapping Geary on the back. Geary laughed, too, slim shoulders convulsing.

"We do learn how to go on," Dudley muttered. "Even the worst of us."

At length, the wait was over, and a quartermaster-sergeant allowed Dudley and his men access to a group of small wooden storage sheds. The sergeant told them, "Take what you need. Just make sure you sign for the lot."

The squad gathered camp supplies, kettles, frying pans, axes, hand saws, spades, shovels and, most important, three days' rations of salted beef and ship's biscuits. While the men loaded the carts, Dudley asked whether there were any new uniforms to be had.

"Uniforms?" the quartermaster-sergeant repeated. "No, Corporal. Plenty o' blankets, but nothing in the way o' clothing. Not yet, anyhow."

Dudley nodded, disappointed. He had hoped to get himself a sergeant's coatee or a sash to display his rank. Now he would have to ask the regimental quartermaster back in camp, though he doubted the regiment had any new uniforms in stock. The Royal Hants had not brought along any broadcloth for repairing or fashioning new garments, either. Dudley suspected he would have to make do with adding a third lace chevron to his corporal's badge.

When the squad finished loading, the men led the two pony-carts through the congested town back towards the road. Four men pulled the third cart, huffing and puffing as they strained to make the hill.

"Hey, Sergeant," Barker said from his place at the third cart's yoke, "how about givin' us a hand, here?"

Barker had volunteered to pull the third cart—both he and Geary—so he had no reason to complain. Dudley replied, "A big fellow like yourself, Barker, ought not to need any help."

Barker grunted and turned back to his efforts.

Dudley watched him and had a change of heart. Maybe it would be a good thing if he did help out. That would show the men he was not above doing what he told others to do.

Moving to the front of the cart, he grasped the wooden yoke and said, "Move over, there, Private Geary."

The men had loaded the cart with biscuit barrels, heaping them so high they threatened to spill. Dudley and his comrades eased the cart up the hill, wary of every bump. One wheel squealed and groaned, but once they reached more level ground, the cart rolled along on its own momentum. Dudley could walk with little effort, and began to enjoy himself, like a boy pulling a toy wagon.

The supply party neared the village of Kadikoi. The cart shuddered, and Dudley glanced back to check the load. The squealing wheel had started to wobble.

"Stop!" he shouted. "The cart wheel's about to come off."

The cart groaned to a halt, listing to one side as the loose wheel bent inwards. One of the biscuit barrels rolled off. It landed with a splintering thump in the dirt.

"Well, so much for that," Dudley said, pushing back his forage cap and scratching his head. "We can't go on with this thing." He kicked the broken wheel.

""What of that old Tartar, standing there with them oxes?" Barker said, nodding at an idle wagon parked in front of a low stone cottage. With the wagon were a team of oxen and a driver.

The driver was a local civilian, but he was no Russian, his head swathed in a dingy turban, a fur robe hanging from his stocky shoulders. He stroked a long, full beard as he stood idle, watching the traffic on the road.

"Excellent suggestion, Private Barker," Dudley said. "We'll see if he'll help us."

Dudley approached the wagon driver. Behind him came the other four men who had been pulling the broken cart.

"Excuse me, sir," Dudley said, "but may we have the services of your wagon?"

The wagon driver nodded his dark head and said, "I give you for money." Many local Tartars had learned a few English phrases, seeing potential wealth in the presence of the invaders. They offered various services for a price.

"He wants payment, I think," Geary said in his nasal squeak, looking at Dudley.

Enunciating every word, Dudley said, "You shall be paid when we reach our camp."

The man shook his head. "Money now."

"I think he wants it now," said Geary.

"Well, then," Dudley began, uncertain what to do next. He suspected the few coins he had with him would not be enough.

The man folded his arms. Dudley heard Barker growl in irritation, and realized this fellow was in no position to demand anything from the army.

"Well, then," Dudley repeated, "we'll just have to shoot his oxen for forage, if he doesn't want to help us."

The man understood the threat. His eyes widened, and he held up his hands, shaking them from side to side.

"No, no," he said. "I take you. Money later."

Dudley nodded. "Agreed."

———✦———

The supply party could see the ordered tent city of the Light Division camp miles before they reached it. The conical peaks of the Second Division camp made another tiny mountain range farther north. Beyond the camps ran the slim gleaming trace of the Tchernaya, its banks choked with spreading trees, guarding

128

the Allied right flank. Above the river's far banks rose a high bluff of sheer-cut cliffs, like a pair of giant steps. Along the top of the bluff were the ruins of the ancient town of Inkerman, nothing but a few tumbled stone walls and partial foundations. The bluff was so imposing many Light and Second Division troops referred to their side of the river as "Inkerman" in its honour.

Dudley's squad arrived with their goods and took them to the quartermaster's depot. The depot was a collection of trunks, crates, barrels and loaded wagons, all surrounding a single tent. The Tartar driver was nervous as the soldiers unloaded his wagon, but he had nothing to fear. The quartermaster had set aside a fund for hiring conveyances, and the quartermaster-sergeant paid the driver without any objections.

His supply detail finished, Dudley took the opportunity to present his written and signed promotion orders to the quartermaster-sergeant, a short man with massive shoulders who was known in the regiment as Sergeant Bull, though that, Dudley was sure, was not his actual name. Dudley asked him whether any of the many boxes contained a sergeant's kit.

"You want a new uniform?" Bull exclaimed, opening his mouth to laugh and revealing several gaps where teeth should have been. "With a sash to boot? Well, we all have our vanities." He waded through the collection of stores, adding, "You're in luck, mate, at least where the coat's concerned."

He climbed into a wagon that was full of discarded pieces of kit, just odds and ends. After rummaging about for a moment, he produced a patched senior NCO's coatee. Three thick gold chevrons adorned the right upper sleeve.

The sergeant explained that the coatee had belonged to a bloke who had snuffed it at the Alma. The fellow's comrades had buried him in his uniform, but he had owned two dress coats, one of finer quality than the other. This one was the other.

"Auctioned his kit in his company after they had a little memorial," the quartermaster-sergeant went on. "No one wanted this old coat, though. You're the first new promotion to come lookin'. The poor bugger's boots and trousers went first."

129

Dudley hesitated, wondering whether he wanted to wear a dead man's uniform. Then again, he was carrying one of the Russian overcoats, which had come from a battlefield corpse. It did not matter. He had a dead man's position, so why not a dead man's uniform?

After slipping his corporal's coat off, Dudley donned the other garment and fastened the first five buttons. The coat was a size too large, but he thought he might grow into it.

"I'll take it," he said.

The sergeant grinned. "Now, then, lad, nothing comes for free in this world. I have to keep account of all transactions, you know."

Dudley frowned. He had not considered payment, though he realized he could not expect to get a double-breasted coat of melton wool for nothing.

"How much?" he asked.

Bull's gap-toothed grin widened, and he nodded toward the Russian overcoat Dudley had dragged over a barrel.

"That's a fine-looking garment. That'll keep you warm at nights."

"I trust it will." Dudley knew what was coming.

"See here, then. They'll take the price of this uniform out of your pay. Or I'll give it to you in exchange for your Russkie rig."

Dudley glanced at the overcoat. It would be missed in the winter, but he wanted a proper uniform.

"Done, then," he said. "A coat for a coat."

That evening, Dudley joined the other sergeants for supper. He had avoided their company since his promotion, afraid he could not meet his old drill instructors as equals. He felt less uncomfortable now that he had a proper coat, but he was still apprehensive when he approached the sergeants' bivouac fire.

The sergeants did not have a mess tent. They sat around the fire on crates, trunks, a few camp stools and the ground, chatting and laughing as they ate salt beef and biscuits. Sergeant Wellman shared a perch with Sergeant-Major Maclaren and a sergeant from the 17th Lancers who was Wellman's cousin. The red-haired Irishman, O'Ryan, was also present, next to the red-faced Colour-Sergeant Onslow. Dudley was the youngest member of the group. His instinct was to attempt to make an impression with humour, but he fought that impulse, for these experienced men might find that childish. Instead, he sat in silence, listening.

The sergeants were a rough bunch, their voices loud and their language coarse. As Dudley had feared, this made him feel even more out of place. He missed Harris, with his quiet manners.

The one character he felt comfortable with was O'Ryan. The Irishman's social persona was a gentler version of the half-amused, half-angry front he displayed on parade. He was cheerful, talkative, and always seemed to have a full flask of brandy at hand. The flask brought a few taunts about what an Irishman was doing drinking brandy, but no one ever refused when O'Ryan offered to share.

Dudley questioned him about the brandy's source, and the other sergeant explained, "I have some friends in the French camp. Us fellow Catholics look after each other. The Frogs know how to treat an army! An ill-disciplined lot, a bit slovenly, but their leaders feed 'em well. They accounted themselves well in battle, too."

"Oh, aye," agreed Wellman's cousin, a round-faced and grinning fellow in the blue jacket and mortarboard cap of the 17th Lancers. "We were not fully engaged, as you know," he said, referring to the Light Brigade of the Cavalry Division, "and I was able to witness the French attack on the Russkie flank. With such zeal, they advanced!"

The others nodded, agreeing the French had done well that day. The conversation then ran to memories of the Alma. Sergeants' mess rules prohibited shop talk, but that did not include tales of battle. No one would dare speak of the humdrum duties that took up most of a senior NCO's time, but reminiscences of war, old stories and new, were common, at least among the sergeants of the Royal Hants.

While O'Ryan passed around his flask, others told tales of war and of extraordinary soldiers. One of them turned out to be Dudley. Much to his surprise, he had become well-known in

131

the regiment for becoming a sergeant despite having only served for a little over a year. Other men had managed as much before, but not many, and none in the Royal Hants. The sergeants knew his rise was due to luck as much as anything else, but it was still extraordinary. They also assured him that, after the Alma, he had every right to consider himself a hardened and experienced veteran.

"You did us all credit back there, lad," Colour-Sergeant Onslow said, putting an arm across Dudley's shoulder. Dudley found it hard to imagine Onslow had noticed him during the noise and chaos of that mad scramble up the heights.

"A hard fight, that," Maclaren intoned with some emotion, speaking in his usual melodic rhythm. "A bigger fight than any of us have ever known. May the memory of those who fell there never dim."

"I'll drink to that," Dudley stated. He took a pull on O'Ryan's flask as the others exclaimed their agreement.

"Silence!" O'Ryan cried, rising to his feet and taking the flask from Dudley. The red-haired sergeant held the flask aloft as if preparing for a toast. The others smirked at each other, then gave him their attention. They knew they were about to hear one of O'Ryan's famous speeches.

"I have a presentation to make," O'Ryan began, "to our gallant young hero. The newest member of our mess, Sergeant William Dudley, a true fire-eater, who should have been born an Irishman but is instead a native of Hampshire by birth."

There were a few chuckles, and O'Ryan added, "Now with yer permission, I shall fetch an object o' great importance."

He turned and walked into the nearest bell tent, which was his own. A moment later, he emerged carrying a knot of red cloth, which he unrolled with great care. It was a faded and worn sergeant's waist sash.

"In honour of the occasion, I present you with this, William Dudley, the symbol of your new rank. May ye wear it with distinction."

He laid the sash across Dudley's lap. Dudley looked at it. He could think of nothing to say.

The others delighted in his astonishment, laughing, cheering, slapping him on the back. His sense of displacement evaporated. These fellows had accepted him as one of their own. More than accepted him—they had honoured him as something of a hero. He knew he wasn't a hero, that these men didn't really know him. O'Ryan had staged this ceremony for the cheer of his fellow sergeants as much as for Dudley's benefit.

But this truth did not detract from the occasion. Dudley was glad to be the focus of that cheer. He was glad to be able to help morale, if in an indirect sense.

The good mood didn't last. In the distance, the guns of Sevastopol began to boom, probing the Allied lines. The sound was a stiff reminder of what lay ahead. The war had only just begun.

***

A week into October, the Allies began the construction of their siege lines. Under the direction of the Royal Engineers, the infantry assisted the sappers in the backbreaking tasks of digging trenches and throwing up artillery batteries. Dudley's assignments included aiding with the supervision of the work parties. He also helped direct armed covering parties for the workers, or led outlying pickets, or fatigue parties off to fetch supplies or forage. This supervision was most often in conjunction with an officer. The officer was usually Lieutenant Coltern.

Coltern hung back while the work went on, smoking one of his slim cigars. He made a few suggestions but left most of the direction up to Dudley or one of the other senior NCOs. Dudley accepted the responsibility. It was surprising how little independent thought he needed if he followed the basic instructions of the engineers. He wondered how capable he would be in a true command situation, in battle. That had always been his dream, to lead men into glory. To lead men to their deaths. He wondered if he could maintain that dream after the Alma.

He had always known war was death and destruction, but knowing was one thing and comprehending was another. Comprehension had dawned when he saw the mangled corpses strewn across the hillside. Now, he understood.

133

Scenes from the Alma often flashed in his memory. In particular, he remembered images and emotions from the aftermath. He could still conjure the dull horror of that time, though he preferred to forget. He preferred to focus on the positive, for it had been an astounding victory, and he had done well. He had not run in terror as he had half-feared. He had stood his ground in the face of the enemy. He had stood and fought and killed. Damn the fact that the enemy were just other men like himself. Damn the fact he had killed men who had dreams, destroying those dreams with a thrust of his bayonet, or a bullet from his rifle.

He often saw their faces. He recalled the terrified eyes of the Russian he had killed with his bayonet near the battle's conclusion. But he told himself Oakes was right—this was a conflict of one professional army against another. Many of the Russians were conscripts, but at least every man Dudley had struck down had been a soldier, and knew the soldier's lot. Soldiers accepted their potential fate before going to war, the fate of joining the ranks of the dead. It was the same for the British Army. For a professional soldier, to die in battle was an honourable death. Private Oakes had said as much. To die in battle was a glorious death, for it meant you had done your duty to the end.

On an emotional level, however, Dudley now found it difficult to accept that philosophy. On a rational level, he believed it completely. He had a desperate need to believe it. If he didn't, he would have to believe Harris had died for no reason, that this war would be horror and nothing more.

But that could not be true. Dudley told himself real glory, true heroism, lay in how one stood up to the horror, how one faced it. Glory lay in how one faced the prospect of death and defeat. A soldier either turned that horror on its ear, overcoming the enemy, or had that enemy strike him down in the attempt, like Harris. If this was not so, then war was nothing but a grand and colossal mistake, and soldiers were not heroes but dupes.

No. Lance-Corporal Reginald Harris and his many fallen comrades had not died for nothing.

Aside from Colour-Sergeant Onslow, there were two sergeants in No. 3 Company who were still alive. One was Dudley, and the other was O'Ryan. Lieutenant Coltern often placed them in charge of work parties together, with O'Ryan leading and Dudley as second-in-command.

Dudley had come to see O'Ryan as a friend. It was clear now that his witty irritation on the parade square was one aspect of his flair for the dramatic. His presentation of the sash had been another aspect of that flair. He seemed to delight in such performances, such grandiose gestures or announcements. On one occasion, he had stood and asked those assembled around the campfire, "What is a fusilier?"

Dudley had struck up with what he supposed was the proper definition.

"A soldier in a regiment descended from those regiments which once carried fusils, light muskets of the matchlock variety."

O'Ryan had laughed and clapped him on the back.

"No no, you young philosopher. That is but the beginning of it. A fusilier is a member of an institution." And he looked around at his proud companions. "An ancient order of brothers who stand together in the face of adversity. Now the enemy has retired into the countryside. We shall be seeing them soon, I think. They will not be content until they have pushed us off this Crimean Peninsula.

"But like our famed predecessors who fought on another Peninsula, and those fusiliers who came before them, and so on back to Marlborough, we shall not let them."

Then he had handed around his flask, refilled from some mysterious reservoir. The sergeants had all drunk to the Irishman's epic words before rushing off to their various duties.

The source of O'Ryan's endless supply of brandy was puzzling, a secret much sought after. For some reason, he chose to reveal that secret to Dudley one morning.

The two sergeants were guiding another work party along the supply road to Balaclava. The sky was gray with clouds, threatening rain. Each of the last several days had been cooler than the last, as if summer were moving into winter without passing through the mildness of autumn.

As the work party passed near a French encampment, O'Ryan stopped, took Dudley by the arm and pointed.

"There she is," the Irishman said, "my little brandy fountain."

Dudley followed O'Ryan's jutting finger. He saw a young woman dressed in the most remarkable costume he had ever seen. She wore a broad-skirted coat, tight-fitting in the body and embroidered with curling leaf patterns. Red silk pantaloons billowed about her legs as she moved through the camp, carrying an earthen jug in either hand.

"Isabelle," O'Ryan said. "She's what they call a *cantiniere*. Lost her husband at Alma, poor darlin'. I knew him, ya see."

"She gives you the brandy?" Dudley asked, continuing to watch her movements.

"Aye. The cantinieres keep mobile canteens, selling wines, spirits and the like. Isabelle will sell you a tot of brandy for a small price. She also keeps a little field kitchen. As I said before, the Frogs know how to treat an army. Every regiment has a cantiniere, on strength! They even wear a sort of uniform, modeled on their regiment's. She's with the Zouaves."

Dudley nodded, now understanding the outlandish, though attractive, costume. The Zouaves were French light infantry units that had originated in Algeria. Europeans, including many English and Irish, had since replaced the Algerian soldiers in most Zouave regiments, but they retained their North African uniform. That uniform consisted of fez caps wrapped in colorful turbans, short embroidered jackets that hung open in the front, bright waist sashes, baggy pantaloons and whitened gaiters securing their boots. Isabelle was dressed in a similar fashion to one of these fellows.

"You know her, do you?" Dudley asked.

"Aye. Well, I know her well enough. Handsome woman, don't ye think?"

Dudley nodded, though he said nothing. He did not want to admit his thoughts, fearing the older man might laugh at his innocence. He did not find the French cantiniere simply hand-some, but beautiful. Perhaps the most beautiful woman he had ever seen. The Turkish ladies he had spied from afar had struck him with their mysterious allure, but this woman almost ban-ished their memory with her dark hair, her high cheekbones, her large eyes like a fawn's…

"Come on, then," O'Ryan said. He looked to his left, down the road where the supply party still marched. "We best be on our way. The boys are gettin' away from us!"

# CHAPTER SEVEN

There is some soul of goodness in things evil,
Would men observingly distill out.

William Shakespeare
*Henry V*

***The supply route*** from Balaclava was now one long train of
oxcarts, wagons, horses, British soldiers, Turkish soldiers, and
civilians, all moving supplies up to the front. Mules laden with
*gabions*—wicker baskets designed to hold earth—and *facines*—stiff bundles of sticks—ambled up to where the engineers
were building the gun batteries. Camels pulled carts loaded with
barrels of beef and biscuits and bags of green coffee beans.
Horses and ponies dragged wagons filled with shot and powder.
Men and women carried burdens on their backs or slung on
poles.

Every vehicle had its infantry escort. Dudley watched an
oxcart lumber by, four men of the 49th Regiment lounging on
top of its load. The soldiers chatted, and puffed on their clay
pipes.

Dudley wished he had time for such relaxation. No. 3
Company was part of a massive work party of more than two
hundred infantrymen and sailors, and they were behind schedule. Lieutenant Coltern and a portly midshipman held joint

command of the work party. Together, they were trying to guide a train of five siege guns to a battery on Victoria Ridge.

Two of the guns had come from one of the men-of-war anchored in Balaclava harbour. These naval guns were cast-iron Lancaster 68-pounders, massive and modern. The other three were Royal Artillery cast-iron 32-pounders. All five guns sat on the right side of the road, halted again. It had been raining for almost a week, and the roadbed was soft, which slowed transport. The heavy guns became stuck in the mud every few yards. One of the 68-pounders was stuck now.

Dudley gazed at the steel-gray sky, looking for a break in the dense clouds. There was none. Just the promise of more rain. More rain, more mud, and more frustrating work. Because of some unidentified administrative bungle, the work party had only one team of horses. The men had to do the rest, hauling the guns with long drag ropes. The guns were heavy, each weighing more than three tons. It was no wonder their carriages sank into the sodden earth.

"Horses!" Lieutenant Coltern called. His voice betrayed no emotion, no hint that he cared about the constant delays.

A Royal Artillery driver led the team to the rear of the column where the stuck gun had settled. Dudley watched for a few minutes then turned his attention to the distant line of the Russian defences. He could hear the thunder of Russian artillery and see the muzzle flashes in the gloomy light. The Allies could finally return that irritating fire. The army and naval brigades had been working for days now, dragging up guns and supplies to build the batteries. The few guns and mortars in place had been banging away at the Russian works off and on, though there had yet to be a concentrated effort.

The three 32-pounders rested on travelling siege carriages. With carriage and limber, each one rolled along on four reinforced wagon wheels. The naval guns did not have mounts of this type. Each 68-pounder came equipped with a common naval carriage, a wooden frame with two flat sides. The naval carriages ran on four small iron trucks, or spokeless wheels. The trucks would have been too small to carry their burdens over the soft earth, so the 68-pounders had been dismounted and loaded onto platform wagons. The platform wagons were designed to carry heavy ordnance and stores, but the 68-pounder was the largest and heaviest class of gun the British possessed.

The horses strained to pull the stalled naval gun free, their hoofs slipping in the muck. Sailors under the midshipman's command strained to help the stamping team, levering the carriage from behind with handspikes. Two other sailors ran ahead and laid planks in front of the wheels.

The wagon began to move, its wheels rolling up onto the planks. When they reached the end of the first two, the men placed another set of planks in its path then snatched up the first two and leapfrogged them forward, thus making a mobile pathway. This continued until the wagon rolled onto firmer ground.

The entire train began moving again, the infantry labouring at their drag ropes. For almost fifteen minutes, the five guns rolled along uninterrupted.

A gap opened between the lighter 32-pounders and the awkward naval guns. Dudley thought that the men on the 32-pounders should slow their pace so the naval guns could catch up. He was about to suggest this to Lieutenant Coltern when the leading 32-pounder ground to a halt.

There was a string of curses, and he jogged forward to see what was the matter. When he came to the leading gun, he saw the right trailing carriage wheel had sunk more than a foot into a trough of watery mud soup.

The team was still dragging the cumbersome 68-pounder. It would take time to unhitch them and bring them forward, so Dudley shouted, "Handspikes!"

Two privates scurried back to the sunken carriage wheel. One thrust a wooden handspike under the axle while the other positioned a lever under the wheel itself. The men on the drag ropes pulled while those with the handspikes tried to rock the carriage. A fine rain began to fall. As the siege carriage rocked, the wheel sank deeper and deeper.

Dudley pushed on the gun barrel where it inclined in the rear of the carriage and limber. When he saw they were doing no good, he shouted, "Stop!"

The drag ropes slackened. The men stood in the rain and looked at him with blank faces.

"Well, Sergeant Dudley, this is a fine fix," Lieutenant Coltern observed. He looked back at the two naval guns, still creeping towards them. "I suppose we shall have to use the horses. I wonder why they don't find us another damned team?"

Coltern tried to light one of his cigars while Dudley stared at the stuck gun. A rider approached from the opposite direction, hoofbeats thumping on the soft roadbed. Dudley and Coltern glanced up to see an old man with a kind face, his empty right sleeve pinned to the front of his coat. A string of mounted officers rode behind him. None of the officers paid any attention to the stalled guns.

"There goes Lord Raglan, the general," a private said.

"Aye," said young Private Geary. "Lost his arm at Waterloo, so he must know what he's about."

Barker was one of the draggers on the stuck gun, and he suddenly roared, "Right, let's get this gun a-moving! You there with the handspikes—on my count o' three, give it one mighty heave. You other lads get ready to pull. Now, one, two, *three!*"

The men followed Barker's directive without hesitation, ignoring Dudley and Coltern. With a chorus of grunts and gasps, they pulled and pushed and started the gun rocking again. The carriage wheels slid forward a few inches, then shot ahead with a jerk, sucking out of the mud. The men on the drag ropes almost fell but gave a small cheer as they regained their balance.

Dudley felt a touch of irritation that it had been Barker who had encouraged the men to get the gun moving. He wished it could have been him. He was ashamed he had such a wish, but could not deny it. It was another example of that foolish and unwanted competition.

He tried to dismiss his envy as the guns crept closer to their destination on Victoria Ridge. The rain continued and then poured harder, the mud growing softer and deeper. The men's wool uniforms became soaked. Weary and uncomfortable, they grew silent and began to drag their feet.

The great forward gun became stuck again, this time within sight of the Light Division camp. Again, the men with the hand-spikes went to work, while the others pulled on the drag ropes. With a jerk, the gun started forward.

Private Geary, who had tugged with all his might on the drag rope, lost his footing in the slippery roadbed. He fell flat on his chest and face in the mud.

"Halt!" Lieutenant Coltern shouted, and the gun slid to a stop.

No one laughed at Geary's comical misfortune. Even Barker managed to refrain from comment. Dudley took this as an indication of how miserable they all really were. They saw no humour in Geary's spill. All they saw was a companion now more miserable than the rest.

Dudley sloshed forward, gripped Geary's hand and pulled him to his feet.

"Thanks, Sergeant," Geary said, rubbing wet earth from his face. He resumed his place on the drag rope. The front of his jacket was brown with muck.

"Don't worry, Private Geary," Dudley said. "If this weather keeps up, you'll get a good washing."

The men managed a feeble chuckle. Dudley took that to mean the rain had not sponged away all their cheer after all. It was just that they were exhausted.

The work party pulled the guns all the way to Victoria Ridge. There, they dropped the drag ropes and prepared for a short rest. Coltern took the men into the Light Division camp for something to eat, though the only food available was ship's biscuits.

"At least the rain's softened 'em up a bit," Oakes commented as he chewed.

The modest meal done, they were back to work. It was growing dark, and they rushed to pull the guns to their desig-nated battery. The guns of Sevastopol flashed and banged in the west, and the occasional long shot would come bouncing along to bury itself in the turf. When the work party reached the bat-tery, they were still outside the normal range of most of the enemy's artillery, but the guns of the Russian ships and gunboats bottled up in Sebastopol's inner harbour could reach them.

"Just hope they don't notice we're here," Dudley said.

The new British battery lay on the edge of Victoria Ridge. It was a wide, shallow ditch with a row of gun emplacements in its western face. Protecting the emplacements was a parapet of shaped earth, gabions, and facines. In the rear, the engineers had constructed earth-and-stone bunkers for the gunners to take shelter from enemy shells.

Each gun emplacement contained a gun platform of wooden planks. Temporary wooden ramps allowed the fatigue party to push the three 32-pounders into place with brute force and handspikes. It was then simple to unhitch the limbers from the siege carriages, roll them off the platforms and take them back behind the bunkers.

Two empty naval carriages were waiting to receive the 68-pounders. The sailors lowered the heavy guns from the platform wagons by parbuckling them, or rolling them down inclined skids with the aid of ropes. The sailors then parbuckled the guns up onto their carriages and pushed the carriages into position with handspikes.

Russian round shot began to rain down forward of the battery as the sailors worked, spraying fountains of earth and mud. When the naval guns were at last in place, a lookout on the parapet shouted, "Shell!"

More than two hundred men dropped to the ground, though a few ran toward the bunkers and crawled inside. With a high whining arc, the shell fell toward the battery. It struck the ground just to the right and exploded, showering dirt and fragments. A lucky long shot for the Russians.

The smoke cleared, and everyone checked himself for injuries. No one was hit, but one of the naval guns had caught the edge of the blast. The shell had blown off its right rear carriage truck.

"Goddamn," Barker grunted when he saw the damage.

One of the sailors hefted an axe and scurried over to the damaged carriage. He raised the axe and hacked off the other rear truck.

"We'll make do, mate," he said with a grin. "Take more'n that to put us out of action."

The sun had set and the day had ended, but the battery was complete. Coltern ordered his sergeants to form the men into squads for the return to camp. Dudley was still shaking from the stray shell, but his jaded mind found the energy to wonder what tomorrow would bring for No. 3 Company.

---

Tomorrow brought rest until the evening. At dusk, No. 3 Company moved out for picket duty. They were to form a covering party for one of the approach trenches. The actual digging had stopped now that darkness had fallen, but the trenches needed to be guarded around the clock.

Dudley and his men filed toward the trench. He had never been closer to the Russian guns, and knew those guns would open up at the first sign of movement in the British lines.

He was right. Before No. 3 Company reached the trench, three bright flashes appeared on the face of the Redan.

"They know the relief comes just after dark!" someone shouted as the company sprinted for the cover of the trench. Shot and shell began to fall just short, and a few men cried out or grunted with the impact of flying earth and shards of rock.

Dudley leapt down into the trench. Lieutenant Coltern was there with the officer in command of the present covering party. Coltern shouted into the officer's ear, "Your men are relieved."

"Wonderful," the officer said. "I think we shall just sit tight for a while. Until the shelling dies down a bit."

The Russian gunners gave up after fifteen minutes. The sky was now almost pitch-black. The relieved officer's men filed away into the dark toward their camps and tents and maybe some salt beef or pork. Dudley's men took their places along the trench parapet.

The infantry could not assault Sevastopol across miles of open ground without being shot down wholesale. That fact made the system of trenches—a combination of parallels and angled approaches—essential. The sappers had already completed the beginnings of that system, having dug several trenches running parallel to the enemy works, forming an offensive line. Other trenches then led off from that line, zigzagging toward the town. When these approach trenches reached a certain distance, the Royal Engineers would construct another series of parallels. They would then continue to dig approaches and parallels until the forward lines were close enough to make an assault on the Redan, Malakoff and the other fortifications.

The trenches were up to six feet deep, their forward parapets reinforced with sandbags and gabions. In many places, soldiers could only climb in and out by way of short scaling ladders. Thanks to the rain, the trench bottoms were ankle-deep in muddy water.

Digging the trenches was now a filthy job, the worst the infantry could draw. Dudley was thankful the company was on covering party tonight, guarding the forward edge of the approach. That meant they probably would not have to dig tomorrow. Hauling the guns up had been a dirty enough job, he thought. The company needed a rest. The men all seemed to have colds, ague or some other minor yet irritating affliction. New sicknesses cropped up every day. The dampness, the sudden cold at night and in the mornings, poor food, and the exhaustion from constant bone-wearying work were taking their toll.

The men of No. 3 Company lay on top of the parapet, six paces apart. They peered into the dark, watching for signs of enemy movement. Dudley looked along their line and realized he knew them all now, though the men from his barrack room were still the most familiar. There lay the silent and strange Private Doyle, while next to him was Johnson, his Minie gleaming every time the slim moon shone through gaps in the cloud. Oakes and Geary lay farther left, then Barker, and Sergeant O'Ryan with his section. These were the survivors, those who had eluded death in Varna and at the Alma, and were not on the growing sick and disabled lists.

Dudley turned from the dim shapes of his comrades and stared into the northwest. He thought he could hear the rumbling of wagon wheels on the Russian supply road that ran from the north. No lights burned in Sevastopol, but he could sense the grim weight of the Redan and the Malakoff. He knew exactly where they were, exactly where to look.

As he looked, he saw a flash of orange light.

Before the sound reached him, he shouted, "Down!" The gun's report came as the men slid or leapt back into the trench, pressing themselves against the forward wall. The round shot struck the lip of the parapet where a man had been a second ago. It shattered a gabion and bounced clear over the trench.

"Jesus!" Dudley heard Barker cry. "That was too close!"

Another round shot landed outside the trench. Men flinched, then heard the sound of two more Russian guns. Seconds later an iron ball bounced over their heads, while the fourth fell in front of the parapet.

No fifth shot sounded. It seemed to be over for the moment, so Dudley peered over the lip of the trench.

He saw another flash. He slid back into the trench as a mortar shell, whistling like a skyrocket, arched toward them. Men waited wide-eyed, and then the shell burst behind the trench, showering fragments of rock and metal.

Someone cried out, then shouted, "Syphilitic poxed bastards!"

"Is that you, Doyle?" Barker said, his voice displaying no concern.

"Yes, it's bloody well me," the usually silent Doyle replied. "A goddamned shell fragment sliced open me cheek!"

Dudley saw Doyle clutching his face with his right hand. Blood ran between his fingers, but the wound was not deep and did not appear serious. Dudley gave him a handkerchief to press over the gash, then said, "This is a historic occasion, boys— Doyle said an entire sentence."

That brought laughter, and the tension of the moment eased. Even Doyle was laughing.

No further artillery attack followed the mortar shell. It had been a typical limited bombardment, designed to harass the

Allied pickets. No. 3 Company knew all would be quiet for a time.

As Doyle made his way to the rear to have his wound tended, the others crawled out of the trench to continue their surveillance. Dudley knelt on a clump of grass, hoping that at least thirty minutes would pass before the next artillery salvo.

He blinked, then rubbed his eyes. He thought he had seen shapes moving out in the dark, against the bluish black horizon. Then he saw them again—dim figures flowing toward the trench like ghosts. There was a splash, like a boot stepping in a puddle. Dudley realized what was happening. The Russian artillery had fired to prepare the way for an infantry raid.

Knuckles white on his rifle stock, he turned to the drummer on his right and said, "Give the stand to."

The drummer put his bugle to his lips and blew. Along the parapet, men tensed and squinted into the darkness. Coltern appeared at Dudley's side and said, "I don't see them, Sergeant."

There was a flash and a bang ahead. A bullet whined past his ear.

"Oh, hell," Coltern said, drawing his Colt percussion revolver. He shouted, "Independent fire!"

A few rifles went off, nervous shots, unaimed and wasted. The dim shapes outside the trench drew closer, becoming a line of Russian skirmishers. They slowed to a halt and raised their muskets.

Coltern fired his pistol, and Dudley raised his rifle to his shoulder. The rifle kicked, though he didn't see if he had hit anything. The whole trench parapet then erupted in sharp rifle fire, while the Russians returned that fire in a chaos of bangs and flashes.

There was sudden quiet as the fusiliers reloaded. The Russians sprinted forward in the lull. Dudley watched them come as he replaced his ramrod. They wore decorous helmets, each with a thick spike sprouting from its crown. Russian grenadiers.

Coltern's revolver banged again, and one of the attackers pitched backward. The other grenadiers struck the line of fusil-

147

iers with a collective grunt. Men stabbed with bayonets, and rifle butts struck helmeted skulls. Dudley knocked a Russian's musket aside with the muzzle of his own weapon, then Coltern shot the man in the chest. The body flopped down in the mud, a groan and a sigh escaping its slackened mouth.

Down the length of the trench there were more gasps and cries. Dudley swung his rifle back and forth, but he saw Russians turning and running, leaving a number of their comrades behind.

He stared at the body of the man Coltern had just shot. The sight did not bother him as much as he thought it should.

The sound of continued fighting came from somewhere on his left. He heard a voice shout, "They're in the trench!" There was the sharp bark and muzzle flash of another shot, and the wooden clack of musket stocks striking together. Dudley realized the grenadiers were in the forward end of the sap. Without thinking, he leapt down into the trench and sloshed through the water toward the noise. A few others followed him.

Fifteen paces on, he found a group of men struggling in the confined space between the trench walls. There were half a dozen combatants on either side. Dudley thrust his rifle over the shoulder of a fusilier and fired point-blank at the lump of grenadiers. The bullet knocked down the foremost man, and the Russians staggered back. With a cry, Dudley pushed through the knot of British defenders, swinging his rifle stock. He felt the weapon smash into a man's head, saw the man's helmet come off and his body fall back in the mud. The other Russians turned and ran.

He pursued them to the end of the trench and stabbed his bayonet into the leg of the last man to scramble up the lip of the parapet. The fellow screamed and kicked, knocking the bayonet free, and escaped.

Dudley maintained a grip on his rifle and stared at the empty trench, at the picks and spades the sappers had left. He heard a splash behind him and turned. A grenadier officer stood aiming at him. As Dudley watched, the officer's thumb reached up and pulled back the revolver's hammer.

He was too far away to use his bayonet, so he dropped down into the mud. The movement startled the Russian, and the revolver went off. The bullet punched into the dirt behind Dudley's head.

The officer cursed and pulled the hammer back a second time. Before he could aim, a meaty paw grabbed his wrist. The revolver fired, the shot went wild, and a huge screaming fusilier lifted the Russian and threw him against the trench wall.

The officer fell, still clutching his pistol. He aimed it at his assailant, but a booted foot caught him under the jaw, snapping his head back with an ugly crack. The officer slumped into the muck, his body losing all rigidity.

Dudley struggled to his feet. Barker grinned at him.

"So you're still alive," the big man said. "Well, you're a tough little bugger, that's for sure."

"That's no way to speak to a sergeant," Dudley said, though without force.

"Beggin' yer pardon, Sergeant," Barker said. He gave a little bow, then added, "I think that was the last of 'em."

Dudley reached down into the water, retrieving the officer's spiked helmet with its golden badge of the double-headed eagle. "At least I've got myself a Pickelhaube as a trophy."

The Russian raid had been a complete failure. No. 3 Company took three prisoners and counted seven Russian casualties. There were also British casualties—three wounded men.

The company had reason for pride, yet the men simply went back to their positions and watched for the flashing of the guns. Dudley resumed his place on the parapet and felt relief and a small sense of triumph. He rubbed his hands and his body to keep warm and wished he had worn his greatcoat. The night air was damp. He had not noticed it before the raid, but now he did.

A few more random mortar shells fell as the night wore on, though none caused any injuries. No. 3 Company settled into place and waited for morning. Sometime past midnight, an orderly arrived from battalion headquarters with a ration of grog for each man. This warmed them a little, giving them the strength to carry on a few more hours.

Daylight began as a gray glow in the east. The relief company arrived, and No. 3 Company marched back to the camp under the lightening sky. In the camp, reveille had sounded, and those companies not engaged in some kind of work party were forming for parade. Dudley was astonished to see how few men there were gathered round the Colours.

There was nothing ready to eat save the usual biscuits, and these were covered with spots of unappetizing green mould. Dudley forced a few down then wandered to his tent. Before he reached it, he began to tremble. First his hands, then his whole body shook. He remembered staring down the barrel of the Russian officer's revolver. It seemed his nearest brush with death yet, despite the constant artillery fire.

Odd that Barker would come to his rescue. Dudley supposed the fellow had simply been doing his duty. Barker did, after all, have a reputation for being a lion in action.

The trembling began to subside. Recognizing the source of the reaction—his close brush with death—seemed to have dealt with it. But it left him feeling exhausted and depressed.

Inside the tent, he placed his trophy helmet against the central pole and lay on the bare ground. Wrapping himself in his greatcoat and blanket, he rested his head on his knapsack and tried to sleep.

Someone stuck his face through the tent flap and shouted, "Buckets!"

Dudley raised his head to see a young corporal looking at him with an expectant expression. Dudley knew the corporal was on water duty and was collecting the buckets from the tents. He and his mates would take them to the little ravine near the Woronzov Road where a tiny spring bubbled.

"It's outside," Dudley murmured. "Put there to catch the rain."

The orderly stared for a second, said, "Sorry, mate," then disappeared.

Dudley again tried to sleep. Not a minute later, another face poked in through the flap, roaring, "Is Sergeant Dudley in?" He looked up again to see an orderly-sergeant staring in, and said, "Yes, what's up?"

"You are for fatigue at once."

The orderly-sergeant disappeared. Dudley remained on the tent floor for a minute, trying to soak in this information. Fatigue duty, without any sleep.

Sighing, he sat up and threw back his blanket.

———•———

Dudley had drawn supply detail again. His party was in charge of several heavy wagons, all with horse teams and Tartar drivers, rough-bearded men in ragged turbans, baggy trousers and tall leather boots.

On the way to Balaclava, the soldiers rode in the wagons, chatting, smoking their pipes, telling jokes. Dudley walked beside them. His body was stiff and slow with weariness, but he did not want to ride. It would be better if the men could see he wasn't lazy, not overeager to take a break. He would fall asleep if he sat in one of the wagons anyway, and was grateful for the ambling pace on the congested supply road.

Off to his right, the guns of Sevastopol cast a few random shots towards the British works. The Russian artillery had plenty of shot and shell, while their engineers continued to throw up new earthworks. It was common knowledge that Russian supplies and reinforcements arrived from the north every day. Meanwhile, the British had yet to receive fresh troops. The enemy grew stronger while the constant shelling and unstoppable cholera reduced the Allied ranks.

Dudley felt the offensive had stalled, that it was taking too much time. He yearned for a larger action. A further battle would wipe away the bitter stain of Alma and prove to him the glory he had always sought could be found. He needed to reaffirm his beliefs about soldiering, to convince himself those beliefs were true and always had been true. Last night's skirmish, though a small triumph, had not been enough. If not for Barker's intervention, the skirmish would have been no triumph at all. It had demonstrated that Dudley had developed an ability to shrug off the emotional shock of war, but that was all.

Being able to shrug off his feelings was not what he wanted. Since the arrival in the Sevastopol theatre, he had become hardened to the sight of the wounded and dead, just as he had become hardened to disease in Varna. But that hardening could not change what had happened at the Alma. A fresh action would allow him the opportunity to defeat the horror he had known there.

In Balaclava, the fatigue party loaded the wagons with wooden crates and barrels containing the usual salt beef and pork, more biscuits, and a load of new wool blankets. The blankets were welcome, for they were getting scarce in camp. Since they offered the only cloth available, many fusiliers had taken to using them to repair their time- and weatherworn coatees. The Royal Hants was beginning to look like a patchwork regiment.

The loaded wagons made their way back toward camp, the men now lounging on top of the piled supplies. Dudley still walked, boots squelching in the ruts.

Before long the little column ground to a halt. An oxcart had become bogged down in front, its Turkish drivers shouting and gesticulating, blaming each other for the mishap. Blue-clad Turkish soldiers, with poles and handspikes, ignored the drivers and tried to free the heavy vehicle, which had sunk low and listed to one side.

Dudley ordered his men to help. As the fusiliers set to work, he noticed they had halted across from the Zouave camp. A few French soldiers, along with wives and camp followers, had gathered to watch the little drama on the road. Dudley recognized one of the spectators. It was O'Ryan's cantiniere, the lovely Isabelle, supplier of brandy to the Irish.

She saw him looking at her, and turned her wide brown eyes in his direction. His instinct was to look away, but he fought it and managed a smile. She returned the smile.

"Bonjour, Madame," he said.

"Bonjour, Sergeant," she returned, a singsong greeting.

A cheer went up on the road ahead, for the oxcart had begun rolling. The two lumbering beasts snorted and slipped in the mud but managed to move forward.

Dudley's wagons began to move a minute later. As he marched beside them, there was a little more spirit in his step. He did not feel quite so weary anymore.

# CHAPTER EIGHT

To count the life of battle good And dear the
land that gave you birth, And dearer yet the
brotherhood That binds the brave of all the
earth.

Sir Henry Newbolt
"Clifton Chapel"

***Dusk settled on*** another day in the trenches. There was no
sunset, no blaze of fiery colour in the west, just an increasing
darkness. The day had been bleak and gray, while the evening
had brought chilling winds and spitting rain.

Dudley and the men of No. 3 Company lay in the wiry
grass along the trench parapet. They huddled in their greatcoats
of thin gray wool and waited for the arrival of the relief company. With them waited a company of sappers dressed only in
fatigue shirts and trousers. The sappers had finished their day's
digging, and now shivered and clutched their picks and spades
as if to squeeze warmth from the wood and steel.

The relief company came marching along the flooded
trench bottom. Lieutenant Coltern and the relieving officer exchanged words, then Colour-Sergeant Onslow formed No. 3
Company and gave the quick march. The sappers followed under the command of their engineers' officer.

When they had all gone about a hundred yards, Dudley heard the Russian guns open behind them. The target was the relief company.

"Poor buggers," Barker said. "A moment sooner, and we'd 'ave caught some of that."

There was a murmur of agreement. Some lamented the fate of those comrades who would have to endure the shelling through the night, but all were glad to have escaped that shelling themselves. The men then tried to forget about what was happening in the trenches so they could enjoy the next hour or so. They laughed and chatted, in high spirits despite the cold and exhaustion of a day of dull picket duty. They still felt the glow of their many small victories over the past week.

There had been a number of raids on the siege lines, but the British had repulsed every one. No. 3 Company had taken part in some of that skirmishing, their accurate Minie rifles leaving a scattering of Russian corpses on the blasted ground before the trenches.

The guns were still firing when the company reached the Light Division camp. There, the men stacked their rifles and crowded around the bivouac fires for warmth and companionship. Orderlies brought food and alcohol rations and passed them round. Dudley ate his insipid hard tack and beef strips with the other sergeants in camp, O'Ryan and Colour-Sergeant Onslow. Oakes and his wife joined them, as well as some of the other veteran privates and corporals.

Someone at another campfire broke into song, delivering a few verses of one of the new compositions that had sprung up in the camps:

> Then Britain's sons may long remember
> The glorious twentieth of September
> We caused the Russians to surrender
> Upon the heights of Alma.
>
> To Sevastopol the Russians fled.
> They left their wounded and their dead.
> The rivers there that they run red
> From the blood was spilled at Alma.

Dudley listened and marveled at the mood of the regiment. Morale had been running high lately, though it should have been the opposite. The men worked to exhaustion every day while the weather grew colder, wetter and filthier. Sickness, raids and shelling caused a dozen casualties every day. The men wore patched jackets and wrapped their feet in straw for lack of stockings.

For all this, they remained cheerful. Morale had made a steady climb since the months in Varna, though conditions had not improved.

Dudley glanced in the direction of the singing. He did not know the singer, but next to the fellow sat Private Barker. After the second verse, Barker threw back his head and joined in.

Dudley shook his head. He was unsure what to think of Barker now. He could not get past the fact Barker had saved his life. The man had changed, had been less of a burden since the landing in the Crimea. In fact, he had been an asset. The reason for the change was unclear. Barker, of course, understood the army would not tolerate any nonsense during time of war, and perhaps this explained his better behaviour. But Dudley was not sure. Barker was a puzzling character.

"That Brian Barker has a fine voice," Hester Oakes commented. Dudley agreed. Barker was a fine singer; he and his partner sang:

> And many a pretty maid does mourn
> Her lover who will ne'er return.
> By cruel wars he's from her torn—
> His body lies at Alma.

For some reason, the song made Dudley think of home. He chewed a mouthful of salt beef and biscuit and wished for one of his aunt's meals, or a ripe apple from their orchard. Even a decent pot of coffee would have been welcome. Sergeant O'Ryan was roasting some of the green coffee beans the army seemed to have in abundance, but the beans had yet to yield a respectable brew.

Dudley grimaced as he swallowed the lump of biscuit. The food was disgusting, but like most of the other men, he refused to voice his discontent. True to his policy, he pretended to be as cheerful as the others, though he was not

Oakes sat with Hester on a cask on the other side of the fire, poking at the coals with a stick.

"The lads may scoff at learnin' and so on," Oakes was saying, "but we all want to better ourselves. You're our educated man, Sergeant Dudley, and we've all seen how that has helped lead to your early rise in the ranks. And my Hester here has suggested that when this is all over you should consider the position of schoolmaster sergeant. The regiment doesn't have one, as ye know."

Dudley had not been listening to the conversation. For a moment, he didn't realize Oakes had directed this comment at him.

"What do you think o' that, Sergeant?" Oakes prompted.

Dudley looked at him blankly, then replied, "I, uh, suppose that would be a logical pursuit for me."

That was true. After all, Dudley had been a teacher already, and the schoolmaster sergeant was a rank on a level with the RSM.

"I suppose I *should* think about that, Private Oakes," he added, and at Barker's camp fire the singing went on:

Now France and Britain, hand-in-hand,
What foe on earth could them withstand?
So, let it run throughout the land,
The victory won at Alma.

It was remarkable, Dudley thought, how Oakes could so easily think of the future.

"Yes," he said, nodding, "when all this is over, maybe I *will* look into the matter."

When Dudley retired to his tent, he did not bother to remove his greatcoat or his accoutrements. He pushed his cartridge pouch to one side out of his way and lay on his back.

There were ten other men in the tent, all snoring. In three minutes, he had joined them, sinking into a deep sleep.

An orderly-sergeant woke him in the morning and put him on fatigue duty. Dudley and Sergeant O'Ryan were to take a foraging party into the surrounding uplands and scavenge for firewood and any edibles they could find. Dudley welcomed the task as a chance to get away from the siege lines.

The army had depleted Careenage Ravine of most of its prime combustibles, so the foraging party ranged far into the barren hills. They looked for any bit of wood or bracken that would burn, wandering away from the camps and out of their sight. Both Dudley and O'Ryan agreed the men needed the space and the quiet of the open country.

Dudley moved apart from the others, savouring the near solitude and the immensity of the landscape. He took a deep breath. Last night's rain had run out, and it was a day of intermittent cloudiness, with bursts of sunshine. In the south, he could see the long ridgeback of the Causeway Heights. He thought he could make out the square regularity of one of the redoubts but wasn't sure.

He took off his forage cap and shaded his eyes with one hand. He had spied an eagle, a winged speck in the vastness of the Crimean sky, soaring in a wide circle. Farther west was a second speck, possibly the eagle's mate.

How did I come to this place? he wondered. How had he come so far from the green downs of Hampshire, so far from all the places he had ever known? What remarkable series of events had brought him to this war, to this other world?

Hampshire—home—no longer seemed like a real place. Dudley had been writing letters since Gibraltar, but he had received none in return. He hoped this was because of the inefficiency of the mail, and not that Jane had ceased her correspondence. She was rebellious, and even if Uncle Robert tried to forbid her to write to him, she would do so anyway. Dudley was confident in her continued affections.

A footstep crunched in the gravel beside him. He turned to see O'Ryan approaching, grinning beneath his mustache.

"Ye've spied the eagles, have you?" the other sergeant said. "I declare ye're a romantic at heart, lad. Are ye truly sure there's no Irish in ye at all?"

Dudley smiled at the other sergeant's preoccupation with his lineage.

"My aunt and uncle never mentioned it, but that does not mean it's not there."

"Ah! They've hidden it from you. An ancient family secret. Perhaps yer grandmother was even a fairy, for all that."

The men in the foraging party began to sing as they made for a stand of cypress and scrub oak off to their left. Dudley and O'Ryan followed at a distance.

"I must admit," Dudley said, "you were rather a fearsome fellow on the parade square, but you're not at all fearsome off it."

O'Ryan laughed. "A sergeant has to behave a certain way with the men, but not with his fellow sergeants."

They waded into the stand of trees with the others. The party gathered what little deadwood there was and cut a few of the trees down, splitting the trunks into small logs. With this greenwood bundled on their backs in canvas sacks, they made their way back to camp.

Their chosen route took them near the Zouave encampment, and as they passed, Dudley commented, "I wonder if your cantiniere is about, O'Ryan?"

"Ah, now that reminds me," O'Ryan said, reaching into his greatcoat and taking out his flask. He looked at Dudley, hesitated, then asked, "I take it ye'd like to meet Isabelle?"

"Yes," Dudley admitted after a pause, "I suppose I would."

"Ye would, eh? Well, would ye mind, William, having her fill this for me? Here, I'll give you the little fee she charges…"

"You want *me* to go?"

"Well, if you don't mind, as I said. I saw the way ye looked at her, lad, and I'm not blind meself. Ye'd prefer to go to her without me taggin' along." He passed Dudley the flask. "And don't worry about lookin' like you're shirkin' your duties. Brandy is forage as far as I'm concerned."

Dudley looked at the flask, then grinned at O'Ryan.

"I shan't be long. Well, not too long."

He left the foraging party and entered the French camp. Some of the Zouaves there greeted him, and he returned their greetings in his best country-school French. He asked for the whereabouts of the regiment's cantiniere, and they directed him toward one of the French mortar batteries, which one of their companies was guarding. That was quite a distance to go, but Dudley thanked the men and carried on.

The journey took him ten minutes. The French battery, the gunners lounging about their idle pieces, looked exactly like a British gun emplacement. He did not know why this should strike him as odd.

He saw the cantiniere as she moved from Zouave to Zouave, selling each man a tot of brandy or rum. He waited at the edge of their line. Several of the French soldiers gave him hostile stares, but he ignored them. When the cantiniere reached the last man, she saw Dudley, and he knew she recognized him. She smiled.

"Are you here for a tot of brandy, Sergeant?" she asked him in her own language.

He thought he detected a sly glint in her eyes, and he froze. He had not expected this, but her beauty held him. All of a sudden, he had no idea what to say.

"Perhaps you do not speak French?" the cantiniere asked.

"Yes, I do," he managed, in French. "In fact, at one point I taught it." He took a deep breath. "In reply to your first question, I have not come for a tot of brandy, but I will take one."

She poured him a cap-full from a large canteen she carried at her side. He did not have any French coins, so he gave her an English penny. She looked at it where it lay in her hand, then lifted her great brown eyes up at him, smiled again, and passed him the cap. He took it. The brandy burned going down, filling him with grateful warmth.

He returned the cap and said, "We both have a friend, an Irish sergeant named Aiden O'Ryan."

Her smile faded. "Yes, I know him. A friend of my late husband."

"I am sorry for your misfortune," Dudley thought it proper to say.

She shrugged. "Such is the nature of war. I married a soldier. What did I expect? But you did not know my husband, and I doubt that you came here to speak about him?"

"No. I—that is, Sergeant O'Ryan asked me to see if you would mind filling this?" He held up the flask. "He gave me a bender—what he said was your usual price."

The cantiniere nodded. "Very well. But I can't fill it here. Come back to my tent."

Dudley followed her back to the camp. It was another long walk across open ground, and he tried to ignore the strange stares the Zouaves cast his way. Doubtless, some of these men did not like to see an *Anglais* with their *belle* Isabelle.

Beside her tent was a table on which rested several small barrels. She filled the flask from one of these, and Dudley paid her.

"Tell O'Ryan," she said, "that this is the last. Do not be harsh about it, but if he still wants his brandy, from now on he will have to give the full price."

Dudley nodded. His business here was over, but he did not want to leave. He wanted to speak to this lovely young woman, to ask her how she had come to be travelling with the French army. He wanted to know who she was, but he did not know how to begin. He stood, feeling foolish, but no appropriate words came to mind.

Finally, he touched the rim of his cap and said, "Well, thank you very much, Madam. I will tell Sergeant O'Ryan what you said."

"It was nothing, Sergeant. You are welcome."

He nodded, then turned to leave.

"Sergeant," she called after him. He stopped, looking back. Her smile had returned. "You may visit me. If you have the chance."

For a moment, he could not believe his ears. Then his face flushed and split into an involuntary grin. All he could do was nod in reply. Then, embarrassed, he turned and walked out of the camp, back onto the supply road.

He jogged along the muddy track, hoping to catch up to the foraging party, which was almost an hour ahead. His heart was racing. Somehow, Isabelle had recognized what he wanted, though he had not really understood it himself. Yes, he did want to visit her. Now he would be able to do what he had wished he could do—talk to her.

Yet, he was not certain how good an idea that really was. A doubting inner voice asked him why he thought it was worth pursuing the affections of a woman from the French camp. He would never find the time to visit her, and even if he did, what then? If he fell in love with her because of her beauty, would he want to marry her? A Frenchwoman attached to the French army?

"It doesn't matter," he said to himself. "It doesn't matter."

Whatever the reality, he felt a warmth in his heart simply from having Isabelle tell him he could come to her. It felt like an achievement of some kind. He wanted to tell O'Ryan.

Under the Irishman's direction, the foraging party had dawdled on the road. Dudley managed to rejoin them, though he was breathless from running when he caught up and delivered the flask.

He told O'Ryan what Isabelle had said about having to pay the full price for his brandy. O'Ryan nodded, sighed and said, "Ah, well, it couldn't last, could it?"

"I suppose not, with supplies as they are," Dudley agreed. Then he brightened and told him what else the cantiniere had said.

"What do you think she meant by 'visit' her, lad?" he asked.

"Well, to visit her. To go and speak with her and so on. Begin a sort of friendship."

O'Ryan laughed. "Are you sure she didn't mean go to her tent with a few pennies in your pocket to pay for her womanly services? And I don't mean laundry, boy!"

Dudley's face flushed for a second time that morning. "What do you mean? You think she...she sells herself?"

O'Ryan shrugged. "Well, I don't really know. But her husband's dead, and she's not yet remarried. Maybe she's earning herself a good wage, selling brandy and a romp in the hay. Or a romp in the mud, given the conditions." He laughed again. "I thought that's what you were after anyhow!"

Dudley's jaw clenched. He had not considered this possibility—and refused to believe it.

"I was not after anything of the sort, and I don't believe she sells herself," he said. "She is not the kind. A lovely and practical young woman."

"Practical, aye," O'Ryan chuckled. "How practical, I wonder?"

Dudley had nothing else to say.

The siege preparations went on. As he had feared, Dudley was so busy he never had a free moment. He never found a chance to visit Isabelle and prove to himself her invitation had been nothing to do with commerce.

Because of the growing sick-and-disabled list, the number of men available was shrinking. Dudley was on duty all day every day, and did not even have time for sleep. Meanwhile, the work was dull and monotonous. Most of it involved waiting, standing guard or watch, always waiting for something to happen.

The waiting at least gave Dudley time to think. His mind, near delirious from fatigue, would race on quiet nights of picket duty, running over the events of his young life. On one such night, he sat in a rifle pit, wrapped in his greatcoat and watching the crest of a low ridge near the Russian defences. His imagination again and again brought forth the image of a woman with huge brown eyes, sensuous lips smiling, smiling at him. He tried to remember Martha and his feelings for her. Even after Martha's betrayal, those feelings had persisted. Now they came to him as impressions of what his life had been before his enlistment, before this war. He no longer ached for Martha. The same longing he had known for her he now felt for Isabelle, a woman he did not even know.

163

He heard a rumbling of wagon wheels coming from the direction of Sevastopol. It was an ominous sound, but he was glad for the distraction from his thoughts of Isabelle and Martha. He had heard that rumbling before, though it was louder this time. Maybe that was because No. 3 Company was closer to the enemy tonight, deployed far out in front of Victoria Ridge. Just west of them was the Russian supply road. The road ran from the north, past the Inkerman ruins, then over the Tchernaya River. After that it passed under the lee of the enemy's northernmost fortifications before entering the town. The Russian supply parties did not use the road during the day because of its exposure to the Allied guns, but they could be heard almost every night, going to and fro.

"They're moving down there again, Sergeant," said Private Johnson, who sat with Dudley in the shallow pit. The other men of the picket were squatting in similar holes, or behind boulders. "Bringin' up bloody reinforcements again, more than likely."

"That doesn't sound like marching men to me, Private Johnson," Dudley replied. "It sounds more like they're rolling up more guns, though it hardly seems possible they need any more. They already have every avenue of our approach covered."

For a fleeting moment, he wondered what Martha would think if she could see him now, but then Johnson exclaimed, "Wait! You hear something funny, Sarge?"

The private sighted along his rifle and squinted into the darkness. Dudley had not heard anything save for the wagon wheels, but he held his breath and listened. He could hear it now—a faint slithering sound, as of men crawling over brush and rocks.

He gripped his rifle and froze. The slithering grew louder, and dark silhouettes appeared over the ridge crest. Men creeping forward at a crouch.

Johnson turned to him and said eagerly, "Stand to?"

Nerves tingling, Dudley nodded. Johnson fired his rifle as a signal then ran back to report to Lieutenant Coltern.

On Johnson's signal, the men of the picket fell back twenty yards and deployed in a skirmish line. The Russians must have heard the shot and the movement, for Dudley could see them start to run, dark smudges scurrying forward. It looked like another Russian skirmish line, maybe of company strength. Another night raiding party.

Lieutenant Coltern crouched low, revolver in hand, and moved from man to man, saying, "Choose a target carefully, now. Wait for my word to fire."

The Russians were close enough that Dudley could see their faces, lighter smudges in the dark. He brought his rifle up and aimed.

A flash and a bang on the far left made him flinch. Someone had discharged his rifle without Coltern's order. A second later, everyone was firing, tense trigger fingers unable to wait. Russians soldiers fell.

There was the usual lull as everyone reloaded. The Russians had balked, and some ran back from where they had come. Others stood their ground but did nothing, as if confused. Dudley heard a Russian officer shouting orders, then four enemy soldiers came running toward his position. He brought his rifle up again, as did Johnson.

The two soldiers in the lead suddenly threw down their muskets and threw up their hands, crying, "Pole! Pole!"

Dudley lowered his rifle.

"More Polish deserters!" Coltern exclaimed. "Let them through."

Oakes and another man rushed forward to take the Poles into custody. The two Russians who had been coming up behind them stopped in their tracks. They looked from side to side and saw they were alone, the rest of their raiding party having retreated. The Russians turned around and began to run the other way.

Johnson aimed at the back of one of the men and fired.

"Oh, bollocks!" he cried in astonishment. He had missed in the darkness.

Slinging the rifle on his back, he leapt to his feet and charged after the fleeing soldiers. He reached one of the men and dove for his legs, tackling him as if playing rugby. The Russian hit the ground and his musket rattled and skidded away.

"Go get that man, Sergeant," Coltern ordered.

Dudley slung his rifle and ran to where Johnson and his opponent wrestled on the ground, grunting and cursing. Johnson had the man by the head and the back of the coat, but the Russian was stronger. With a sharp cry, he slipped from Johnson's grasp and scrambled to his feet. A second later, he was running back toward his own lines.

Johnson sat on the ground and watched the man go. As Dudley approached, the private said, "Well, at least I got his cap."

He held up the Russian forage cap, which had remained in his hand when the other soldier had wriggled free.

"And I have his musket," Dudley added, stooping to where the weapon lay, discarded and forgotten.

They returned to the picket line with their trophies. Dudley displayed the musket with pride. It was a heavy smoothbore weapon marked "1834." The reinforcing bands and cap lock were loose, further reducing the musket's quality.

"Probably loosen them to get a good dramatic rattle and crash during drill," Dudley speculated.

The rest of the night was uneventful. At dawn, No. 3 Company returned to camp and heard some of what the two Polish deserters had said to their new British saviours. The daily life of a soldier in the Russian Army was not a pleasant one. The Poles said their officers and NCOs beat the men with their fists, and with sticks and canes. This was for both punishment and "encouragement." Their officers had also told the Poles that, if they deserted, the Allies would cut off their ears.

They had not believed that story.

By October 17, the Allied guns were all in place, seventy-three British and fifty-three French. The batteries were ready to strike at Sebastopol's defences while the British and French navies would add their fire from the sea.

It was none too soon. If the bombardment and assault did not come now, the Allies would have to endure a bitter Russian winter in the trenches and camps. If all went as planned, such a fate would be averted, for Sevastopol would fall within the day, or the next few days. The guns would pound the fortifications, reducing them to rubble. The French would then make the assault, their trenches being nearer the Russian lines than those of the British. The British infantry would provide support for the storming French troops.

The Royal Hampshire Fusiliers stood on the right of a line of six batteries known collectively as Gordon's Batteries. They were named after the officer of the Royal Engineers who had overseen their construction. To the right rear of the fusiliers was the detached five-gun battery No. 3 Company had helped to build.

The infantrymen sensed the contained power of those silent guns and fidgeted in impatience. After reveille that morning, the quartermaster had issued each man fresh powder and ball ammunition. Lieutenant-Colonel Freemantle then relayed the orders from Brigade that the regiment was to form in column, minus greatcoats and knapsacks. The same orders went out to the other regiments. Now, the entire army waited for further orders, words that would send them forward to the trenches in the wake of the artillery's destruction.

Dudley stood with his company alongside Barker and Geary, Oakes, the silent Doyle, and the twenty-five others still fit for duty. He was the only senior NCO present—Sergeant O'Ryan had made the sick list that morning with a mild fever and cramps, while Colour-Sergeant Onslow had been on the sick list for days. The only other company authority was Lieutenant Coltern. He stood apart from the column and spoke to the Royal Artillery officer in charge of one of Gordon's Batteries.

Coltern chuckled at something, then left the battery and came over to position himself next to Dudley. The artillery officer, a captain, was now sighting on Sevastopol with a brass-furnished telescope. After a moment, he clapped the telescope shut and pulled out his watch. With a look of satisfaction, he put the watch away and said, "Nearing six-thirty, lads," then shouted in command, "Target at six degrees elevation, with five rounds round shot, load!"

The sergeants in charge of each gun then cried, "Load!" Their gun crews sprang into action, sponging their guns according to the drill, then loading charge, wad and shot. Gunners carried out these same actions all along the line of Gordon's Batteries, and in Chapman's Batteries farther left, and in the five-gun battery. Dudley imagined the same activity in the other detached batteries, such as the so-called Sandbag Battery in front of the Second Division's camp. In his mind's eye, he saw the host of soldiers and sailors preparing to do their duty in every gun position along the British and French lines.

The men in the nearest battery ran their guns up, then inserted friction igniter tubes into the vents. Each sergeant then announced to the captain his gun was ready.

"Number One gun," the captain called, "Fire!"

The No. 7 man on the first gun pulled his lanyard. The great 32-pounder crashed and recoiled on its massive siege carriage. The noise was deafening, and when all of the guns in the battery had fired, Dudley's ears were aching.

There was to be no escape from the din. The air became filled with a constant roar and thunder as more than a hundred guns, French and British, began a constant rolling fire. Dudley gazed in amazement at the black specks of round shot as they sailed aloft. He could see them fly at their target, then crash into the Russian works below the Malakoff, spraying earth and debris. The mortar shells were even more impressive, whining and whistling, trailing smoke as they flew. They burst on-target, tearing down the Russian walls and reducing the squat White Tower to complete rubble, its heavy guns silenced and dismounted.

The bombardment continued all morning. By the middle of the afternoon, the enemy fortifications were crumbling. Dudley decided the Russian casualties must have been high, for their return fire was sporadic and had done little damage to the Allied positions. Two small Russian steamers, turning circles in the inner harbour, managed to score a few hits on the five-gun battery, but the huge Lancaster guns soon sent these gunboats limping for the north shore.

"We'll be going soon, just you see!" Johnson shouted over the noise. His eyes lit with glee, and he was trembling in anticipation.

Dudley was also excited. He was nervous, but glad to be striking a major blow at the enemy, the blow he had so wanted. Johnson was right. It seemed likely they would attack this very day, given the effectiveness of the bombardment.

He looked to his left, over the heads of the infantry and toward the French lines. That was where an assault would begin, and he studied it for signs of troop movement. He saw none, but did notice the Russian fire was a bit heavier there.

As he watched, there was a bright flash of light that covered the entire sky. Seconds later, a monstrous clap, like thunder, sounded over the roar of the guns. A large mushroom-shaped cloud of smoke began to rise near the rear of the French siege line.

"Christ," Barker breathed, "their magazine's blown."

A lucky Russian shot, Dudley thought, gaping at the monstrous cloud. It was an uncanny sight, and gave him a strange sensation in the pit of his stomach. A disaster like that could delay the assault.

Minutes later, there was a second huge explosion, a sight as spectacular as the first, and just as shocking. A second French magazine had blown up. The infantrymen groaned and shook their heads.

"Bloody Frogs!" an officer in another company cried. "You can never rely on 'em for anything, save incompetence."

The bombardment in the French sector began to slacken from want of ammunition. Barker let loose a string of curses, and Dudley shouted at him to mind his language. The reprimand allowed him to relieve some of his agitation.

There was still a slim chance the attack could go ahead as planned, for the British artillery continued its work. But as the hours went by and the men waited, no orders came. Evening approached, and the French batteries stopped firing altogether.

By then, Dudley was beginning to feel a sense of resignation. There would be no assault today after all. Perhaps it would have to come tomorrow.

At dusk, the British batteries ceased firing. The stillness that followed was eerie, somehow foreboding. Dudley did not like the feel of it.

The infantry received orders to return to their camps. In the night, the Russians could be heard repairing their works. The morning showed the enemy fortifications returned to their former condition, almost as if there had been no bombardment.

The British batteries resumed their fire, and again it continued until dusk. On the third day, the French had solved their problems and joined in again.

The bombardment continued as the weather grew worse. The heat and stillness of the initial landing in the Crimea seemed a distant memory under these gray skies. Now there was a constant howling wind that brought rain and sleet and wet snow at night. Dudley felt the morale of the men begin to dip, this sudden frustration defeating what he had thought was an invincible good nature. Every day, they saw the Redan and Malakoff blown to pieces, and every morning saw them risen anew.

After almost a week of constant thunder, the Allied guns fell silent. Everyone knew there would be no assault. Word spread that Lord Raglan had wanted to attack on the first day, but the French misfortune had made it impossible. Now Raglan did not believe his force was strong enough.

Rumours circulated the main Russian force had returned and was lurking somewhere inland. Intelligence reports also told of 25,000 enemy troops massing in the north beyond the Tchernaya, poised to strike at the British right flank near Inkerman. In light of this likelihood, there could be no assault. There were not enough able-bodied men left to make the attack and defend the siege lines at the same time. The army would have to wait for reinforcements.

The night after the ceasefire was the coldest yet. This seemed an added insult in the wake of the failed bombardment. In the morning, Dudley found the water in the bucket outside his tent half-frozen. The sight seemed a warning of things to come now that the siege had stalled.

An orderly sought him out and told him he was on supply duty. The routine would continue. Dudley nodded as the orderly explained that new blankets were waiting in Balaclava. He knew the sick and wounded were in desperate need of those blankets.

With a party of twenty men, he set out for Balaclava. He marched in their fore and said nothing. The men did not share his gloom, and cracked quiet jokes as they marched. To his relief, they had already shrugged off the failed bombardment and regained some of their cheer.

A rumbling of cannon fire came from the southeast. The men paid it no heed at first, for it was nothing unusual. The Turks in the redoubts along the Causeway Heights often exchanged fire with Russian patrols.

"Turks and Russians playing at long bowls again?" Barker suggested.

There was a murmur of agreement, but after a few minutes the fire increased, becoming regular and heavy. Then a party of mounted staff officers dashed by on the road, kicking up dust. Dudley began to feel uneasy. Those officers were in a hurry for some reason.

When the work party reached the uplands, they came upon a crowd of spectators gathered on the side of the road. Traffic had halted. The spectators were gazing in the direction of the noise, over the Heights and the hills and the plain.

The work party stopped, the men chattering in a mixture of excitement and confusion. Dudley turned to a French officer, a portly fellow in a gold-laced kepi who resembled an English bulldog. He saluted and asked, "Excuse me, sir, but do you know what is happening?"

The officer rolled his eyes in Dudley's direction, touched his cap brim with one lazy hand and said, "I will tell you what I know."

A large Russian army had appeared early in the morning, the Frenchman explained. It came from the east rather than the north, and attacked the redoubts. The Turks had put up a valiant struggle for an hour and a half against overwhelming odds, but the four redoubts had fallen.

Now, the Russian army stood in formation, facing the British. Massed Russian cavalry stood along the captured Causeway

Heights, with infantry behind them. In the shallow valley north of the Heights, the enemy had massed their field artillery. Behind the artillery were more dark columns of infantry and rank upon rank of cavalry.

Facing the Russians was a British force of scattered units. Most of them were from the Cavalry Division. On the left sat the Light Brigade, drawn up in even lines of man and horse. On their right, the Heavy Brigade had also formed in line. Behind them, all along the Sapoune Ridge, was a French force of four infantry regiments and two cavalry.

On the far right, protecting the supply road that ran past Kadikoi and on to Balaclava, was a regiment of Highlanders and a few companies of Turks. On *their* right was a six-gun field battery of the Royal Artillery. Someone said the Highlanders were the 93rd, and that they and the Turks and guns were under Colin Campbell, an able and experienced commander.

Dudley thanked the French officer and ordered his party to stay together. It was impossible to continue on their way, and he didn't want his men to become dispersed among the gawking crowd of soldiers, wives, civilians and camp followers.

"What's this little drama we're about to witness?" Oakes wondered aloud. Because of the sharp cold, it was a clear day, the ground was dry and the visibility excellent. "The big fight we've all been waiting for?"

"Russkies trying to cut our supply line," Barker rumbled. That was obvious. Russian artillery on the Causeway Heights was shelling the supply route near Kadikoi, forcing the line of Highlanders to retreat to the rear face of the little hill they had occupied. The Turks fled, their distant forms resembling scurrying ants as they ran.

Dudley felt a pang of distress. Here he was with an unarmed party while a major engagement was in progress. He was missing it.

But many others were missing it, too, and he said, "It seems the infantry divisions are to be left out."

"Our camps are too far away behind us," Oakes said, "and unaware of what's going on. Save for those Highlanders. Look!"

Four squadrons of Russian hussars had suddenly broken away from the main body of enemy cavalry. They thundered toward Kadikoi and the hill behind which the Highlanders had taken shelter.

As Dudley's men watched, the Highlanders advanced, returning to their place along the crest of the hill. The Russian cavalry found themselves facing British infantry in line. The hussars dug in their spurs and thundered forward, perhaps sensing an easy victory over these exposed men on foot.

"Why don't they form square?" Barker exclaimed, for it seemed the Highlanders would be outflanked and cut down. The British field battery fired at the Russian squadrons, the 6-pounder guns making a steady thump-thumping, but the horsemen kept coming, straight at the infantry.

With a blast of smoke, the Highlanders fired a volley at long range. No horsemen fell, but the enemy wheeled to the left.

"God bless the Minie rifle," someone said, and Dudley heard Private Johnson cursing and crying, "Someone give me a rifle! Someone give me a rifle!"

The hussars aimed for the Highlanders' right flank. That flank wheeled back with parade-square precision, moving like a door on a hinge. Another great volley of rifle fire burst forth. Horsemen fell in a twisted mass of men and animals.

The hussars turned and galloped the other way. The field battery kept up its fire, blasting round after round into the crippled squadrons. On the road where Dudley stood, people cheered. The Highlanders had repulsed the Russian charge.

"Amazing," Oakes said. "Infantry in line defending against cavalry? Unheard of!"

"It's not over yet," Dudley said.

The Highlanders had been successful, but they were still just part of a thin screen defending Balaclava. That screen had to be reinforced.

From the British center, four squadrons of the Heavy Brigade of cavalry began to move toward the right. The Heavy Brigade was made of big men on bigger horses, most of its units garbed in red jackets, like the infantry. They would offer support for the Highlanders.

Above the British horsemen, sitting on the Causeway Heights, the main body of Russian cavalry edged forward. The Heavies saw this movement. Their flank exposed, they wheeled left to meet the new threat.

"Oho! What are we going to see now?" Oakes said with glee.

"Madness," Barker said. "Their cavalry outnumber ours four to one."

Dudley knew the commander of the Heavy Brigade was Brigadier James Scarlet. Scarlet seemed oblivious to his numerical inferiority, and halted his squadrons to have his officers dress their lines. Then the trumpets sounded, and the Heavies moved forward as one, at the trot. They advanced in two lines, men of the Inniskillings, Scots Greys and Dragoon Guards, now moving uphill. At the crest of that hill waited the huge black-and-gray mass of the enemy—Cossacks and ten squadrons of hussars.

The other British squadrons of Heavies must have seen what was happening, for they galloped to the aid of their fellows. Before they could arrive, Scarlet's four squadrons struck home.

The first British line sank into the Russians, engulfed. A collective gasp went up from the spectators around Dudley and his men. They could see every Heavy as a red coat amidst the dark mass of the enemy, their sabres rising and falling. They were so few, and the Cossacks were riding around the flanks to surround them.

It was then that the other Heavy Brigade squadrons caught up to their comrades. One squadron of Inniskillings charged into the Russian left flank, piercing it like an arrowhead, unhorsing Cossacks in great bunches. Then a squadron of Dragoon Guards struck the Russian right flank. Finally, the Royal Dragoons arrived, charging into the melee. The huge Russian formation began to fray, to unravel, and then broke, scattering to its left rear. Gray-and-brown horsemen fled, leaving behind the milling and disordered ranks of the victorious British.

The spectators cheered as they had cheered for the 93rd Highlanders, while down on the plain the Horse Artillery managed a few shots while the Heavy Brigade rallied.

"The good old Union Brigade!" Oakes cried, referring to the fact the Heavies included English, Irish and Scottish regiments.

"What are the Lights doing?" Johnson complained. "This is the perfect time to pursue, while the enemy's running!"

But the Light Brigade was just sitting there, holding its ground.

The main Russian cavalry force retreated over the Heights, and the battle seemed won. Though the enemy had captured the redoubts, the British had saved their supply route from two successive attacks. A third attack was possible, for the Russians remained on the Heights and in the shallow valley, but they seemed uncertain what to do next. Dudley's men sat tight, chewing on bits of dry grass and waiting, discussing the morning's action in excited voices.

It was close to eleven o'clock when the Russians began to stir again; the French officer let Dudley have a view through his telescope. Dudley focused on the enemy in the captured redoubts. They were limbering up the guns the Turkish artillerymen had spiked and abandoned there. The Russians were about to carry the guns away, which could mean they were about to withdraw.

"Someone should clear those buggers off that ridge," Johnson said. He seemed disgusted that he was unarmed and could not be part of this fight,

"I think someone is," Dudley said, for the Light Brigade of cavalry had at last begun to move. These were smaller and quicker steeds, the men all in blue-and-gold. They advanced in three lines of two ranks, moving at a moderate pace. Behind them, the re-formed Heavies followed. Dudley assumed they were off to attack the Causeway Heights and recapture the redoubts.

But they didn't. Something strange was happening: They were not riding towards the redoubts.

"I think our cavalry is going the wrong way," Barker said. He sounded amused. "It'd take an infantryman to point 'em in the right direction."

The Light Brigade was riding into the shallow valley north of the Causeway Heights. At the far end of that valley was an enemy field battery of eight guns.

"Surely, the Lights aren't going to attack massed artillery from the front?" Dudley said, astonished. It would be useless—and impossible. The battery and the crossfire from the Heights and hills opposite would cut them to pieces.

The spectators watched, breathless. Dudley's men were now climbing to their feet to see. Oakes watched with a wrinkled brow, a sprig of dead grass protruding from his lips.

The Russian guns on the Heights and hills opened fire. Russian riflemen also opened fire. The Light Brigade began to gallop, leaving the Heavies behind in a cloud of dust. The Heavies halted; they were already taking casualties from the crossfire, and now could not keep up with the Lights. There was nothing for them to do but withdraw, which they did, moving back out of the valley.

The Lights went on, taking hit after hit. Dudley could see horses and men falling. But the three lines kept going, galloping on and on, toward the battery.

"They'll be slaughtered," someone murmured.

Most of the spectators stood in hushed silence. Dudley looked at the faces in his fatigue party, saw big tears rolling across Oakes's cheeks. Johnson stared at the Lights in admiration, shaking his head. Barker frowned, while Geary looked puzzled. Doyle betrayed no emotion at all, though he watched with as much interest as the rest.

The Light Brigade had reached the guns. The guns fired, almost in unison. Grape and canister shot swept away both men and horses. The gunners reloaded and fired again, and the smoke and dust hid everything from view.

Then riderless horses began to emerge from the smoke. Behind them came men on foot, staggering, scattered. Soon a few riders began to appear, sabres in their hands, sitting as proud as statues in their saddles.

One-by-one, those who had escaped death and capture returned from the battery. Still under fire from the Causeway Heights, they gathered and began to form in line again. It looked to Dudley as though less than a third of the brigade had survived.

He turned to Oakes. The old veteran made no action to hide his grief at so many British soldiers cut down for no apparent reason. Why had they charged the battery?

Dudley said to Oakes, "I think someone has made an error."

The remains of the Light Brigade were filing along beneath him. He saw Sergeant Wellman's cousin, the sergeant in the 17th Lancers, sitting erect, his cap gone, his lance in his right hand. Somehow, he had survived.

Dudley ran down the slope to meet him.

"We watched the entire drama unfold," he said after they had exchanged greetings.

"Well put!" the cavalryman exclaimed. "Drama, indeed. A wild, mad dash that was. I don't know how we managed to reach those guns, but we did. And we gave them a whack or two as well! Something to write songs about, wouldn't you agree?"

Dudley found himself smiling. The man was beaming with happiness, his face lit with the glory of the impossible thing he and his comrades had done.

"Surely, though, there has been a mistake?" Dudley said.

The other sergeant looked thoughtful. "Well, it seemed mighty strange to all of us, but that is all done now. We have done what was asked of us, and can do no more. I suppose it will all come out in the end."

Dudley waved farewell and rejoined his men at the top of the slope. The battle had ended. The Russians still held the Causeway Heights, but their main force had withdrawn. The supply columns were moving again, and it was time for Dudley's men to resume their march to Balaclava.

The fatigue party trudged along the road. As they passed, French soldiers shouted at them, *"Bon Anglais! Bon Anglais!"* They had seen the Light Brigade's charge and judged it to be magnificent:—such bravery, such steadiness under fire, such dash and discipline all at once.

Though the work party had not taken part in the fighting, Dudley could not help feeling a sense of pride. The Light Brigade's charge had been mad bravery. Mad, deadly, wild bravery. He was uncertain how to feel. It had been a mistake, of course, charging those guns, and a disastrous one, but the cavalry troopers had played no part in that. They had simply followed the orders of their commanders.

Which had been greater, after all, the tragedy or the triumph? He found his instinct was to believe in the glory of the act. He wanted to believe in it.

But he had not been there, had not seen that maelstrom of men and horses up close, and so could not make a proper judgment.

A profound disappointment settled over him at not having played a part in the battle at all.

"When are we going to get our chance?" he heard Johnson repeating. "When do we get our chance?"

# CHAPTER NINE

But search the land of living men, Where wilt
thou find their like again?

> Sir Walter Scott
> "The Lay of the Last Minstrel"

***Dudley crouched behind*** a low barrier of piled stones. From his hiding place he could not see the forts and buildings of Sevastopol, but he could see the tops of the masts of the Russian ships trapped in the inner harbour. The masts resembled the crooked crosses of a dozen churches and made him think of the church bells he had heard in the town that morning.

There had been church bells and cheers. He had thought perhaps the enemy was celebrating two days of fine weather, for the morning—the morning of October 26th—had been beautiful. Even now that afternoon was upon them, the sky was full of ragged clouds and patches of deep blue. It was calming to lean back and study the vastness of that sky, to do nothing but look for eagles, mind wandering, and slip into a doze.

He forced himself awake, shaking his head and rubbing his eyes. He had lost count of the sleepless nights, but he could not allow himself to succumb to the fatigue. No. 3 Company was guarding the edge of Victoria Ridge above Careenage Ravine. The five-gun battery was on their left, the huge and silent Lancasters waiting for the next chance to speak. The company was part of a line of other pickets, companies from the Light and Second Divisions, protecting the northwestern perimeter. Not even one man in one picket could grant himself the luxury of sleep, and as a senior NCO, Dudley had to be an example to the others.

He heard the sharp report of a rifle, far away on his right. With a groan, he sat up. Other men in the company were doing the same. A rifle shot usually heralded the beginning of a raid.

He searched the landscape for enemy movement. All he could see were the tiny forms of the British pickets about a mile away. Behind him, Lieutenant Coltern had his little spyglass extended. The officer was studying the Inkerman Heights, over beyond the Second Division's camp. More rifles were firing now, a distant popping sound, like a skirmish line in action.

"Ah, there's something happening down there, all right," Coltern stated. As he said it, Dudley spotted the cause of the excitement—three columns of Russian infantry had appeared over the crest of a hill known as Shell Hill. With the columns came a battery of field guns, carriages and limbers painted green in the Russian manner. Three more columns of infantry stood behind the first three. All were difficult to see from this distance, their brown overcoats almost blending into the terrain.

"The pickets of the Forty-ninth, I think, have engaged them," Coltern reported, still peering through his telescope. "Their ammunition cannot hold against such a large body, I fear."

Dudley nodded, for it was the largest Russian sortie he had yet seen. They must have come out of Sevastopol, marched along their supply road then turned right to come at the Second Division lines from the north.

The Second Division pickets were putting up a furious fight. They countered the enemy's skirmishers and sniped at the Russian gunners unlimbering the field pieces. Dudley could also see gaps appearing in the enemy columns as men fell. Russian soldiers dropped one-by-one, but the ranks closed and the columns came on, forcing the British defenders back.

Coltern was right—the British picket's sixty rounds per man would not last much longer at this rate. Soon, the weight of the enemy raiding party would overwhelm them.

"Sir?" Dudley said, though his expression communicated more than that single word.

"Aye," Coltern agreed, "we shall go to their aid. Bugler?"

The drummer boy at the officer's side put his bugle to his lips and sounded Assembly. The men of the picket came running from their various positions and formed into two ranks at close order.

Dudley took his proper place on the right of the line—he was still the sole sergeant left in the company. O'Ryan and Colour-Sergeant Onslow were still on the sick list and would have to be evacuated back to the hospital in Scutari.

"Sergeant," Coltern said, "fall out and form a skirmish line."

"Sir," Dudley responded. He took one pace forward, did a right face and stepped off, wheeling in behind the company. He took a deep breath, filling his lungs and trying to relax, for he did not have a strong voice for shouting commands. It was even worse if his chest and throat muscles were tense, as they were now, thanks to the impending danger.

"Company, tell—off!"

From the right, each man in the front rank shouted his number, beginning at "one" and ending at "twenty-four." That meant there were forty-eight able-bodied men left in the company. At the beginning of the campaign, there had been almost twice that many.

Next Dudley called, "Company will extend six paces from the center. Ex—tend!"

Half the men did a right-face while the other half did a left. After a pause, the men marched away from the center, counting their paces. Each pair took six more paces than the last, halting at a different interval from the center. When the line finished extending, the company now covered a frontage of 120 yards.

The procedure seemed to take too much precious time. Dudley's nervous voice cracked when he called, "Skirmishers will advance in line, by the center, quick—march!"

The long line started forward, snaking over the rough ground. Dudley ordered them to bring their rifles to port arms. Every man had already loaded his weapon before going on picket.

They clambered down into a narrow section of Careenage Ravine then ascended the far side. The noise of rifle fire grew louder, and they could hear shouts and groans, the clash of swords and bayonets. When they emerged from the ravine, the first line of British pickets had retired through the gaps in a second British skirmish line.

Three more companies from the 30th Regiment comprised this second skirmish line. They advanced against the Russian formations, but those formations did not seem intent on stopping. The men in Dudley's company surged forward, almost at the double, eager to help the men of the Second Division, who were still a painful distance away.

Blood racing, Dudley shouted, "Independent fire when we get there, boys!"

On his left, he heard hoofbeats and rolling wheels, and turned to see a battery of the Light Division's field artillery rattling up from the rear. The blue-clad men of the gun crews sat on their limbers and rode their horse teams, faces set with determination. The guns were a welcome sight, given the numbers of the enemy.

Dudley's men were advancing on the Russian columns at a slight angle, on the far left of the British line. They would have a nip at the enemy's right flank.

"Halt here and take cover!" he called, and his men hit the ground, diving behind boulders or clumps of brush. The Russians did not seem aware of them yet.

"Commence firing!" Lieutenant Coltern suddenly bellowed, and a rifle banged. Dudley smiled to see that Johnson had been the first man to fire. More shots sounded, one man in each pair of skirmishers firing as the other loaded. Men along the sides of the closest Russian column began to fall.

"Hurray for the Royal Hants!" someone shouted, and Dudley looked to see an officer of the 30th grinning and waving his sword. Dudley waved back.

The Russian columns kept coming. A section of the closest formation broke off and began a steady, ponderous advance toward No. 3 Company's position, their own skirmishers fanning out ahead. A bullet whined past Dudley's ear. A man barked a strange laugh as the bullet struck him and knocked him backward.

The 30th began to retire, ammunition spent. Now without support, Coltern called No. 3 Company back as well, back to find new cover and turn again, loading and firing as fast as they could. Russian skirmishers went down, but the main body pressed forward. As Dudley reloaded his rifle, he saw the second enemy line was drawing nearer. He knew No. 3 Company did not have enough cartridges to stop them.

There was a sudden burst of cannon fire to his left rear. The men of the Light Division field battery had unlimbered their 9-pounders and 24-pounder howitzers. Now that the British skirmishers had fallen back, the range was clear for the artillery. Shot and shell began to scream toward the enemy, mowing great lanes in the ranks of the fresh second line, or bursting overhead and knocking down clumps of Russian soldiers.

Dudley let go a great whooping cheer of relief. The second enemy line was already breaking up in the face of this murderous barrage. One battalion disintegrated, while the others turned and ran, disordered, back over Shell Hill.

Their fellows routed, the first enemy line decided they had seen enough. They turned and began to retire in good order.

The men of the 30th were cheering, as were Dudley's men. Back on Victoria Ridge, there was a louder bang as a single naval Lancaster opened fire on the retreating Russians.

"Now's our chance," Coltern said, and Dudley was surprised to detect a rare hint of excitement in the officer's voice. "Fix bayonets!"

Members of the 30th and the light company of the 95th were charging forward in triumph. The men of No. 3 Company fixed their bayonets and charged after them, wolfish grins on their faces.

They caught a few stragglers from the Russian rear guard, but could not go far. The guns of Sevastopol loomed ahead and opened up with a few shots of their own, causing the disordered British to dodge back out of close range. The bayonet charge could go no farther, but they had done their work. Another enemy sortie had failed.

The guns continued to boom, but the withdrawing pickets slowed to a walk as they neared their own lines, battle energy spent. They gathered their wounded to help them back to the camps, their dead for burial. The Russian dead they left on the field. They would deal with them later.

Dudley stared at the enemy corpses. There must have been close to two hundred.

"The bastards," Oakes was saying, face purple with rage. As they had retired, the Russians had stopped to bayonet the British wounded. Those wounded had been men of the first picket engaged, men who had held on until their ammunition had run out.

Oakes kicked the body of a dead Russian. "Fucking whoreson bastards! Savages! I thought we were fighting a Christian nation, not a race of murderous heathens!"

"They did that at Alma, too," Dudley said.

This appalling behaviour on the part of their opponents had taken some of the excitement of the moment away from him. At the same time, it had strengthened his sense of moral superiority.

"Our foe is worthy of destruction. This is not simply a war of politics, of defending Britain's trade routes and the freedom of a foreign nation. The influence of such a barbarous people in Europe and the East must be broken."

"Aye," Oakes said, nodding. "Well, they won't try tangling with us again soon, after this."

"Perhaps not," Dudley replied.

That possibility left him with a sense of disappointment. He could not share the jubilation of those around him. Most were glad for their little success, and did not join Oakes in his anger. Even the wounded—in particular the wounded—continued to cheer. They walked or hobbled with pride despite their hunger, fatigue and injuries. Dudley warmed to see them so, but he felt he had little right to joy himself. The artillery and the pickets of the Second Division had taken the brunt of the fighting, and it had been their show.

This had not been the major action he'd hoped for. Maybe that action was nothing but a fantasy. Maybe the Russians would not come again after this little drubbing, and that was fortunate, with the dwindling numbers of French and British. At least there had been few British casualties in this skirmish, with twelve men dead. Those twelve seemed a shame, though, good men wasted on repulsing another raid. A large raid, but just a raid, nonetheless.

Dudley again studied the Russian dead on the field. They lay in contorted heaps, the heavy, conical Minie bullets having rent and smashed their limbs. They had carried entrenching tools on their backs, as if they had planned to stay awhile this side of Sevastopol.

But six battalions and a few artillery pieces? That wasn't a major push, he thought. More like a reconnaissance, a test of the Allied defences.

"What are you two standing there for?" Barker's voice thundered. He strode up behind Dudley and Oakes. "There's work to be done!"

He stooped over the nearest dead Russian and rummaged in the man's haversack, coming up with a loaf of hard black bread. He grinned and stuck the loaf on the end of his bayonet. A moment later, the men of No. 3 Company were going from body to body, stripping them of valuables. The bread was the most prized item found. Food in the British camps was getting scarce, and some soldiers hadn't eaten in a day.

Dudley made his way back to Victoria Ridge, chewing on a dry loaf. It was some consolation for their losses. It had been a small action and possibly insignificant, but the bread now seemed the true taste of victory.

The next morning Dudley and the company made their way back to camp under a sky that had gone gray again, threatening further hostility from the climate. He didn't have the energy to care or worry about the weather. His body was giving in to exhaustion in the wake of what was now yesterday's action. He flopped down in his tent, the dirt floor looking as inviting as any feather bed.

Having slept a few hours, he took another foraging party into the hills and ravines. As part of the never-ending quest for fuel, the party again cut stunted trees and brush to feed the campfires.

As they were returning, Dudley realized here was an opportunity to do what he had been unable to do for almost two weeks. He could visit Isabelle in the Zouave camp.

His mood lifted. He decided he would visit her. Maybe she could provide him with a bottle of something. The others in the shrinking sergeant's mess would appreciate that.

He told his men to wait at the edge of the French camp. They were glad to do so, taking the time to rest and chat with the Zouaves in a mixture of signs, broken French and broken English.

Dudley remembered the location of Isabelle's tent and canteen, and he made for it. As he approached, he saw her come out of the tent. He felt a mixture of joy and anxiety.

Then a man also emerged. He wore the sky-blue coat, tall red shako and baggy red trousers of the Chasseurs D'Afrique. The Chasseurs were a dashing cavalry regiment that had helped cover the Light Brigade's return from the guns during the battle near Balaclava.

The fellow buckled on his sabre. He turned to Isabelle and bent to give her a kiss.

Dudley halted. The chasseur moved off into the camp, and Isabelle stood with her arms folded, squinting up at the steely sky.

O'Ryan had been right, it seemed. Dudley's throat constricted. He wanted to turn around and leave the camp, but a sudden burst of temper compelled him forward. Isabelle noticed him as he approached, and she recognized him. She smiled, though to Dudley it looked more like a smirk.

Though he knew it was rude and not in his right, he demanded, "*Qui est cet homme?*"

He must have looked sympathetic in some way to Isabelle. Her face was soft and somewhat melancholy as she reached out to touch his arm.

"My poor young sergeant," she said, "how upset you look. You do not like what you have just seen?"

Her touch brought a sense of reality—and instant shame. Dudley tried to clear his throat, but the constriction remained. He forced himself to change his tone, asking, "Forgive me, but I am simply curious about who that man was. The chasseur."

"Why, he was my new husband. I married him three days ago."

Dudley stared at her. Her new husband? He swallowed, but his throat would not clear.

Isabelle shrugged. "He was my best offer, a sergeant of cavalry. He has arranged for me to leave these Zouaves and work for his regiment. These fellows will miss me, but he is a good man." She paused, studying Dudley's face. Then she asked, "Did you fall in love with me, my little Englishman?"

Dudley's shame turned to embarrassment. I am a complete fool, he thought. He knew he should have heeded the mental warnings he had tried to give himself. Did he really think he could fall in love with this woman he did not know? A woman he had only spoken with once before? And of course, she would have had dozens of offers of marriage, a widow of a comrade, and one with such good looks.

Isabelle sighed, and to Dudley's surprise, she put her arms around him and pressed her head to his chest. He felt her softness through his greatcoat, and that brought a bitter memory of Martha. It was an unpleasant reminder of old dreams that had never come true.

Yet there was comfort in Isabelle's embrace. He could sense it was a friendly gesture, one that contained true affection.

She released him and stood back.

"Boys do fall in love easily, I find, and you are just a boy, aren't you, despite that sash about your waist." She reached out and touched his cheek, and her hand was rough. The hand of a woman who worked hard for her living. "Would you have married me and taken me back to England?"

The question surprised him, for though it had crossed his mind, he had not pursued it. He had steered away from it.

"I don't know."

"And what if you *did* wish to?" she went on. "What if I did not want to go to England? Did you think of these things?"

"No," he admitted. "I started to, but then…I didn't think of anything." He took a deep breath. "I must seem very foolish to you, Madame. I'm afraid I was guided by my feelings alone."

"I understand that. But life is not so for me. I must think of realities."

Dudley drew himself up, trying to regain his dignity.

"I must apologize. I behaved very improperly just now. I had no right to come barging up to you and making demands. I am quite ashamed."

She nodded. "I accept your apology."

There was a moment of silence, and then he asked, "I also came hoping you could provide me with a bottle of something for my mess."

"Alas." She looked forlorn. "There are no supplies. Those in charge are very lax in getting us what we need. We have been waiting for days."

So, it was to be nothing but bad news.

"Well, then, I must take my leave. Get back to my men."

"Farewell, then, my little sergeant," she said. "Do not be downhearted."

I am simply a complete ass, Dudley thought as he made his way back to the foraging party empty-handed. He knew now how naive he had been in his attitude toward Isabelle. That, more than the fact she had remarried, was what upset him. His embarrassment went deep.

When he reached the fatigue party, cold drops of rain began to fall from the sky.

A steady rain pounded the camps for the next few days. The men did their duties soaked through to the skin, greatcoats and coatees weighted with water.

But the work went on, and when November arrived, a rumour spread that the Generals were again planning to bombard and attack the town. Most of the men discounted this, for no reinforcements had yet arrived, while the Russians still had a sizable force in the north. The Allies would have to deal with that force if the campaign was to be a success. When that would happen was anyone's guess, private or staff officer. Most of the men were prepared to wait out the winter.

Dudley dreaded that winter and the hardship he feared it would bring. This fear was reinforced on a dark morning when he found himself in charge of a column of sick and wounded. His fatigue party was to escort the disabled to Balaclava so they could board the ships waiting in the harbour. The ships would then take their human cargo across the Black Sea to Scutari, where they would enter the cavernous Barracks Hospital.

Dudley's men walked alongside a collection of creaking wooden carts. In the carts rode the sick and wounded who could not stand, those too feverish to keep their balance, and those with shattered limbs and other debilitating injuries. Those capable of walking did so, with Dudley's men giving support if need be.

He found it a wretched, depressing duty. He saw no hope in the cadaverous faces of the sick men, who stared into the distance with vacant eyes. The wounded, on the other hand, remained cheerful, but he knew they joked to hide their pain, and perhaps their fear of what would happen to them now. Many would have to leave the army, discharged with only their small pension when they returned to Britain.

One of the sick was Sergeant O'Ryan. Dysentery had weakened him until he could barely move or speak. He lay in one of the carts, head propped on his knapsack, his face blank and colourless. Dudley walked beside him, now and then providing a few words meant to comfort, such as "You'll get to spend the winter in a warm hospital bed, and in the spring you'll be as right as rain and back among us."

O'Ryan's face wrinkled in a grimace, but he saved his strength and did not even groan in reply.

When they reached Balaclava, the fusiliers and a group of sailors helped load the convalescents onto the boats. Dudley helped O'Ryan from the cart but was unable to get him down to the wharf without help. O'Ryan could not walk so much as a single step.

"Could someone give us a hand?" Dudley called to his men.

A soldier came forward and took a grip under O'Ryan's right arm. The soldier was Barker.

Dudley nodded, and together he and Barker lifted the Irishman down to one of the boats, Barker saying, "There you go, Sarge."

"You boys save a few Russians for me, will ye?" O'Ryan said with great effort, voice weak and trembling.

"We'll try," Dudley replied.

The boats began to move away, oars dipping and rising. The members of the escort stood on the small rickety wharfs and watched. Dudley was sorry to see O'Ryan go, and hoped the Irishman would recover. In fact, he feared for the red-haired man's life. He did not like the thought of losing another close comrade, another friend.

"Those poor buggers," Barker said, staring after the boat. "And I don't mean the wounded. They received their wounds with honour. But to die of sickness is such a waste. Better to die in battle."

Dudley looked at the big private, studying his hard and weathered face.

"I have never heard such sincere words from you, Private Barker. Nor such warlike sentiments."

Barker shrugged then turned and began walking along the wharf, back toward the village. Dudley rounded up the rest of the men, and they all started back.

On the road, Dudley caught up to Barker.

"I never thanked you for saving my life that time, weeks ago. From that Russian officer."

"I didn't save your life, Sergeant," Barker said without looking at him. "I knocked a Russian on the head. I was doing my duty."

Dudley felt a rush of irritation at this display of Barker's old defiance. "Have it your way, then, Barker."

He was about to move away when Barker said, "You think I hate you, don't you, Sergeant?"

Dudley hesitated, considering that statement. As an NCO, it did not matter whether Barker hated him or not. But in the grander scheme, for the good of the company, it did matter.

"Perhaps in the way that you hated poor Corporal Manning."

Barker chuckled, though there was no humour in the sound.

"I didn't hate Manning. He was my friend. Maybe the only true friend I ever had."

Dudley was skeptical. "I find that a strange assertion, given the manner in which you two socialized."

"You mean that we liked to fight? Maybe that's not friendly for you, but you're a scholarly type. For Manning and me, it was our little game. Our game, and no one else's. I never had a truer friend than Manning." He paused, then said, "You see, Sergeant, men either hate me and are too frightened of me to do somethin' about it, or they follow me and lick me boots, because they want to be like me, big and strong and not afraid o' anything, not authority and not the enemy. Or they simply fear me, too, and follow me to avoid my anger." He looked at Dudley, whose face was an empty mask, and added, "You did neither, and I grew to respect you for it."

Now it was Dudley's turn to chuckle. "Am I supposed to feel appreciation for that?"

Barker shrugged, as he had on the wharf. "You can take it or leave it, Sergeant. I merely thought you ought to know that I don't hate you. That I'm not here to give you trouble. Though I know that some of our trouble—some of it—has been what arises between an NCO and a bothersome private, a private who thinks he knows better than anyone else. I know none of that trouble was personal on yer part. Well, it weren't personal on my part, either."

Dudley weighed this for a moment. It was an immense oversimplification, but true in a sense.

"Thank you, then, Private Barker. I can see the validity in your statements. But if you know you are a bothersome private, why do you not take more steps to correct that fact?"

Barker smiled. "That's a long story, Sergeant."

"Ha. We have a bit of a walk ahead of us, and a story would take my mind off the rain."

They walked in silence for a moment, boots squelching in the mud. Behind them, someone was humming a song. A horse whinnied, and a group of civilian wagon drivers began a heated argument in an unfamiliar dialect.

"The army is something special to you," Barker said at length, "ain't it, Sergeant? It's treated you well, for the most. It's where honour and glory go hand-in-hand with loyalty and duty?"

"I like to think so," Dudley answered.

"Well, that's everything I believed at one time, too. But then I learned the hard way that it can all be a sham, and by that I'm not referring to the hardships of war. War is what we're in for. If we don't like it, then that's hard luck. A soldier learns to accept it and find the good in it. But that good can be destroyed, too, you see. And that's shameful."

"What are you talking about, Barker?"

"Tell me, Sarge, how do you like our officers?"

Dudley thought for a moment. "Captain Clarke was a fine man, as is our dear old Colonel Freemantle. Our generals seem a brave lot, Sir George Brown and Brigadier Codrington."

"Well there you have provided only four examples, and one's dead." Barker's face clouded, his dark-rimmed eyes growing darker. "I'll tell you—our officers are a useless lot of treacherous trumped-up bastards who bought their way in, steppin' on the backs of the working folk, who they use for their own means."

"Those are pretty strong words, Private." Dudley had heard similar things said in the barrack room, but never with such emotion.

"Strong words, maybe, but true. You want to know my story, Sergeant? I know you do, that you have for a while. Well, let me tell you that I grew up in a workhouse, a place of bad food, harsh discipline, rats, pestilence and cold winters." He laughed.

"Very much like here, only worse. I wanted to escape, and I was willing to work my way up to something respectable. So it was that I joined the army at fifteen, rather like our young Geary over there." He jabbed a thumb in Geary's direction. "And I worked. I did me duty, and in time, I was promoted to sergeant."

Dudley gave him a dubious look. "You were a sergeant?"

"Aye, that I was, in this very regiment you love so much. I joined with my best mate, Bob Manning. We'd grown up together, on the streets of our great capital of London. We both had high hopes of improving ourselves. My goal was to be sergeant-major, the man I thought truly ran the battalion. And I wanted to own a silver-tipped cane and a watch and fob.

"Simple dreams, maybe, the dreams of a poor boy. The fact is, I was well on my way to achieving those dreams. Manning, too, for he made it to sergeant just behind me.

"Then came our downfall, and it came because we were honourable men." His voice was harsh with enmity, and he paused for a moment, frowning. "You see, Sergeant, there was a pair of officers in the regiment, whose names I shall not mention for it no longer matters, who disliked a particular young captain. This young captain was something of a celebrated person, having campaigned in India and made a name fer himself.

"These other two resented his experience. They were fancy soldiers, y' see, men who'd learned their job from books and manuals and mess tales. They were eager to rise, they were, and saw this young captain as a threat to that, as well as to their authority, manhood, and everything else. Jealous types, and treacherous as mad dogs.

"These two cornered Manning and myself one evening. They had a task they wanted us to perform. That task was twofold. One, they wanted us to provide them with information about this young captain's doings, his comings and goings and associations—"

"They wanted you to spy?" Dudley exclaimed, appalled.

Barker nodded. "Aye, spy, indeed. And that weren't all. They also concocted this scheme whereby, through this captain's batman, a corporal we knew, we would plant certain objects in this fellow's quarters at the depot. Things from the mess, you see Sergeant, that mysteriously went missing. Bottles, mostly."

Dudley shook his head, uncertain whether to believe this incredible tale.

"And I take it you refused?"

"Refused, aye, as politely as we could. These officers could not order us to perform these illegal acts, but we had to be careful. They controlled our destinies, you see, Sergeant, just as others control yours. But we told them we couldn't oblige 'em, on account of our Christian values, you understand.

"They were put out by this, o' course. But I was confident they were in the wrong, and us in the right. I was a young fool, you see.

"Before long I began finding myself on report for little things, one after the other. I was being scrutinized, and Manning as well. The good I did went ignored. My previously spotless record was suddenly very spotty. Nothing great, mind you, but enough to know I was being watched, and persecuted, and if I did anything improper at all, that could be the end of me.

"Well, it *was* the end of me. I was brought before a court-martial on trumped-up charges, concocted by none other than our two delightful officers. Neglect of duty. The actual situation doesn't matter much. I had delegated a particular task to a corporal so I could rescue a comrade from an awkward situation, which involved a woman and her husband and a few bottles o' rum.

"My comrade was drunk in the woman's residence, and in danger of a good beating as well as a charge of desertion, so I made it my business to retrieve him. I suppose now I should have left him to his fate, for it was his own fault, and it gave those two treacherous villains the fuel they needed to burn me.

"My sentence was reduction to private. Manning was up on similar charges soon after, and met the same fate. I suppose we were lucky, for it could have been worse. But the fact was, we hadn't done anything at all, you see, and it was difficult to make our supposed crimes look too serious. No floggings by that time, Sergeant. No dismissal from the service, though that might have been a blessing.

"And do you know what truly bothers me, Sergeant Dudley? Not that two worthless lumps o' horse dung did their best to ruin myself and my friend, but that everyone else listened to them and believed I was no good. No one came to my defence.

"My company officers, it is true, weren't convinced of my guilt, but they didn't shout this loud enough for anyone to hear. No one looked at my whole record, but saw only those minor infractions and reports, and listened to the rumours I was lazy, and believed with their whole hearts I deserved my punishment.

"Well, in the last few years Manning made it back to corporal, but the drink did him in, as you well know. I didn't see the sense in trying again. I saw I was stuck for twenty years of service with the Colours, which I had once worshipped though now saw as tarnished."

Barker said nothing more, and Dudley thought about the story. Though he was reluctant to believe it, much of what Barker had said rang true. Either the man was a great actor, or his disgust with the army was genuine. Oakes had also provided snatches of these events in things he had said in Barker's defence.

But whether true or not, Dudley did not feel the events excused Barker's own behaviour.

"So," he began in an accusing tone, "you became the company bully and behaved dishonourably. You do everything the two officers once accused you of doing, though now you do it on purpose."

Barker did not deny that. "Perhaps I have made a mockery of what the army is said to stand for because I no longer believe in it. Where was the loyalty shown me? Where was the honour of my own officers? Where was the glory of the famous Royal Hampshire Fusiliers?"

"It's there," Dudley insisted. "And if it has been compromised, it can be renewed. You said to me once that a soldier fights. What does a soldier fight for? Certainly, he fights the enemy, but does he not also fight for honour and justice elsewhere? I say that he does, or should, from the lowest private to the highest marshal. And sometimes a soldier loses a battle, but unless he is destroyed, the soldier keeps on fighting after that battle. You lost a battle, Private Barker, and then you surrendered."

Barker said nothing for a long time. They were nearing the Light Division camp, and he stared ahead at the little mountain range of tents.

"I have not surrendered yet," he said at length, his voice little more than a whisper.

Barker's tale haunted Dudley for the rest of the day. He asked Oakes if there was any truth to the story, and Oakes said it was true enough, that only the men in the ranks had seen what was really happening.

"But no one would listen to us," he said. "And now many of the boys who were around back then are gone, having paid off or gone where all good soldiers go in the end."

"A discouraging story," Dudley said. "But only one story, I think, out of many that make up what this army truly is. After what we have all achieved here, in this muck and misery, how can you believe that honour and glory are all a sham?"

Oakes grinned. "I never believed that, Sergeant. There are fools and blackguards in all walks of life. Barker got stung by a few. But there's a lot of heart in this regiment. There's a lot of good boys here in this barren place, and many more who are buried in it. I honour them all."

As do I, thought Dudley.

That thought stayed with him and gave him strength the next day as No. 3 Company guarded the trenches. The men stood knee-deep in the muck and water, the skies pouring rain and the Russians pouring fire. The enemy barrage was heavier now. Every few minutes, the fusiliers had to dodge one of the huge incoming mortar shells they had dubbed "Whistling Dicks." The shells made a high-pitched whine as they fell, and the men always laughed when they missed. Laughed and shouted insults towards the Russian gunners, who were too far away to hear.

Perhaps there was an undercurrent of fear—perhaps there always was, to some extent—but as usual, no man displayed discouragement. There were no complaints about the mud, nor the rain, nor the enemy fire. Dudley could see them all as they huddled in the trench—his men, under cover from the shelling. He smiled to himself, realizing they would all make "dirty parade" now.

Their greatcoats were frayed and full of holes, their belts turned gray or brown. Now that the army had allowed beards, many had let them grow, and they were beginning to get long and tangled. Every man was ragged, scruffy or filthy, cheeks sunken from lack of sleep and food. They should have been sullen, hopeless, ready to give up, but they crouched in the trench and smiled and chatted and made jokes. Someone began singing a song that Dudley knew as "The Death of General Wolfe."

> Bold General Wolfe to his men did say,
> "Come, come, my lads, and follow me
> To yonder mountains that are so high,
> All for the honour, all for the honour
> Of your king and country."

Dudley stared in amazement, for the singer was Doyle. The others laughed and joined him. Dudley looked at their grinning faces, at Johnson and Oakes, Barker and Geary, and all the others in No. 3 Company. He thought of what they had all been through together—the voyage to Turkey, the waiting and disease, the heat, the Alma, the work, the bad food and lack of it, the wet, the mud, the cold, the Russian sorties, the shelling and bombardment. All of this they had endured.

When their relief arrived at dusk, these men would return to their muddy camp with its mud-floor tents. There, they would continue to sing songs and spin yarns and tell jokes. If the enemy was to attack again, these men would triumph. They truly had done great things in the face of horror. They had won again and again.

Dudley knew he was not much like these fellows in character or temperament, but at that moment, he felt closer to them than to anyone he had ever known. Closer than to Isabelle, closer than to Martha. Closer even than to his family.

He looked off to his right, into the veil of rain. Somewhere beyond that mist was the Tchernaya River and the ruins of Inkerman. A large Russian force had been waiting on the far side of that river since before the battle near Balaclava. That force had marched in a grand review today, despite the weather. The review had been visible from the British lines, and many had seen a bright yellow carriage in the Russian camp.

Everyone assumed someone important was visiting, and the Russian army had staged that review for him or her. It seemed something was brewing, something larger than just another sortie.

Dudley once again surveyed his comrades. If he was to go into battle again, as he wished, he was glad he would be going with them.

# CHAPTER TEN

We few, we happy few, we band of brothers; For
he today that sheds his blood with me Shall be
my brother.

William Shakespeare
*Henry V*

So all day long the noise of battle wild
Among the mountains by the winter sea.

Alfred, Lord Tennyson
"The Passing of Arthur"

*Sometime before dawn* the rain stopped. A heavy mist settled
and thickened into a dense fog. In Sevastopol, church bells tolled
a solemn round while Dudley and his company returned from
the trenches, leaving behind another sleepless night. Dudley
marched to the bells, the slow clatter and bong sounding a
weary cadence for his men as they tramped through the mud.
The bells were a melancholy reminder that this November 5th
was a Sunday.

"Well, Wellington," Dudley whispered to the charm that
still hung around his neck, "on this holy day, we should give
thanks that we are still alive, and that we will eventually conquer,
I have no doubt."

He realized he had not spoken to the tin soldier for some time. Months, perhaps. Not since they had landed in the Crimea.

He shivered. The rain had soaked him through to the bone. The rain had soaked the entire company through to the bone. The men needed the warmth of the campfire, the satisfaction of a hot breakfast. But when they reached their camp, there was no fire burning, and no one had yet served out rations. The bugles had sounded, and the battalion was beginning to stir. Orderlies were collecting water buckets and assigning fatigue parties, but the camp was too weary to move with haste.

Dudley found his tent. His fingers and toes ached with cold, and he could feel the months of grime and filth on his body. As usual, he longed for sleep—sleep in a comfortable bed. He longed for the smell of his aunt's kitchen in the morning.

He heard a rifle shot somewhere to the north. He waited, and a minute later heard another shot. This one was more distinct. It seemed to come from the direction of the five-gun battery.

Pickets shooting at shadows in the fog, he thought. He turned to enter the tent, but the crash of a squad or company volley made him pause. After the volley came isolated firing, a regular and continuous crackle.

Men who had come off picket and trench duty were gathering to look into the fog, muttering about the disturbance. Dudley squinted into the darkness and wondered if maybe this was another large Russian sortie like the one on the 26th. Either that, or a small raiding party had provoked an overzealous reaction from the tired pickets.

"They're sure shooting at something," a young private said.

"Don't care whether it's the czar himself and a herd o' Cossacks," said another, "I want a crack at 'em!"

Dudley thought of the great host of gray-and-brown troops massed on the far side of the river. Those troops had paraded in triumph yesterday. What if they had made an advance in the last hours of the night, the darkness and fog covering their movements?

The light was beginning to brighten in the east, but the fog was so thick Dudley couldn't see twenty yards in any direction. He could barely see halfway down the line of tents. An attacking force would be invisible until it had advanced to within spitting distance.

He started to move away from his tent, stomach clenching with the cold certainty he knew what was happening—the Russians were making another push.

A bugle chirped out the order to *stand to your arms*, the clear notes carrying through the camp. Dudley started to run. The bugle then called assembly.

Dudley's rifle was still in his hand, and there were fifth-eight rounds in his cartridge pouch. He made his way to the parade area, fatigue and hunger no longer important.

The noise of firing increased as the Royal Hampshire Fusiliers gathered round their Colours. The men formed a double line of gray greatcoats and dirty crossbelts. The shot-torn flags hung limp in the still-damp air. The regiment looked miserable and shrunken.

Dudley took his place with No. 3 Company. Some of the men were muttering in ranks, speculating about what might be happening.

"Silence, there," he called.

The muttering ceased.

"Good morning, Sergeant Dudley," someone said.

He turned to see Colour-Sergeant Onslow approaching.

"Good morning, Colours," he replied, surprised to see him. "I thought you'd been sent away to hospital."

"I refused to go," said Onslow. He blew his red nose into a handkerchief. "Told 'em I'd recover, and I have. And just in time. Looks like something nasty's brewing."

Most of the firing was coming from the right now, near the Second Division camp. There was the deeper thud of field guns as well, though it was impossible to say whether the guns were British or Russian.

Colonel Freemantle sat his horse behind the regiment. He looked down at Sergeant-Major Maclaren and said, "Have the men fix their bayonets, Sergeant-Major."

"Sir," Maclaren replied, then sang out a series of commands: "Rear rank will take open—order! March! Rear rank, dress! Eyes—front! Battalion will fix bayonets. Fix! Bayonets!"

The drill movements of the men were calm and precise, as though the clamour of battle was not so near at hand. A moment later Maclaren called, "By the center, quick—march!" The battalion advanced, moving to take up their position with the rest of the Light Division.

Dudley marched in the front rank on the right of No. 3 Company. His heart pounded in his chest, but he was grateful he didn't feel the chills and nervous discomfort he had experienced before the Alma. He had seen too much since then.

An aide thundered up with a message from Brigadier Codrington to the commander of the Royal Hants. The aide was a typical young officer of his sort, a privileged son of a privileged family with a plum position thanks to that family's connections. He was blond-haired, blue-eyed, and wearing a scarlet light infantryman's uniform that appeared brand-new despite the hardships of the campaign. Dudley heard him say the general wished Freemantle to deploy his men near the southeastern edge of Victoria Ridge to watch the Careenage Ravine below. Freemantle acknowledged the order, and the aide sped away.

The regiment marched until it reached its assigned position, where it halted. The men loaded their rifles and waited. The day was growing lighter, though the fog showed no sign of thinning. The noise of artillery fire had increased, and now and then an enemy ball would come bouncing along, striking the ridge and plowing a furrow in the wet turf.

Dudley stood easy and fidgeted in his place. He wanted to know what was going on, how this fight was shaping, how large the enemy force was and where they had struck. He could sense Lieutenant Coltern standing behind him, and heard the officer puffing on a cigar. For some reason, he found this irritating. How had Coltern come by so many cigars when conditions had forced so many men to go without food for days at a time?

The blond-haired aide again came riding up to Colonel Freemantle, his horse blowing and sweating. Dudley heard him say, "Brigadier Codrington's compliments, and he says the enemy has apparently come out in force. He is concerned one of their columns could slip along this ravine unnoticed in the fog and attack the Second Division's flank. He directs you to take your battalion to the southern end of Careenage Ravine and prevent the enemy from using it in this manner."

Freemantle's reply was muffled, but a moment later, the regiment was moving away to the right in two files, towards the sounds of fighting.

The Royal Hants marched eastwards, down the slope of Victoria Ridge. When they reached the post road, they turned left and headed due north, toward the Second Division camp.

The Careenage Ravine narrowed here into another ravine called the Wellway. The Wellway was a direct route from the Russian lines to the British, like an open tunnel linking the combatants. An enemy column had used that tunnel during the skirmish on October 26th. It was logical to assume the Russians would try to use it again, this time with the cover of the fog.

Dudley could see the mouth of the Wellway as it drew nearer on their left. Low brush and the debris from many woodcutting expeditions covered its floor and steep sides. Coming over that debris, toward the Royal Hants, was another regiment. The fog was too thick for Dudley to make out who these soldiers were, but he thought they were marching in column.

The other regiment emerged from the fog. It was a battalion of soldiers dressed in gray coats and round caps with dull red bands.

"By Jove, there they are!" Freemantle cried, turning his horse, which rose up on its hind legs. "Come on, my brave lads!"

The colonel drew his sword. Only then did Dudley realize the advancing column was Russian.

There was no need to think, no need to wait for further commands. The Royal Hants turned from file into line on its own, the men doubling toward the Russian column with bayonets leveled. The Russians halted in dismay at this silent and unexpected charge, and then the British line crashed into them.

Dudley drove his bayonet deep into a man's belly. The man crumpled and fell, dragging him forward. Dudley tried to remove his bayonet, but it was stuck. For a second, he panicked, but no one took advantage of his helplessness. The Russians were already turning and running.

Dudley freed his weapon and watched them go. Rifles were barking around him, the bullets finding the backs of the fleeing Russians. A volley boomed to his left, and he saw a company of Guards standing on the lip of the ravine, firing into the Russian flank.

"Reform!" Coltern cried, and other company officers took up the call. Dudley helped dress the ragged line. He was breathing hard, excited from the sudden charge and the little victory.

"We shall continue to advance," Freemantle declared. "Sergeant-Major?"

Dudley wondered if perhaps it would be more in accordance with Codrington's orders if they remained where they were and guarded the ravine from further enemy incursions. But the Guards company was there, and other small groups of British—half-battalions and companies—were now marching up from the right rear. Freemantle left the Wellway to them, and the Royal Hampshire Fusiliers moved toward the front of the action.

The Second Division camp was an utter ruin when the Royal Hants reached it. The British regiments had just begun to strike their tents when the Russian artillery caught them unawares. Some of the tents still stood, and others lay in shapeless heaps. Russian round shot had thrown up great chunks of ground between the tents. Dead supply ponies lay amidst the heaped wreckage of ruined carts and smashed wagons. Dead men lay where they had fallen. Some of those men were in their shirtsleeves, caught as they rose to meet another day in the Crimea.

Beyond the camp lay a rise of ground known as Home Ridge. The ridge ran west to east, and it had guarded the Second Division camp. Along its crest, Dudley could see the dull shapes of British infantry units as they stood and fired. None of the units was of battalion strength. Shells burst among their ranks, but those ranks closed and kept fighting. The enemy was invisible, but Dudley could feel the weight of their presence. He had his proof this was no mere sortie. He was certain this was it—the big push, the Russians' largest attempt yet to drive the British and French from the Crimea, perhaps larger than the attempt near Balaclava.

Dudley made a quick calculation and decided the Russian host he had seen yesterday must outnumber the British by at least three-to-one. He had no doubt the Allies were facing that host, a horde that could roll over them and push them into the sea. And in the fog, the generals could not see to direct a proper defence. The danger was greater than it had been since the landing in Calamita Bay. Today, the Allies faced the possibility of defeat.

Yet, here was also the battle Dudley had been waiting for. Here was the chance to fight on a grand scale, to reclaim the glory from the horror and misery, from the loss and deprivation. Here was the chance to reward the men for their good humour and supreme efforts, reward them with victory despite over-whelming odds.

Victory, if that were possible.

He wasn't sure it was, but he would do his best. He would fight today.

Sergeant-Major Maclaren, striding along on his long spidery legs, bellowed the order for the regiment to deploy from file into line. When the men had finished the move, they advanced through the ruined camp and up the southern slope of Home Ridge. They would cover the left flank of the British line.

The Royal Hants reached the top of the ridge and halted. Dudley expected to see the enemy at once, but all he saw was a white wall of fog and powder smoke. The Russians lurked somewhere within. He could hear the crunch of their boots and the shouting of their officers.

A brown-coated mass appeared ahead, a Russian battalion in a column of companies. Three companies marched in front, each in two ranks, and a fourth company marched behind these. It was a looser formation than the usual Russian column, but one that allowed for more firepower.

The column approached Home Ridge at an angle. It would have struck the British line in the flank if not for the arrival of the Royal Hants.

Sergeant-Major Maclaren saw the threat and barked a few quick commands. The Royal Hants wheeled on their center to face the enemy. The sergeant-major then cried, "Volley fire as a front rank kneeling, rear rank standing, at forty yards, ready!"

Dudley and the others in the front rank dropped to the kneeling position then pulled back the hammers of their rifles. Each man reached into his cap pouch, took out a percussion cap and fitted it in place. No one flinched or fumbled. With the calm of well-drilled soldiers, they adjusted their rear sights to forty yards.

The men of the Russian column began to howl and scream as they surged forward, goose-stepping, bayonets leveled, hidden drums pounding. They came closer, the forty-yard gap now reduced to thirty.

"Front rank, pre—sent!" Maclaren called, and in quick succession, "Fire! Rear rank, pre—sent! Fire!"

The smoke from the two volleys curled and mingled with the fog as Dudley stood to reload. He could see men dropping from the enemy column, part of its front rank crumbling back. The column halted, the close-range fire having decimated the center company.

Smoke and flame burst from the two Russian flank companies. Men in Dudley's rank cried out and fell. He struggled to ignore them and listen to Maclaren's commands.

"Battalion will fire a volley and charge! Pre—sent!"

He aimed into the smoke. "Fire!" came the word. The volley crashed. The rifles came down to the charge, and the sergeant-major screamed, "Charge!"

Dudley screamed and leapt forward. The rest of the battalion ran with him. The Russian column, like the other they had charged, fell back, crowding into the tightly packed ranks of a second column advancing behind it. Then the British bayonets struck home.

Dudley faced an officer. The officer swung his sabre in a downward arc. Dudley blocked the blow with his rifle's stock then smashed the rifle butt into the officer's head. As the officer's body fell, Dudley stepped over it and saw the enemy was edging back.

The first column had broken, but the second about-faced, turning in good order. The second column marched away at a walk, retreating into a ravine Dudley didn't recognize.

"Follow them, my boys," a voice said behind him, a voice weighted with strain. Dudley turned to see Colonel Freemantle slumped in his saddle, blood staining his left armpit where he gripped his coat with his right hand. Freemantle looked down at Maclaren and said, "Sergeant-Major, carry on. I shall not leave you."

The regiment moved forward on its own as Freemantle spoke. Men who had not slept or eaten sprinted ahead like agile schoolboys on the track, running after the retreating Russians. Dudley raced after them, dodging through the low brush. He could see the fellows of No. 3 Company ahead, still showing some adhesion, commanded by Coltern and Onslow. He didn't want to be left behind.

The Russians from the second column had lost some of their order now. Individual soldiers were halting and firing as they retreated north. The dispersed companies of the Royal Hants did the same. Coltern was blazing away with his revolver, and Dudley halted next to him to reload, oblivious to the Russian bullets whizzing by his head.

The Russians who had been firing turned and retreated again. Coltern said, "Come on, lads," and moved away out front.

"Let's go," Dudley added, though the company was already moving. He heard Barker shout a wordless war cry as he ran. More than half the company cried and screamed with him.

There were orange flashes in the fog ahead, and with a note of alarm, Dudley realized they were facing artillery. They must have run all the way to the Russian gun line. He knew where they were now—there was the dim shape of Shell Hill, and on its crest were the shapes of Russian cannons, gouting flame and hot metal.

The Royal Hants could go no farther. They halted in disarray just under the guns, the fleeing enemy column having made it to safety.

"Down, down!" Coltern shouted, and he crouched, revolver in one hand and sword in the other. Dudley dropped to his knees, the shot rushing overhead. Behind him, a bugler was calling for them to retire and reform the line. Coltern waved his sword toward the south, and shouted, "Go! Go!"

The company ran at a crouch. Dudley heard the artillery booming behind him. He did not like the feeling of turning his back, and he jumped as a round shot struck nearby and bounced high in the air.

An unearthly shriek rose over the roar of the guns. Dudley looked back to see Coltern writhing on the ground. Something had torn the officer's right leg off at the knee, and blood gushed from the stump. Coltern's face contorted in agony, his teeth biting into the cigar that still smoldered in his mouth.

Dudley scrambled back to help him. Grabbing the lieutenant under one arm, he lifted him with one heave and bore him along to where the regiment had reformed not far away.

"Lay him on the ground," Colour-Sergeant Onslow said. The lieutenant was now unconscious. Onslow bandaged the bleeding stump with the officer's own cravat, saying to Dudley, "I have the company now. You're with me behind the ranks."

"Aye, Colours," Dudley replied. The Russian guns banged away on his right.

Lieutenant-Colonel Freemantle sat behind his reformed regiment, his face pale. He ignored the fact they were still taking fire and spoke with another officer, an aide or messenger who had ridden up from Home Ridge. As the aide galloped off, Freemantle said something to the sergeant-major. Maclaren then addressed the battalion in a voice that carried over the sound of battle.

"We're going to retire a bit farther, boys, back to that ravine we chased that last bunch through. It's called the Mikriakoff Glen. We're going to hold our position there, guarding the left flank of the British position from further attack. You've done well so far, boys! Let's show 'em that *we* don't tire easily, either. Let's go!"

A few moments later, the regiment had turned and retired in line, back the way they had come.

They waited at the edge of the Mikriakoff Glen with elements of the Connaught Rangers and a wing of brother fusiliers, the old Royal North British Fusiliers. The battle continued to rage on their right along Home Ridge and beyond. In their front, things were also heating up. The fog had thinned a bit in areas of higher elevation, and they could now see the Russian gun line they had stumbled against, muzzles flashing in the distance. The guns stretched along Shell Hill and to either side of it, positioned to fire over the heads of the massed Russian infantry.

Dudley watched as some of that infantry advanced along the post road from Shell Hill, the leading columns descending into the fog and fading from view. A moment later, he heard screaming and musketry mingled with the clash of steel and the loud banging of cannons.

"It's the fog of battle, all right," Colour-Sergeant Onslow growled. Then he laughed at his joke before asking, "How can the generals know what they're doing? Everything's a muddle."

"They can't," Dudley said. "We simply have to find the enemy and fight them where they stand. Though it seems someone must be in charge on Home Ridge, to be sending messengers about."

"Fight them where they stand, that's the ticket. And here we sit idle in case some of the buggers show up."

There was a rattle of boots on stone, and a double file of British infantry appeared behind them. The commander of this battalion, a major, rode to where Freemantle wobbled in his saddle and said, "Sir, you are relieved here."

"Relieved?" Freemantle said, confused. "Where shall we go now?"

"Why, to Home Ridge. General Pennefather wishes you to return to Home Ridge. Though he believes the Mikriakoff must still be guarded, so he has sent us."

Pennefather, Dudley knew, was commander of one of the Second Division's brigades. So, he was in charge back there.

"Sergeant-Major Maclaren," Freemantle said between gasping breaths. "March the battalion to Home Ridge."

The regiment formed a column and made its way to the next position. Dudley could hear the fierce fighting along Home Ridge but saw only shadows. From the noise, he decided a large volume of artillery fire was striking the ridge.

When the Royal Hants reached the ridge top, they found it empty of all save heaps of dead, both Russian and British. The Russian artillery had forced the remaining defenders to take shelter on the south side. The nearest friendly unit was a French regiment in line. Line was a formation the French army did not often use, and the regiment's men seemed uneasy, their officers and NCOs raging at them to hold their ground.

Maneuvering from column into line, the Royal Hants formed on the left of the French regiment. With the new and reassuring presence of the British, the French soldiers seemed to gain confidence and steadied.

The Royal Hants were still dressing into position when the enemy appeared. Another Russian battalion emerged from the mist and came tramping over the heaps of bodies. The column was ragged and had taken hits from its own artillery, its men stumbling, clutching their hats, looking right and left. When they saw the solid line of French and British, they halted. For a second, it looked as if they would stand and fight, but then they turned about and scattered back into the fog.

"That was easy," someone joked, and a few men chuckled.

"Quiet there," Dudley said, though without much force. These men had fought hard today, proved themselves, and did not need harsh parade discipline on this field of fire.

With a dull thumping of hoofbeats, a gentleman in a blue frock coat appeared and reined in next to Colonel Freemantle.

The fellow had a gray beard and a peaked forage cap, and he said, "Colonel Freemantle, you will fall back and keep your battalion here in reserve. And don't fret—you will surely be needed sometime soon."

This was General Pennefather himself. The battalion fell back and waited once more. The men stood easy, their rifles loaded.

Dudley watched in fascination as a combination of French and British troops beat back another Russian attack. Then these Allied battalions advanced out of sight beyond the ridge. It was still difficult to see what was going on, but he could hear the French musicians sounding the *pas de charge*, the martial call of drum and bugle that had so stirred Bonaparte's men. It was strange to think of that music now coming to Britain's aid.

As the *pas de charge* faded, the sound of horses and rattling wheels grew louder. A large contingent of Royal Artillery arrived, their two-horse teams pulling a pair of heavy 18-pounders mounted on siege carriages. The artillerymen unlimbered the two guns on the right of Home Ridge. The muzzles faced northwest, toward the Russian gun line.

"There we go, boys," Dudley heard Oakes say. "Our gunners will show 'em a thing or two."

"About time," Barker growled.

The big guns were a welcome sight, something to counter the constant and deadly fire from the Russian artillery. The Russian gun line was the greatest threat to the Allied position, far greater than the hordes of infantry. Shot had struck the Royal Hants three times since the regiment's arrival at Home Ridge, and the attacking British battalions would be taking worse.

Dudley watched the first 18-pounder crew take a ranging shot, pitching a ball at a Russian battery almost two thousand yards away. The ball fell short. The next ball, fired from the second gun, scored a direct hit. A Russian gun fell silent. The artillerymen cheered.

The arrival of the British guns caused the Russians to redirect some of their fire. An artillery duel began, fought between two spurs of high ground above the fog. For thirty minutes, the

Royal Hants witnessed the death of many a British gunner as solid shot plowed through the Royal Artillery positions. But no shot struck the guns themselves, and relief gun crews arrived to replace the killed or wounded. Other gunners armed with spades began to throw up low defensive walls of earth, complete with gun embrasures, to deflect the incoming fire.

The 18-pounders were running low on ammunition, their commanding officer calling for resupply, when a messenger came to Lt. Col. Freemantle. The commander of the Royal Hants was now as pale as his starched shirt, the wound in his bandaged arm still seeping blood.

The messenger was another young aide, though this one seemed harried, and his scarlet coat was disheveled and stained.

"Sir," he shouted, "General Pennefather needs a company to go forward to The Barrier and reinforce Captain Haines. The right wing of the Twenty-first is holding out all by itself with hardly any ammunition. It would be best, too, if you could send a group of expert marksmen."

"Take us!" Dudley heard Johnson shout. Johnson was staring out from his place in ranks, expression pleading.

"Sir!" Colour-Sergeant Onslow said, scurrying over to Freemantle. "Number Three Company volunteers. We have several of the best shots in the battalion, including Privates Johnson and Barker, and Sergeant Dudley."

Freemantle grimaced and gave Onslow a weak nod, waving his approval. Onslow hid his delight and called No. 3 Company to attention.

"Where and what is The Barrier, sir?" Onslow then asked the messenger, who was a young captain of the 49th.

"Straight north up this road from Home Ridge," the captain replied, wiping his brow with a filthy handkerchief. "It is a low wall of loose stone blocking the road just as it dips into Quarry Ravine. The Second Division constructed it weeks ago as an obstacle for enemy artillery that might come up the road. It commands the approaches to Home Ridge, and the Russians took it this morning.

"But the Twenty-first have recaptured it. They are now beset by infantry attacks and heavy fire from the enemy guns, and cannot hold much longer without ammunition and rein-forcement."

"We shall do our best, sir," Onslow said grandly, then re-turned to the company. Dudley, surprised and touched at being named as one of the best marksmen, took his place on Onslow's left.

"Company will advance in line," Onslow shouted, "by the right, quick—march!"

No. 3 Company detached itself from the battalion and marched over the crest of Home Ridge, then down into the hollow where the fog and the fighting was thick.

The Barrier was more than a hundred yards wide and formed a half-circle across the road. Behind it, the British soldiers of the 21st huddled around their ragged Colours. In front of The Bar-rier, the road dipped down into Quarry Ravine then continued on towards Shell Hill and the enemy gun line.

The slope from the ravine was covered with the bodies of Russian soldiers, in places four and five deep. British casualties were also heavy, the dead strewn about, the wounded either still fighting or lying apart, their comrades having made them as comfortable as possible.

Howitzer shells burst around them as Dudley's company doubled into the shelter of The Barrier, taking their position on the left. The Russian batteries were close here, and down in Quarry Ravine he could see Russian infantry. They crouched behind bushes and rocks, and the muzzles of their muskets flashed as they fired.

Colour-Sergeant Onslow found Captain Haines, saluted, and said, "We're here to reinforce you, sir."

Haines stood with one hand on his hip. He had a regal bearing and a clean-shaven face dominated by an enormous nose. His cap was regulation, but his coat was civilian, plain and brown and stained with dust.

"How many?" he asked, calm and collected despite the fragility of his position.

"One company, sir. But we've each still got about fifty rounds. Full pouches, sir."

"And you have rifles, too, I see. That will have to do. The Russians are only sniping at us now, but they will make another attempt to retake this position soon. You may as well stay where you are and cover our left flank."

Onslow made his way back to his company at a crouching run, bullets smacking into the wall as he went. He found Dudley and said, "These fellows are still armed with Old Brown Bess. Those muskets haven't got the range to reach the batteries. I think we should try, those guns being too close for my liking. I didn't like 'em the first time we ran into 'em, and I like 'em even less now."

Dudley looked up toward Shell Hill.

"We're about a thousand yards away. A tough shot."

"I can do it," Johnson boasted from where he lay against The Barrier.

Dudley grinned. "Do your best, Private Johnson."

Most of the men in the company were firing down into the ravine. Johnson took careful aim at the Russian gunners. Before he could fire his first shot, someone screamed, a sound of rage more than pain. Dudley saw Private Doyle clutching at the bloody stump of his left ear. A musket ball had grazed the side of his head, taking the ear with it.

"Damn, damn," Doyle was saying over and over.

"Conserve your ammunition!" Onslow shouted, ignoring Doyle and standing upright so he could be heard. "Don't fire at shadows and boulders. Wait until you have a clear target!"

The Colour-Sergeant suddenly pitched backwards, blood spurting from one eye. He landed on his back and did not move. Dudley scrambled to his side, but Onslow was dead. The bullet that had entered his eye had blown away the back of his skull.

"Did we lose him?" Private Barker said, crouching next to him.

Dudley stared at the blood and bits of gray matter on his hands—Onslow's blood and brains.

"Yes, I'm afraid so."

"Then you have the Company, Sergeant."

Dudley wiped his hands on his greatcoat and took up his rifle. Yes. He had the company. There was no time to allow that fact to become overwhelming. There was only one thing to do here —stay and fight.

"Then, my first command," Dudley said, "is a repeat of the Colour-Sergeant's last. Spread the word, Barker—no indiscriminate shooting. One can go through fifty rounds in twenty minutes, and I feel we shall be here longer than that."

"We can hold here all day, Sergeant," Barker said with determination, then went off to follow Dudley's instructions.

"Sweet Jesus!" Oakes exclaimed. "Here they come!"

Dudley was on his feet and behind the company, shouting, "Form back in two ranks, kneeling. Quickly! Do it now! Independent fire by file. Wait for my command to commence firing!"

A column of Russians was charging up out of Quarry Ravine. The 21st conserved their fire and waited, but a company of Rifle Brigade blazed away. Russians dropped, but the column didn't slow.

Dudley waited until the enemy was within sixty yards then called, "Commence firing!" His front-rank men, steadying their rifles on the wall, all let loose at once. Russians fell, and their comrades marched over their bodies. Then Dudley's rear-rank men, firing over the shoulders of the front, blasted their volley. The Russians ignored their losses and did not stop. They kept charging up the rocky slope, some of them firing as they ran and stumbled.

The Russians reached the wall. The sheer weight of their massed ranks drove the foremost men into the British bayonets. The rest screamed and crawled forward, stabbing and firing.

All along the wall men struggled. Dudley saw Barker swinging his rifle like a club. A Russian prepared to thrust his bayonet under Barker's ribs while his arms were raised. Dudley fired, and the Russian fell back. His body knocked over those advancing behind him.

Dudley stepped forward to the wall to cover a gap in the line. He felt a bayonet graze his leg. The man wielding the

215

bayonet could not regain his balance after his thrust, so Dudley stabbed him in the neck.

As he withdrew his bayonet, he saw Oakes grappling with a Russian officer and Doyle screaming like a madman, "doing the lunatic" for the benefit of the enemy. The blood from Doyle's shorn ear covered the left side of his contorted face. He was lifting rocks over his head and throwing them down the slope, crushing skulls.

The Russians broke off, flowing back down into the ravine. A shell burst in the air as they went, scattering hot fragments. A group of British defenders fell. Dudley pressed against the wall and watched the enemy column regroup below. They would come again in a moment.

"This is a little more than we bargained for," he heard Oakes say. So, the old man had beaten the officer. Good.

Dudley made a quick count of the handful of tattered defenders at The Barrier. Maybe there were two battalions'-worth here, maybe not. He saw men of the 21st leap over the wall to retrieve the ammunition from the pouches of the enemy. Many also took up Russian muskets. They were resorting to the use of anything they could fight with.

This seemed to be the front line of the battle now. Far to the right, a constant chorus of firing announced another fierce struggle was taking place, a struggle against overwhelming numbers of guns and men. The 18-pounders on Home Ridge had not fired in some time.

With a sense of calm resignation, Dudley understood they were fighting for their lives. They were fighting for their very existence. There had been some success today when they had beaten the Russians back from the ground they had captured, but how long could that last? It was true the enemy seemed incapable or unwilling to exploit their successes; they threw them away once gained. But sooner or later, they could force their way through by sheer weight of numbers, and then the right flank of the British siege lines would crumble.

We won't let that happen, Dudley decided. We will stand here to the last man.

He moved along the line of his company—*his* company, he realized again with something close to shock. He came to where Johnson crouched and continued to take shots at the enemy gun line.

"Well, Private Johnson," Dudley said, "we're finally getting our chance, eh?"

"Yes, Sergeant!" Johnson replied with enthusiasm. Dudley studied him for a moment. Johnson was enjoying himself, even though he stared death in the face.

A screaming cheer issued from Quarry Ravine, like the exultation of a pack of drunken revellers. Dudley saw the Russians coming again, charging up the slope. He found a place behind Private Doyle then loaded and fired two rounds in quick succession.

The Russians refused to stop. For a moment, he admired their bravery, for they came on despite their heavy losses. But there were not enough British rifles to end their charge, and soon they had clambered over the slain and were again thrusting their bayonets across The Barrier.

Dudley stood behind Doyle and reloaded his rifle a third time. Doyle thrust forward with his bayonet, screaming and stabbing a man in the guts. His bayonet caught, and three men ran him through with theirs at the same time. Dudley shot one of the men. The Russian fell back, leaving his musket still hanging from Doyle's body. The other two turned on Dudley. One stabbed; Dudley deflected the blow with his rifle stock then smashed his rifle butt into his attacker's face. He then turned to the second fellow, but he had already fallen, Barker's bayonet through his neck.

The Russians broke off again but refused to withdraw. They retreated a few paces then halted below the wall and formed a rough line. They stood not more than ten paces off and began firing up at the defenders.

"My ammunition is running low," Dudley said as he rummaged in his cartridge pouch. A musket ball ricocheted from the wall and plucked at the side of his coat.

"You're bleeding, Sergeant," Barker said, coming to Dudley's side. Dudley looked down and saw that blood had soaked his right trouser leg. There was a long gash in his calf. Barker tied a piece of a dead man's shirt around the wound.

"No time to worry about that," Dudley said, moving back to the wall.

The Russians were not advancing or retreating, just held their ground. It was nothing but a big shooting match, except that few British rifles and muskets were firing now for lack of ammunition. Men instead threw discarded bayonets, rocks, anything that came to hand.

"We'll have to push them back," Dudley said. He stepped up on top of The Barrier. It seemed the best thing to do, so he shouted, "Come on," and charged down at the Russian line.

There was a whir of bullets in the air, but none hit him. Behind him, the rest of the company followed without hesitation. Even men of the 21st and the Rifle Brigade charged after him, howling. The Russian line broke before the British wave could strike it, falling back into Quarry Ravine.

"Hold here!" Captain Haines shouted, trying to restrain his men. They heard him and scurried back behind The Barrier, just as Russian round shot began striking the slope, bouncing high over their heads.

Perhaps because of the closeness of their own troops, the batteries on and around Shell Hill had not been firing at The Barrier for a while. Now that the Russian infantry had again retired into Quarry Ravine, the guns resumed their assault.

A ball smacked into the wall, showering bits of rock. Dudley heard a bellow and saw Oakes screaming with a splinter in his eye. Dudley ran to his side, ducking low as he went. Oakes lay on his back, face covered in blood, though he was still conscious, still breathing. Without thinking, Dudley pulled the splinter from the wound. Oakes howled, and blood and fluid gouted, but the splinter had only ruined the eye and had done no life-threatening damage.

"You'll be all right, old fellow," Dudley reassured him. "You're still breathing."

He turned to another private, said, "Look after him," and went looking for something to bind the wound. Before he had gone two paces, he found himself facing Captain Haines.

"Who's in charge of this company?" Haines demanded.

"I am, sir. Sergeant Dudley."

"Well, then, Sergeant Dudley, listen to what I have to say. It is my opinion that the enemy infantry have had enough and will not attack in such force again. It's those blasted guns that worry me now." A shell burst behind him, but he ignored it. "I have ordered those groups of men armed with the Minié rifle to get closer to the guns and harass the gunners. I want you to take your company and bring fire on the westernmost battery."

Dudley's hand snapped against his cap in salute, and he said, "Yes, sir."

Haines did not elaborate on his orders, returning to the center of The Barrier.

Crouching down next to where Oakes lay, Dudley said, "You lie here, Private. We'll be back for you." Then he stood and shouted, "No. 3 Company!"

His men looked at him from where they now huddled with their backs to the wall. Shot struck nearby every few seconds, and their eagerness of a few minutes ago seemed to have evaporated. They could deal with the enemy infantry, but the guns were another matter.

"Get up and follow me," Dudley ordered. "We're going to attack the guns. Private Matheson, leave him, he's done for. Come on!"

He motioned for them to follow him to the left, out from behind the protection of The Barrier. They travelled in two ragged files, crouching low and scrambling through the brush and over rocks. The Russians must not have seen them, for they managed to go some distance before Dudley motioned for them to squat in the meagre shelter of some low bushes.

Dudley pointed at the western battery of three 9-pounders. The battery was five hundred yards away, the gunners busy blasting at The Barrier.

"We're going to take that," he said.

The men looked at him, but no one said anything. A ball struck the turf five yards to their right. Several men flinched, and others fell flat on their chests.

"Come along," Dudley said, moving forward.

He had gone three steps when he realized only two men were following—Johnson and Barker. Turning back, he saw the rest of the company still crouching, hesitating. Some lay looking as if they wished they could burrow into the ground.

Dudley saw their exhaustion, their reddened eyes and smoke-blackened faces. How much more of this could they take? Had they reached their limit? He looked towards the guns. They had to be taken or destroyed; this was no time to be giving up.

*Please don't let me be wrong about them. Please don't let me be wrong about any of this...*

"I'm with you, Sergeant," Barker said. His voice betrayed his disgust for the others.

A man disengaged himself from the sluggish majority and scrambled over to Dudley's side. It was young Geary.

"I'm game, Sergeant!" he cried.

Dudley turned to the rest again and said, "This is no time for hesitation. Come on!"

He trusted them. He knew they would follow.

Turning his back, he advanced across the open ground, while ahead the batteries kept up a steady fire. He felt an eerie sense of loneliness, but when he had gone about ten paces, he looked back.

The rest of the company had not abandoned him. They had found their second wind, had scrambled to catch up with Barker, Johnson and Geary. They moved with caution, strung out in no formation at all, but that was, perhaps, wise. He felt relief and satisfaction. These fellows would not let four of their company go it alone. Even if they were all at the point of dropping from weariness, even if they believed the action foolhardy, they would find the strength to go on.

Though he should have done it before, he ordered the company to halt here in the open so he could split them into three sections. They fell to their chests again, listening as he shouted his plan in full view of the guns.

"These two sections will circle around the left and come at the battery from the flank," he said. "The rest of us will take it head on."

"I'm with your group, Sergeant Dudley," Barker insisted.

"Me, too," Johnson said, scowling.

"Right, then," Dudley said, "off we go."

This time there was no hesitation as the three sections moved off. It would take the flanking parties longer to reach the guns than his section, Dudley knew, but the gunners would see only the frontal attack, so the flanking parties would come as a surprise.

Rifle at the port, he ran. His men ran with him, straight at the battery.

The ground began to slope, and the wound in his leg burned. He started to slow, his breath rushing in his ears.

The gunners saw them. Russian voices shouted exclamations and commands. Dudley saw the muzzles of the guns trail around, shifting their aim from The Barrier and lowering their elevation. He saw the gunners loading, rammers thrusting the shot home. The guns seemed to point at him. Not at his men, but at him.

The guns were three hundred yards away and growing nearer. One fired. A ball skipped by, but the attacking group was too spread out. The ball missed.

Dudley felt a wild exhilaration, a glee that had been building ever since he and No. 3 Company moved off Home Ridge. Now, it was reaching its crescendo. Here in the midst of battle with death all around, he felt more alive than he ever had. He knew with clear certainty this was his moment of glory. This was his moment, leading these men in this wild dash, the seeping wound in his leg forgotten. If he should die now, he would die with honour. He thought of the Light Brigade of cavalry, and knew now why Wellman's cousin had been so joyful, even though so many of his comrades had fallen that day.

The attacking group scrambled up the hill, gasping and clawing, some on all fours. The guns seemed almost close enough to touch. Dudley saw the crews loading canister shot, metal cylinders filled with musket balls. He saw the smoke and flame as the guns went off, felt the hot wind, but for some reason he did not hear the blast. Men cried out as the shot tore their flesh, but the guns were silent.

He didn't see which of his men had fallen. They were in loose order, so it could not have been many. It didn't matter anyway, for now they had a precious respite from the fire as the gunners reloaded.

With a loud bellow and a pumping of his thick legs, Barker ran past, rushing up the slope toward the center of the battery. Dudley took up the war cry, and a second later, he was dodging between two of the guns. His men were with him.

For a moment, all was chaos, a chorus of rifle shots as the attackers fired at close range, a confusion of long gray coats, Russian and British, swirling around the guns, men screaming and grunting, thrusting with bayonets, striking with rifle butts. There were more artillerymen than Dudley had thought there were, but he saw some of them running for their horse teams to flee.

He raised his rifle to seek out a new target, but Barker moved in front of him. Barker had pinned a man to the ground with his bayonet. Dudley saw an artillery officer aiming an old-fashioned dragoon pistol at Barker's back. Dudley fired first, and his shot blew the officer backward.

Barker freed his bayonet in time to see what had happened. He glanced at Dudley once then ducked as another gunner swung a rammer at his head. Barker slid his bayonet between the man's ribs as Dudley moved forward, looking for someone else to fight.

It was then that the flank attack appeared, screaming and charging, taking the remaining Russians almost from behind. Rifles banged, and those not killed ran. The fight was over.

Dudley stood amidst a pile of dead and wounded, looking for further resistance. Understanding slowly sank in. He had done it. They had taken the battery. They had done it. He felt light-headed.

But there was no time for reflection. The other batteries were still in action a few yards away. Haines had sent out other attacking parties, but they were firing at the guns from a distance. A few of the Russian gunners saw Dudley's men, and they shouted in warning. Their unease made him wonder if this successful attack could be carried any further. Perhaps they could turn these captured guns on the flank of the other batteries.

Something heavy struck the ground near his feet, throwing up dirt and pebbles. A second later he heard a deep-throated thumping from Home Ridge. Another ball came roaring in, hitting the barrel of one of the guns. The barrel rang like a cathedral bell.

"Eighteen-pounders back in action, Sergeant!" Barker said.

"Take cover!" Dudley cried, for the heavy shot were as much a danger to them as to the enemy.

No. 3 Company scrambled back down the slope. Above them, more shot struck home, though farther east as the British artillery swept across the Russian gun line. A gun limber in the next battery exploded in splinters, the horses screaming as they died.

Coming on the heels of Dudley's attack, this was too much for the Russian artillerymen. Officers shouted orders, and he saw the guns limbering up. Two more rounds came in from Home Ridge, tearing more horses and men to pieces. The remaining Russian batteries ceased firing and began to pull out.

With cheers, the rifle parties sent out by Haines ran up the slope of Shell Hill. When they reached the summit, the guns were gone, leaving behind ruined limbers and carriages, and the dead.

Dudley's men rose to their feet and moved back into the battery they had attacked.

"We took it for nothing," someone said.

"Took it for nothing?" Barker exclaimed. "You bloody fool, we've captured three guns!"

He was right, Dudley realized as he moved between the three dull-bronze trophies. It was almost as big a triumph as capturing an enemy regiment's Colours.

Whether they could keep those guns was another matter. Looking north, beyond Shell Hill, he could see the Russian reserves. Four regiments in dense columns lay in wait. None had yet seen any fighting today.

Barker saw them, too.

"Bloody hell," he said, shaking his head.

Their fears did not come to pass, for the Russian artillery had begun a full retreat. One-by-one, the remaining batteries pulled out, covered by the four Russian reserve columns. One of those columns began to advance to attack, but the 18-pounders shredded it, and it fled in disarray.

When the gloom of mid-afternoon arrived, the last Russians had fled back to Sevastopol. They left the British and French alone on the bloody field.

Dudley and the remnants of No. 3 Company wandered back along the post road. They left the captured guns where they stood. The Royal Artillery could carry them away later.

There was nothing Dudley's men could do about the guns anyway. With the battle's ending, the true weight of their exhaustion and wounds began to settle on them. Some hobbled with the support of comrades, while others had to be carried. Dudley did not need support, but his right leg had begun to ache, and he could not walk without a limp. There was a dull pain in his left side, too, though he did not remember anything hitting him there.

Twisted corpses—many of them the victims of artillery fire—littered the field. Groups of Russians and British lay with their bayonets through each other. Everywhere were the ghastly remnants of eight hours of savage fighting. Piles of dead lay in every posture, killed by sword or grape or round shot or shell. In some places, men lay in ranks as they had stood, while the Russians lay in column, dead hands and faces like wax. The air shivered with the cries and groans of the wounded, some pleading with God, some crying out for loved ones far away, and some for a simple drink of water. Somewhere, a poor dog wailed, having found the body of its master.

"William? William Dudley?" a wavering voice said.

For a moment, Dudley thought he was hearing things, that the voice had been that of his aunt. But it was not his aunt. It was Hester Oakes, who was picking her way through the debris, looking for her husband.

"We have him," Dudley told her, "but he's been hurt. Lost an eye, I'm afraid."

The gray-haired woman clasped her hands together as if in prayer, and tears rolled down her plump cheeks.

"Lost an eye? Lost an eye? He has another, don't he? At least he's alive—alive." Then she saw him, old Private Oakes, coming along with the help of another man, and she ran to him with an "Oh!"

Dudley didn't hear what they said to each other, for he was watching the other wives as they moved here and there among the corpses. Now and then one turned a body over, looking for a familiar face. It was an entire company of widows. Or a battalion.

The British and French buried their dead in individual graves on the uplands, filling the cemeteries that held so many who had died from disease. The Russian dead they heaped in great pits and covered with earth. Once again the enemy had shown no mercy to Allied wounded, and once again the Allies gave no respect to the Russian fallen.

Back in the camps, the bugles were calling for assembly. The cleanup and grave-digging paused while the divisions mustered by battalion. Dudley stood next to No. 3 Company, his fellow fusiliers, men he had led in battle, if only for a few hours. He was weak, and wobbled on his feet, though he was glad to see Lieutenant-Colonel Freemantle still sitting on his horse. The battalion commander looked somewhat better and wore a clean bandage.

Freemantle, the grandfather of the Royal Hants, followed an orderly-sergeant who held a pencil and a list of every man who had been able-bodied before the battle. The sergeant went down the line, checking off whether a man was present, dead, wounded or missing. Many of the wounded were in ranks, standing with pride or leaning on their neighbors. Overhead, the regiment's Colours fluttered in the light wind.

When the colonel and orderly-sergeant came to No. 3 Company, Freemantle said, "Sergeant Dudley, I hear that you led your company at The Barrier, that you took an enemy battery?"

"That he did, sir!" Barker piped up, improper to the last.

"Yes, sir," Dudley said. He was proud of that achievement, but his voice came out weak.

"My God, man," the colonel cried, seeing the blood leaking from Dudley's leg and from the gash in his side. "You are seriously wounded!"

Dudley opened his mouth to reply, but he had been fighting a grayness for some time, a grayness that threatened to close over his eyes. As Freemantle spoke, the grayness attacked.

I must not give in, Dudley thought. I must not fail. I must hold this position.

But the grayness conquered and turned into black.

# EPILOGUE

Soldier, rest! thy warfare o'er,
Sleep the sleep that knows
    not breaking,
Dream of battled fields no more,
Days of danger, nights of waking.

        Sir Walter Scott
        "The Lay of the
          Last Minstrel"

The four-day sea voyage to Scutari was one of pain and delirium. Dudley could not feel his leg, and feared it had fallen to the surgeon's butchering. His mind was not clear or rational enough to confirm whether this had happened or not.

His senses did not return until he had been in Scutari Hospital for some time. To his immense relief, he discovered his leg was still there, swaddled in white bandages, though the pain was a trial at times. His bandaged side ached, too, though not so much it could not be ignored.

The hospital was in no way an ideal haven. It had once been a Turkish barracks, and though vast, the sick and wounded had overcrowded its shabby walls. Dudley had a dim memory of lying for some time in a narrow corridor, his bed a cold stone floor, and staring upward at a cracked plaster ceiling.

Then, at some point, he had been moved, though he did not know when. He had simply awakened in this new location, a rectangular room with high windows along one side and two internal doorways on the other, each doorway opening into, he presumed, that same corridor. The room had cracked plaster walls and a ceiling that appeared to have been very recently white-washed, and it housed two neat rows of iron-framed cots, each containing a straw-stuffed mattress and a wounded soldier.

He found it a depressing place but did not complain. He saw no need to, given the options. It was healthier to lie in a cot with a straw mattress than to lie in a sodden greatcoat in the dirt. His only real misgiving was the food. It was as bad as the stuff they had in the field, or worse. The butter was rancid, the bread mouldy, and the beef like moist shoe leather. Mealtime was nothing to look forward to.

Straw mattress and poor food aside, Dudley was determined to heal and to return to the Crimea, return to the company of his fellow fusiliers. He had already survived the infectious fever and did not plan to stay in hospital long. A simple bayonet wound, he reasoned, should not become an excuse to shirk his duty, however painful that wound sometimes was.

He thought about the battle at Inkerman often, and dreamt of it at night. He remembered the deaths of Private Doyle and Colour-Sergeant Onslow. He remembered Oakes's maiming. He remembered the bodies of men who had fought their last battle scattered across miles of open ground.

These were sorrowful memories, and horrible, yet they existed side-by-side with recollections of the successes, the triumph over great odds. The defence of The Barrier, the charge he had led, the taking of the field battery—these were good memories. Though the battle had been hell and fire and death, just like the Alma, he had been able to bring something alive out of it.

He wondered if that meant he had learned to love war, or had forced himself to love war in order to survive. If so, he did not love everything about it. This war was no game, but a serious business, and he longed for its conclusion. But he also longed to return to that group of men he had led for such a short time. He wanted to fight alongside them again.

In the meantime, he would use this convalescence for some much-needed rest. He would try to relax despite the dismal hospital setting, to read. An officer had brought him a bundle of letters that had been held up in the mail, most of them dated weeks or months ago, all from his cousin Jane. Their appearance had been proof of his confidence in his cousin's continued affections.

The letters were precious to him, and he read them over and over. Jane wrote of the mundane events at home and wished him well. She explained she had enjoyed his fascinating accounts of his travels, but the letters written from the Crimea had been quite frightening. She hoped he was safe. Auntie Bronwyn also sent her love, though Uncle Robert, regretfully, had not yet softened. He considered Dudley something of a family traitor.

Dudley was beginning to believe his uncle would never change his mind.

One of the doctors had also found him a few books. Dudley kept these on a little shelf above his cot, next to the bundle of letters. Weighting the letters down was the tin Wellington, trailing his silver chain.

One morning as Dudley sat reading, one of the new female nurses came to him with a message. The nurse was one of almost forty others who had arrived in Scutari on November 4, the day before the battle. They were under the supervision of a young woman named Florence Nightingale. Miss Nightingale theorized that improved sanitation would increase the survival rate of those in the hospital. Though she and her party had much work to do yet, other patients swore to Dudley she had already made vast improvements.

Most of the army surgeons refused to employ the women in an official capacity, but the majority of sick and wounded saw them as a blessing. Not only were they making advances in the hospital's structure and organization, but they helped bathe and clothe the men, offered words of encouragement, and made for a comforting presence. Many a man claimed to have survived with the clasp of a warm hand, the whisper of a concerned feminine voice.

The nurse who came to Dudley offered none of those things now. She told him he had a visitor. Puzzled, Dudley could not think of who that could be.

The answer to this question was startling.

"Lieutenant Sackville?" Dudley gasped in surprise as a young man in a fine uniform approached his cot.

"Er…Captain Sackville," the fellow replied, frowning. "Have we met before, Sergeant?"

Dudley said nothing for a moment, studying the officer's face. It was the same man, though he had been promoted, it seemed. Apparently, he did not recognize Dudley or remember him.

"Uh, no," Dudley said at length. "I was told that a Sackville was coming to see me."

"Oh," Sackville replied, looking perplexed. "How odd. But news such as I carry is hard to keep down, I suppose, and I am very pleased to carry it, Sergeant." He laughed that foolish laugh Dudley remembered.

"News? What news is that, sir?"

Sackville produced a document from a valise he carried.

"Following the glorious events near the heights of Inkerman, a Royal Warrant has been issued by Her Majesty in appreciation of the gallantry displayed in that action. If I may read to you a part of the warrant…" He cleared his throat and read, "The Queen has been pleased to command that, as a mark of Her Majesty's recognition of the meritorious services of the noncommissioned officers of the Army, under the command of Field Marshal Lord Raglan, in the recent brilliant operations in the Crimea, the Field Marshal shall submit the name of one Sergeant of each Regiment of Cavalry, of the three Battalions of Foot Guards, and of every Regiment of Infantry of the line, to be promoted to a cornetcy or ensigncy for Her Majesty's approval."

Sackville fixed Dudley with eyes that held an odd sense of personal triumph and announced, "For the Royal Hampshire Fusiliers, your lieutenant-colonel has submitted your name, Sergeant William Dudley. Or should I say, Ensign William Dudley? Ha-ha!"

With a bit of a flourish, he presented Dudley with the signed commission. Dudley looked at it, not understanding what it meant. It was dated the 5th of November, 1854.

"I am an officer," he said after a few minutes.

"Er...yes," Sackville replied, a little disappointed with Dudley's reaction. "Congratulations, sir."

"Thank you," Dudley eventually managed. "Thank you, Captain Sackville," and he shook the hand of a man he had once knocked to the ground.

After Sackville left, Dudley lay in his cot, leg throbbing, and read the commission several times. With it was a letter explaining that he was assigned to No. 3 Company, 1st Battalion Royal Hampshire Fusiliers.

"My fusiliers," he whispered. "When shall I return to you?"

He folded the commission and placed it with Jane's letters, on the shelf above his head, weighted down by Wellington and his length of chain.

### *End of Empire and Honor Book 1*

# ABOUT THE AUTHOR

At the tender age of five, HAROLD R. THOMPSON was inspired by a primer and wrote his first two works. He completed his first novel seven years later, and has been writing ever since.

While attending university, he spent his summers working at the Halifax Citadel National Historic Site, a Victorian-era fort in his native Halifax, Nova Scotia. There, he was a member of the 78th Highlanders, an historical re-enactment of the fort's British Army garrison. The job reminded him of his love of history, particularly military history, and he started writing again. After two years of law school, he realized that the lawyer's life was not for him, that he loved storytelling above all else, and so he quit to write. The original edition of Dudley's Fusiliers was published in 1996.

He is now a fulltime employee of the Halifax Citadel Regimental Association, a contractor with the Canadian government. He designs and supervises public programming for visitors to the site, which he sees as another form of storytelling. He has also indulged a love of film-making and has shot a few documentaries about the Citadel, including a staff recruiting video.

"I plan to pursue more film work, but there isn't really enough time in the day. I have a wife and two children aged six and three (as of this writing, but they keep growing), and what with spending most of my non-work waking hours with them, writing has become a midnight pursuit. But I keep up the chase."

# ABOUT THE ARTIST

GARY TROW has worked as an artist since graduating in 2003 with a First Class honors BA in Illustration from the Arts Institute at Bournemouth.

He began by working part-time at magazines before moving on to 3-D visualization and computer games. Now, he's finally producing book covers, the reason he went back to university as a mature student, ("Well, I say mature...") and is also working towards putting together his first exhibition of paintings. Please feel free to visit and comment at http://gary.trow.artistportfolio.ne.

8658711R0

Made in the USA
Lexington, KY
20 February 2011